Buck Spade

Never Date a Cowboy Billionaire

Buck Spade

Never Date a Cowboy Billionaire

by Sophie Devon

Buck Spade - Never Date a Cowboy Billionaire by Sophie Devon

Published by Thady Publishing.

Copyright © 2022 Sophie Devon

More books in this series by Sophie Devon

Buck Spade - Never Date a Cowboy Billionaire

Morgan Spade - Help! My Boss is a Cowboy Billionaire

Follow Sophie on Tiktok:

www.tiktok.com/@sophiedevonbooks

Get notified when new books in this series are published here:
www.writtenbysophie.com

Chapters

Chapter 1

"Table for two, please."

Buck Spade smiled at the friendly restaurant greeter and turned to clap his lawyer on the back. "Come on, Eugene. Let's go have a beer and you can tell me how much trouble I'm in."

The waitress had huge green eyes and long red hair tied up in a ponytail. She smiled back at him and he got a glimpse of dimples before she turned to lead the way to the private dining room of the brand-new Stonebridge Steakhouse.

Buck's first impression, as he followed, was that he liked the place. It had been built in an old warehouse and still had the bare lights and original brick walls. Somewhere in the main dining room somebody was playing a piano, and the sweet scent of grilled steak made his stomach growl.

The place was the buzz of Sandy Creek, Texas, and was the nicest chow house the town had seen since the legendary Rio Catfish Camp had closed down in 1965. The new place felt fun and inviting, and since he was being sued at the moment, Buck figured he could use a little loosening up.

Buck caught the waitress's eye again. Her eyes were the color of the Texas sky on a hot summer's day, and her gleaming hair was the most luxuriant red he'd ever seen. He'd say she was in her late thirties, maybe forty, but she was better looking than most women half her age.

Eugene's harassed voice yanked his attention back to the present. "Buck, I'm afraid the news isn't good," he fretted, and mopped his brow with a handkerchief as they walked into the private dining room. "Buster Hogan is claiming senior water rights to the Big Sandy."

Buck sat down at the big table and snorted, "That's ridiculous!"

"Would you like a drink menu?" the redhead suggested, and clasped her manicured hands together.

Buck glanced up and waved a hand in the air to dismiss her. "No, no, thank you," he muttered abruptly. "We'll order in a little while. We need to talk business right now."

She arched an eyebrow, but he didn't see any more of her reaction, because he turned in his seat to tell his lawyer, "You can tell Buster that he ain't gonna get one drop of water from the Seven, and that if I catch anybody from the Lazy H on my ranch, *trouble* is going to be an understatement!"

His lawyer set a briefcase on the dining table and opened it. "Here's the complaint," he sighed, and handed Buck a sheaf of papers. "Buck is claiming senior water rights to the Big Sandy. He says that your grandfather sold the rights to his father."

"That's a lie!" Buck fumed. "Our father hated old man Hogan. Old man Hogan was an even bigger idiot than Buster."

"That may be," Eugene sighed, "but their lawyer has documentation. It's attached at the back. Appendix A."

Buck flipped through the sheaf of papers and dug a pair of glasses out of his shirt pocket. He stared through them in frowning outrage.

"This is the first time I've laid eyes on this," he muttered. "That's because it's a stinking forgery, hatched up by Buster and that shyster lawyer of his! Buster discovered his 'water rights' because of this drought," he growled. "But it should be easy enough to prove it's a lie. Just check the records at the courthouse!"

Eugene gave him a long, dry look over his glasses. "Thank you, Buck," he drawled. "I thought of that, too. Unfortunately, we can't check, because the old courthouse burned down in December of 1988. They still used paper records then, and they were all lost."

Buck glared down at the papers, then tossed them onto the table with a contemptuous flick of his wrist. "The only thing Big Russ would've given old man Hogan was the toe of his boot. Water rights, my—"

The redhead's soft voice interrupted him again. Buck looked up to see her smiling down at him. "Can I get you gentleman a pitcher of beer?"

Buck frowned at her, still battling with the disaster unfolding before his eyes. "I thought I said we'd order later," he reminded her irritably before turning back to Eugene. "It's hard enough to water our own cattle in this drought. I'm not giving up one drop to that snake. I'll fight him to the last penny!"

Eugene shuffled papers. "Yes, I think we've established that," he muttered. "Well, we can certainly challenge the authenticity of his documents. I'm going to need the original water rights documentation from you."

Buck waved him away. "I'll put Carson on it. He knows where all those things are. He'll call you this week."

"Thank you," Eugene sighed, and reached for the glass of water at his right elbow. "I always enjoy dealing with your brother Carson."

"You think the judge'll throw it out?" Buck demanded, and Eugene put the glass down and shook his head.

"You know I don't predict," he replied. "It all depends on what the court thinks of these documents."

"They're toilet paper, and any judge worth his salt'll know it!"

The waitress appeared again, this time holding a tray with a pitcher of beer and two empty glasses. She set the tray down on the table in front of them, and Buck's glance flicked over her impatiently.

"I thought I told you we'd order later," he snapped, just as she was bending over the table to pour the beer. He glimpsed a split-second of fire in her expressive eyes, then the whole pitcher of beer landed abruptly in his lap.

"Hey!"

He jumped up from his seat. The pitcher clattered to the floor, the whole front of his trousers was sopping wet, and he found himself standing in a puddle of pilsner.

"Oh, I'm so sorry," the woman replied, but the smile at the edge of her lips told him it hadn't been an accident. She shook out a napkin for him, but he snatched it out of her hand and swiped his pants leg.

"What the—if this is how you treat customers, you ain't gonna have this job for long, woman," he told her tightly.

Her eyes flashed, and this time the angry look in them was unmistakable. "The name's Kate, cowboy," she told him softly. "This is my place. And you're free to leave it any time you like."

Buck threw the napkin onto the table angrily and stormed out of the room, grumbling as he went. He burst out of the big main doors of the restaurant and stomped down the front steps past other staring diners.

He caught a glimpse of one of his friends standing among them, and heard the laughter in the man's voice as he sputtered, "Buck, what happened, buddy? Did you fall into your beer?"

A soft chorus of laughter followed him as he stalked out to his red truck, yanked the door open, and climbed in. He cranked it to a roar and sent it scratching out of the parking lot in a spray of gravel.

He was furious, but Kate's rudeness was only the cherry on top of a rotten day.

The steaming main dish was Buster Hogan and that infuriating lawsuit; and he vowed to himself that Buster was going to rue the day he tried to steal water from the Seven Spades Ranch.

Chapter 2

Kate Malone turned apologetically to the frazzled-looking man still sitting at the dining table, and the two of them exchanged a startled look.

But only for an instant. The bushy-haired man with the glasses and suspenders merely closed up the briefcase on the table, set it on the floor, and told her: "I'm ready to order now. I'd like the porterhouse steak with herbed potatoes and a stiff double martini."

"Coming up," Kate replied smoothly. "I'll get someone in here to clean up the beer."

She pivoted and breezed out, but she was laughing as she went. The look on the other man's face had been priceless—that big, brash, six-foot cowboy with the big mouth and the bigger attitude.

Kate's lips curved up. He was a good-looking heathen, though. His face was as brown and angled as a mountain ledge. He had dark, stick-straight brows, and vivid blue eyes and high cheekbones under them. He had a proud nose and a square, stubborn jaw.

He was big and broad-shouldered, a head taller than every other man in the room, and handsome in a cowboy way: all muscle and a little rough around the edges.

Just the kind of man she admired.

But he'd looked as shocked as he deserved to be when she'd poured that beer over him. She'd crossed paths with lots of rude guys like him in her life, and they were sadder and wiser men for having met her.

She blew past an owl-eyed waitress watching from the doorway of the private dining room, and the girl trailed after her all the way to the kitchen.

"Kate, I know you did *not* just pour a pitcher of beer all over that guy," the girl hissed. "Do you know who he *is*?"

Kate walked into the kitchen and leaned over the counter to hand the order to the chef. "I know what he is."

The little brunette propped herself against the wall and crossed her tattooed arms. "That's Buck Spade. He's just the richest man in this county," she drawled. "He owns the Seven Spades Ranch. He and all his brothers are billionaires with a big fat 'B'. Their ranch is 250,000 acres wide!"

The girl tilted her head and shot her an arch look. "He's so hot, too! *I* wouldn't dump beer on the most eligible bachelor in Texas, I can tell you that."

Kate shot her a withering glance, then opened a cabinet to pull out a box of fine Cuban cigars. "He's the most eligible something in Texas, I'll give you that," she agreed. "Right. I have to get back to his friend. At least *he* seems to have decent manners."

"That other man is Eugene Clemmons," the waitress informed her. "He's the Spade's lawyer. You see him on the news sometimes, because they bring him in to comment on the big cases. Do you remember the baseball player who sued the league last year and won?"

"I don't follow sports."

"Well, that was Eugene's client. He got the guy twenty million dollars!"

Kate propped her hands on her hips and gave her waitress a quizzical look. "You seem to know a lot about these people and their friends," she drawled.

"Everybody around here knows the Spades," the girl replied earnestly. "They run this town! And I'm telling you, if they like you, you're made. If they don't, you're sunk!"

Kate resisted the impulse to roll her eyes. "This isn't feudal England. I'm not going to put up with that type of behavior in my restaurant," she objected. "Right. I'm going to make it up to the other guy for ruining his meeting. You did say his name was Eugene?"

The girl gaped at her, and seeing that she was speechless, Kate stepped around her with the cigar box in her hands. Just about every man in Texas loved cigars, and it was her policy to go the extra mile to make her guests happy.

That policy extended even to celebrity lawyers who counseled entitled jerks.

She walked back to the private room, knocked softly, and peeked in. The man was now talking softly on his phone, but he hung up almost immediately.

Kate smiled at him. "I'm sorry to interrupt," she murmured, "but I thought you might like a cigar before dinner." She walked over and placed the box on the table.

To Kate's amusement, the older man's face brightened a bit, and he fumbled in his jacket for a lighter. Back in Denver, most of the men she knew wouldn't touch tobacco, but Texans were a different breed.

"Thank you, Miss—"

"Kate," she smiled. "Kate Malone."

The man lit one end of his cigar. "A pleasure, Kate. Most people around here call me Eugene." He glanced up at her, and the keen glint in his eye gave Kate's skin a warning prickle. He stuck the lighter back into his jacket and added, "Are you new here? I never forget a face, and Sandy Creek's a small town."

"Brand new," she replied pleasantly. "I used to live in Denver, but my late husband had family here. North Texas suits me down to the ground. My daughter and I love horses."

"Well, this is horse country all right," he replied briskly, and blew a spiral of smoke into the air. "There are five big ranches outside of town, and three of them raise world-class horses. The Lazy H, the Chatham Ranch, and of course the Seven Spades. The Seven is mainly cattle, but they raise racing thoroughbreds as a sideline."

Kate raised an eyebrow, but the arrival of an employee with a mop interrupted her train of thought. She turned back to her guest.

"Would you like a different table, Eugene?"

The older man shrugged. "Let him do his job," he murmured. "I've eaten in buses, on planes, and on horseback. A mop doesn't faze me."

Kate's mouth curved up. She liked down to earth people, and in spite of his glittering clientele, Eugene seemed to be down to earth.

But her amusement faded when he sputtered cigar smoke into the air and added, "And thank you for the entertainment. I must say, I admire your attitude. You're the first person I've ever seen win a fight with Buck Spade."

She opened her mouth to tell him exactly what she thought of Buck Spade, but the mischievous glint in his eye as he gazed up at her made her curl her lips into a sour smile instead.

"I'll just get your martini, Eugene."

As she walked away, Kate was reminded that it was useless to argue with an attorney. And if the man wanted to talk about Buck Spade, it was the end of the conversation in any case.

Chapter 3

Buck sent his truck under the big ranch gate and down the mile-long drive to the Seven ranch house. Well-tended green pastures stretched out on either side of the dirt drive, and his truck kicked up dust as he gunned it on the flat.

Delores used to say that he was a horse's butt when he was mad, but she always ended up making him laugh. Now that she was gone, it was just one more thing that he missed about her. She'd always been able to get him down from his tree.

But this time, even Delores would've had a time getting him down, because he was mad enough to drive over to the Lazy H and tell Buster Hogan what he really thought of him. He grumbled under his breath, tightened his fingers on the wheel, and jammed his boot down on the accelerator.

The air blasting in through the open windows made his wet pants feel especially cool; but he told himself that when you were getting slapped with a lawsuit, a lap full of beer was just one more annoyance. Buck scowled and made a mental note to never visit that redheaded woman's place again. He went to a restaurant for food, not drama.

He glanced down at his trousers. They were still damp, and he could count on it that somebody in the house would see him before he could get upstairs and change.

That was one of the drawbacks of having six brothers, and living in the same place with five. You couldn't get anything by them.

The ranch house loomed up ahead as he drove. It looked like a resort clubhouse, and Buck stared at it in distaste. If it'd been up to him, they'd have a big, plain clapboard house like God had intended ranchers to build, but Delores had flown in some Italian designer who'd worked his last nerve and built them a hotel.

The main house was a three-story stone building with a mostly glass front, complete with a big wooden door that had been carved someplace in Germany, a paved courtyard, and a fountain with two naked cherubs that he was going to tear down when he could get around to it. Someday he was gonna have the whole thing changed back to look like it belonged in Texas; but now he had to drop everything else he was doing to protect their access to water.

Buck pulled the truck up in front of the house so short and sharp that the tires squealed, and he yanked the keys out of the ignition and burst out of the truck. He crossed the courtyard, blew through the front door, and was halfway across the atrium when a laughing, relaxed voice called, "Well, Buck! Did you forget to close the windows in the car wash?"

"Zip it," he grumbled, and turned to glare at his smiling brother Carson. That day, Carson looked like a member of the Rat Pack with his dark, slicked back hair, his tailored shirt and jacket, and his creased trousers.

"I'm not in the mood today," Buck warned his urbane brother. "And I've got a job for you. Buster Hogan is trying to steal our water, and I need you to find our rights agreement and send it to Eugene."

A gold watch flashed on Carson's arm as he lifted a glass to his lips. "You have to say one thing for Buster. He's consistent," he mumbled into his drink.

"He's a throbbing pain," Buck growled and headed for the main staircase, just beyond the marble-tiled foyer. "Just get those papers to Eugene. Where's Morgan?"

"Where is he usually?" Carson took another drink, and he grinned as Buck turned on the stair to glare at him. "Out on the back forty, playing cowboy."

"I'm gonna tell him to have our hands ride guard all along the river," Buck growled. "I don't put it past that crook to cut the fence and drive his stock over our property line!"

Carson's amused eyes flicked over his trousers. "Looks like we still have some water left, anyway."

Buck scowled and turned to stomp up the stairs. "I got a pitcher of beer poured down my pants by the woman who runs that new steakhouse," he grumbled. "Just one more thing to go bad today! Well, I'll never darken that woman's door again, that's for sure."

Carson threw his head back and shouted with laughter, and his dancing eyes gleamed over the rim of his glass. "I was wondering what had happened!"

Buck paused again with his hand on the stair rail. "Mind your own business, Carson."

"Temper," Carson chuckled, but Buck didn't stay to talk with him. He jogged two flights of stairs, gained the topmost hall, made a sharp left, and stomped all the way down to a heavy door on the end.

It was the door to the master suite of the house, and it belonged to him.

Buck threw the door open, and a huge, high-ceilinged great room opened up before him. Three wrought-iron chandeliers hung from that ceiling, each ten feet across; and 250,000 acres of Texas river valley stretched out beyond, because the entire southern wall was made of glass.

Buck walked over to a polished wooden bar, poured himself a glass of whiskey, and drifted over to the window to gaze out over that blue-green vista. Endless meadows rolled away to the horizon, punctuated now and then by stands of oak and mesquite trees.

In the middle distance, a double row of those trees lined the banks of the Big Sandy, their only source of water for 10,000 of the finest Longhorn cattle in Texas. Buck grumbled under his breath, tossed back his drink, and slapped the glass on an antique table.

His cell phone vibrated in his back pocket, and he reached for it.

"Yeah."

Eugene's dry voice swam up to him through a babel of background voices and the tinkling of a piano. "You missed a great meal, Buck," he said. "I just enjoyed the best porterhouse I've had in years."

Buck's nerves prickled in annoyance. "You can have it," he barked. "Are you still over there?"

"I figured since I was here, I might as well enjoy my lunch," his attorney drawled.

Buck bowed his head and kicked at the floor. "Look, Eugene, I'm sorry for stomping out on you," he mumbled.

Eugene's tone was resigned. "It's all right, Buck. We've known each other for years now. I can't claim to be surprised."

"Just call me an idiot and be done with it, Eugene," Buck sputtered. "You are going to come over and spend the night with us, aren't you?"

There was a soft *clink* on the other end, and Eugene's voice murmured, "That's enough, thank you," before it turned back to him and added, "I'd like to, but I have to be back in Dallas tonight. I have to meet a client at seven in the morning. One of those lean and hungry heathens who likes to talk business over breakfast, heaven help me."

Buck chuckled and shook his head. "I'll send Carson down to Dallas next week with the papers," he promised. "You need anything else from us?"

"The original contract is the main thing, but you know I'll take everything I can get," Eugene told him.

Buck narrowed his eyes. "Since you're still there, Eugene, remind me. What's the name of that woman who dumped beer over me?"

"Kate Malone," his friend murmured gently. "The owner of the restaurant. Lovely woman."

"Really!" Buck snorted. "You saw what she did to me!"

"Yes," Eugene murmured. "I saw how you treated her, too. You know you're short with people when you get stirred up, Buck. She's not the only one around here who's got a wildcat temper."

Buck rubbed the back of his neck, and his ire cooled down a bit. "Well…"

Eugene laughed softly. "Send Carson down to my office next week, and we'll get this thing with Buster straightened out. I'll talk to you later, Buck. I have to be going if I want to get back home by nightfall."

"Thanks for coming, Eugene. Come back when you can," Buck told him and added dryly, "I'll try to be fit for company next time."

"That'll be the day," Eugene sputtered, and the line went dead.

Chapter 4

"Night, Kate."

Kate stretched to work the kink out of her back and called, "Night, Roxanne. Thanks for staying behind to help me get the place buttoned up."

"Sure, I got you. And I need the money," she added dryly. "See you tomorrow."

Kate watched as her head waitress walked out of the restaurant. The keys clanked in the door as she locked it behind her, and Kate turned and walked from the greeter's lectern in the foyer, past the kitchen door, to the dark, empty main dining room. All the tables were clean and bare and topped with upside down chairs. The parking lot lights threw ghostly white blocks across the wooden floor, and Kate felt almost like a ghost herself as she crossed the deserted space to the industrial staircase. She unhooked the little rope that blocked it off and climbed the wooden steps to her loft apartment on the second floor.

She walked the length of the upper hall, past the brick wall covered with antique rodeo posters and local artwork. That walkway was open to the first floor, and from the top she could see the whole of the main dining room below.

Kate unlocked her apartment door, and homey golden light flooded out. She smiled and called, "Molly, Mommy's home!" She kicked off her heels, set her bag down on the little table beside the front door, and walked out to the living room.

The red brick walls were bare except for a few striking pieces of modern art, but the ceiling-high warehouse windows were covered with cloth blinds. Kate glanced at them and sighed. She loved big, bare windows, but she'd covered theirs up for the sake of family privacy.

Kate flopped down on the long, low couch and flicked on the remote. The wall-mounted television flicked on and had no sooner started to mumble than her daughter Molly came running into the room.

Kate held out her arms, and her six-year-old daughter climbed into them and snuggled against her. Kate stroked Molly's auburn hair absently as she watched a rerun of the late-night news. The story was about something in Colorado, and the screen behind the announcer displayed the Rockies.

"Look, baby," Kate murmured. "It's Colorado."

Molly turned just enough to glance at the screen. "I wish we were still there," she pouted. "I miss the mountains. I miss my friends."

"Aww," Kate murmured, and gave her daughter's smooth cheek a kiss. "We'll make new ones here. You're going to love Texas. It's where Daddy's family is from."

Molly grew still. "I miss Daddy," she whispered sadly.

Kate hugged Molly close and murmured, "I do, too, baby. But this is where your father grew up. He loved this town. I feel specially close to him here."

She pulled back from Molly's unhappy face and added, "It's way past your bedtime, chickadee. Are you ready to say your night prayers?"

Molly nodded silently, and Kate sat up and juggled her daughter in her arms. "All right then. Close your eyes." She watched in indulgent affection as her little daughter squeezed her freckled face into a knot and clasped her hands together.

"Now I lay me down to sleep, I pray the Lord my soul to keep, if I should die before I wake, I pray the Lord my soul to take," Molly murmured.

"Amen," Kate smiled and gave her a peck on the cheek. "Run and change into your pajamas. I'll be there in a minute to tuck you in. Run on."

She watched as Molly clambered out of her arms and trotted off to her bedroom. When her daughter had disappeared, the smile faded off Kate's face, and she rolled her head back on the couch and stared up at the warehouse ceiling, twenty feet overhead.

She didn't see open duct work and metal sheeting. She saw Kevin's tanned face and sharp brown eyes. Her husband had been a handsome man, a great doctor, a wonderful husband, and a tender father.

Why do the best things never last? she wondered sadly. It was the only prayer she had the energy for that night, and she forced herself up off the couch and went to tuck her daughter into bed.

Kate walked down the side hall to her daughter's bedroom and poked her head in. "Are you in bed, Molly?"

Her daughter's head raised up off her pillow, and Kate smiled and slipped into the dark room. "All right then." She sat down on the side of the bed, tucked the quilt up under Molly's chin, and leaned down to kiss her. "I'm proud of you, Molly," she whispered. "You're a smart, strong girl. Sleep tight, sweetheart."

"Night-night, Mamma."

Kate brushed her daughter's silky hair back from her brow and slipped out of the room. She padded down the hall to her own bedroom, then shut the door wearily.

Her own bedroom had potted plants lining the red brick walls and a big clay fountain whose soft trickle of water soothed her to sleep every night. Her bed was a stark, simple, Swedish canopy bed piled high with faux fur pillows, and a huge Lichtenstein with a cartoon blonde hung on the wall behind it.

Kate sighed and changed out of her dress into a silky pink, floor-length nightgown, then clicked off the light with a remote. The room went dark, and she turned to climb into bed; but a flash of light through the blinds made her frown and drift toward the window instead. Her bedroom window overlooked the back parking lot of the restaurant, and it was late.

No one should be out there at that hour.

Kate walked to the window and pulled one of the blinds aside. The security lights showed the lot clearly. There were two cars in it with only their parking lights on.

Kate frowned. She didn't like random people in her back yard after midnight, but anyone could pull into the restaurant parking lot. It could be people turning around, or people who were lost and asking directions, or…

She narrowed her eyes, because the two cars were pulled even with one another, and the drivers were talking to each other through the open windows. She couldn't see who they were, but she didn't expect to know them.

That better not be a drug deal, she frowned; but the thought had no sooner crossed her mind than the headlights came on and the cars pulled out of the lot. She watched as they drove off into the darkness, the first in one direction, and the second in the other.

Kate stood there until the lights faded into the distance and disappeared. She let the blind fall back into place, then sought her own rest, thinking:

It was probably nothing.

She walked to her bed and tossed back the down-filled coverlet. She slipped in, set her alarm, and snuggled into the pillow. A dozen memories of the day swirled in her mind as she settled in, but one stuck out above all the others.

The memory of Buck Spade's outraged blue eyes as ice-cold beer soaked his lap; and Kate giggled softly to herself as she slowly drifted off to   sleep.

Chapter 5

The next afternoon Kate raised her hands in a calming gesture and glanced from her furious head waitress Roxanne, to her furious head chef, Sebastian Claude. They were in the restaurant kitchen, and she was trying to defuse a fight before the customers in the dining room noticed the shouting.

"I told him that the order was wrong and the customer sent it back," Roxanne cried. Her eyes were blazing with fury, and she turned to point an accusatory finger at the chef. "He said that it was better *his* way and wouldn't fix it!"

Kate's eyes moved from Roxanne to Sebastian. Sebastian was an inspired chef, but she was quickly learning that he was also a prima donna.

"It wasn't a mistake. It didn't need to be *fixed*!" he yelled, and threw a pot down on the counter with a shattering *clang*. "Filet mignon is *supposed* to be served rare. It's not my fault if the customer was too stupid to know it!"

"You're supposed to cook it like *they* want!" Roxanne shot back, and Kate stepped in and put a calming hand on her shoulder.

"It's all right, Roxanne," she murmured, and her aggrieved waitress turned to appeal to her.

"But the customer got mad and walked out!"

"It's all right," she whispered, and the girl huffed and stalked out of the kitchen. Kate watched her go, then turned to the chef. He was a tall man with dark hair slicked back from a high forehead, and his needle-sharp eyes challenged her as she approached him.

"Sebastian, why don't we take a few minutes to talk," Kate suggested. She was trying to keep her tone light, but she was struggling to keep her temper under control. Her new chef was good, but he wasn't so good that she could afford to lose customers because of him.

Sebastian crossed his arms and looked away. "I suppose you're going to tell me I have to follow orders like a slave," he complained. "What's the point of getting my expertise if you don't use it?"

Kate wrestled with herself, then replied evenly: "I know that you used to work at a cutting-edge restaurant, and that had to be exciting," she began. "But this isn't Austin, Sebastian. This is a small town, and the people here have conservative tastes." She raised an eyebrow and continued, "Believe me, I understand that you miss Austin. I miss Denver. I miss the open-mindedness and the sense of adventure." She paused and sighed, then forged on: "But I understand that to be successful, I have to give our customers what *they* want, not what I might want."

She raised her gaze to Sebastian's face and stared him dead in the eye. "I expect *you* to understand that, too."

His eyes blared with anger. "Fine," he snapped, "I'll stamp out these steaks on an assembly line if that's what you want. No nuance, no artistry.

Bland, boring, *conservative*!" He slapped a pan across the stove with a *bang*.

Kate bit her lip and looked down at her tightly-clasped hands. "Thank you, Sebastian," she replied softly. "I know I can count on you to be a team player."

She turned on the words and walked out, but the sound of slamming and banging followed her until the kitchen door swung shut behind her.

Roxanne met her in the hall outside and hissed, "I hope you fire that idiot. He shouted at Trisha this morning, and she ran out in tears. He's a—"

"I'll deal with it, Roxanne," Kate assured her evenly. "Sebastian is brand new in this job, and Sandy Creek's a big change from what he's used to. It's an adjustment. I'm sure he'll settle down."

"He better," Roxanne growled, and stalked off.

Kate watched her go in consternation, then put a hand to her brow. They were only thirty minutes into lunch, and already she had a throbbing headache.

She returned to the hostess station in the foyer and busied herself at the little computer console. When she looked up again, to her surprise, there was a man standing there.

He was smiling at her.

"Welcome to Stonehouse," she said brightly, and pasted on as welcoming a smile as she could muster on a trying day. She glanced past his shoulder, but the foyer beyond was empty. "Table for one?"

"For two, I hope," he replied smoothly, and flashed a set of beautiful white teeth. Kate raised an eyebrow. The fellow was exceptionally good-looking, tall and dark and slick and smiling and very nicely dressed. Her eyes flicked to his wrist. He was wearing a Rolex.

And unless she was much mistaken, he was flirting with her. She smiled and looked a question, and he laughed and took her elbow as smoothly as if they'd known one another for years. She pulled it out of his grasp just as pleasantly.

"I was hoping you'd have lunch with me," he told her. "My name's Carson Spade. I hear my brother was less than polite when he was here yesterday. I'd hate for you to think that all the Spades are Philistines."

Kate smiled in spite of herself. She had to admit, Carson Spade was a smooth talker, and he was making himself as pleasant as Buck had been rough.

She was tempted to take him up on his offer, if only out of curiosity.

"Oh, it's all right," she replied softly. "I'm not angry. I always give as good as I get. Your brother and I understand one another now."

He nodded and laughed. "Yes, you do," he agreed. "But you have to have lunch with me, I insist." He turned laughing blue eyes on hers, and Kate's mouth curled up in a smile.

"All right," she murmured. Carson Spade looked like he'd just stepped off the cover of *GQ*, and she had to admit, having lunch with a handsome man was a welcome prospect after such a difficult morning.

"Good," Carson beamed, and took her elbow again. As they turned toward the dining room he leaned in to give her cheek a quick, light peck. It was over so quickly that Kate felt she had no choice but to be gracious.

Not that it was hard to be gracious.

He piloted her to a cozy, secluded table in an empty corner of the dining room. Carson pulled out a chair for her, and Kate slid in behind the little table.

He settled in opposite her and smiled big. "Well! What's good today, Kate?"

She propped her elbows on the table, laced her fingers together, and smiled at him over them. "The filet mignon, if you like it rare," she drawled.

"*Mmm*," he growled, "That sounds perfect! Shall we make it two?" Carson glanced over his shoulder for a waiter, but Roxanne was already at his elbow, smiling big and pretty.

Kate pulled her mouth to one side. Roxanne's goofy giggle and dazzled look meant that she knew exactly who Carson was. Every other diner in the place was staring at them, too. It looked like she and her handsome companion had just made a bit of local news. Kate caught the eye of a gaping older woman and winked at her.

"What would you like to drink, pretty lady?"

Kate turned back to see Carson's amused eyes on her. "Tea for me," she murmured, and Roxanne giggled again and went bustling back to the kitchen. She had no sooner disappeared than Molly came hurrying through the dining room to their table. Molly had the run of the restaurant most days, and Kate reached out and pulled her daughter to her side.

"Well, is this young lady yours?" Carson twinkled, and Kate turned to Molly and smoothed her silky hair.

"Yes, this is my daughter Molly," Kate told him proudly. "She helps me run the restaurant."

"It's a pleasure Miss Molly," Carson smiled, and Kate noticed wryly that even her six-year-old daughter seemed fascinated by Carson's beautiful smile.

"Hello," she dimpled, and swayed back and forth with her finger in her mouth.

"My name's Carson." Carson stuck his hand out, and Molly shook it shyly.

Carson turned to her. "You know, we have a whole stable full of ponies," he told her brightly. "Why don't you two come out to the Seven tomorrow and let Miss Molly ride one?"

"Oh, I don't think—" Kate began, but when she glanced at Molly, the hopeful look in her daughter's eyes made her voice trail off into silence. Molly had been a little blue and lonely since they moved to Sandy Creek; and of course she was missing her father.

It might not be a bad idea to take Molly on a fun outing, even if it was to the Seven Spades Ranch. Carson promised to be a gracious host, and as long as she didn't run into his surly brother, she had no objection. Carson seemed to read the thought right off her face.

"If Buck shows up, I'll punch him in the nose," he told her with a wink and a grin. Molly giggled, and Kate joined in spite of herself.

"All right," she smiled. "And thank you, Carson. It's very gracious of you to make the gesture."

"Oh, it's my pleasure," he assured her warmly, and leaned back to let Roxanne lean down and place a fragrant, sizzling steak on the table in front of him. Kate watched as Roxanne came over to set another platter in front of her; and once her back was to Carson, Roxanne shot her a goggling look over her shoulder that said, *Girrrlll, you go,* as plain as any words.

Kate almost burst out laughing at Roxanne's silly expression, but she controlled herself and shook out her napkin. She turned to her daughter and murmured, "Do you want me to make you a plate, Molly?"

Molly shook her head. "No, Mamma. I don't like steak. I had a peanut butter and jelly sandwich. I just came by to say hello."

Kate's heart melted as she gazed into her daughter's sweet, freckled face, and she leaned over to give her a peck on the cheek; but she didn't have a chance to do more, because Molly skipped away and disappeared through the crowd.

"Molly's a cute little girl," Carson observed, and took a sip of coffee. "She's very pretty.

"Just like her mother."

Kate raised a tawny eyebrow and buried her reply in her tea glass, because Carson's beautiful eyes were on her. They were a deep sapphire blue, with thick, short lashes, and she glanced away to keep from getting snared by them.

You sure are a smooth one, Carson Spade, she thought wryly, *but that's all right. You look like a lot of fun.*

And I could use some.

Chapter 6

Buck rubbed his horse's neck and gazed out across the westernmost range of the Seven range. The low hills rolling off to the horizon were dotted with hundreds of brown and white Longhorn cattle, surrounded by faster-moving riders on horses. One of them was his brother Morgan, and even from a distance, Buck could tell which one.

Morgan always wore a black Stetson, he was on a beautiful black quarter horse, and he was a head taller than any of their hands.

"Come on, Ajax," Buck murmured, and asked the horse forwards. The big dun trotted down the low hill and off toward the other figures moving across the distant grassland. The riders were herding the cattle down to the river to drink, and Buck nudged his horse again, because they were moving away from him.

Buck glanced up. The sky was a beautiful deep blue, with billowing white clouds sailing high overhead; but it was barely ten in the morning and already blazing hot. The grass was dry and sparser than it had been in years, and they were having to supplement their cattle with more feed than ever before.

The whole county had been baking in a punishing drought, and Buck's bright eyes crinkled up as he grimaced up at the sky. There were plenty of clouds, but none of them were rain clouds; and that made the water in the Big Sandy more important than ever.

One of the riders looked up, wheeled around, and came riding out to meet him. Buck urged his horse into a trot and called, "How are they looking?"

His brother Morgan looked like an Old West gunslinger as he came riding closer. His eyes were shadowed by his cowboy hat, and only his dark shoulder-length hair, fierce moustache, spade beard, and stubborn chin were visible under it. He was wearing a white shirt, black vest, and battered jeans, and his horse was a magnificent black stallion with a flowing mane.

"I don't like it," Morgan's gravelly voice called back. "They're getting the water they need for now, but the river's low. If it gets any lower, we're going to have to start shipping water in on trucks."

Buck pulled his horse up as Morgan came riding to meet him. "They look a little thinner to me," he observed, and scanned the cattle slowly moving down to the river. "They're getting less forage. We're going to have to up their feed."

"Yep. More money," Morgan agreed glumly. "And some of the cows are starting to get dehydrated. They're producing less milk for their calves. We're going to have to cut them out and make sure they go to the head of the line for water."

Anger bubbled in Buck's blood when he thought of that. He set his jaw and demanded, "Any sign of stealing? Any broken line?"

Morgan stared down at his gloved hands, crossed over the pommel of his saddle. "Well, now that you mention it, Buck—"

The anger bubbling in Buck exploded as suddenly as a scalding blast from a caldera. "I knew it!" he cried, "Buster's sending his stock over the line to get our water! Where?"

"The fence's been cut down on the border with the Lazy H," Morgan rumbled. "The grass has been tramped down all the way to the river, and there's hundreds of hoof prints stretching a half-mile on the western bank. It's fresh. I'd say last night, or night before."

"I want trail cameras put down there every hundred feet," Buck replied tightly, "and a bunch of hands with Winchesters standing guard! You tell them, they see cattle coming across that line, they blast 'em!"

He turned his horse's head around and urged the horse forwards, and it bounded off like a rocket. Morgan's deep voice called after him, followed by the sound of following hoof beats.

"Buck! Buck, hold up!"

Buck growled and slowed his horse down long enough for Morgan to catch up with him. He glared at his brother as he urged his own mount up beside him. Morgan's shadowed face turned toward him, and his tone was sharp.

"Where you going?"

Buck's face twisted in fury. "I'm going straight over to the Lazy H for Buster Hogan!" he roared. He jabbed an angry finger back toward the herd of cattle drinking at the river. "Here we are, barely able to keep our own cows watered, and talking about having to ship water in on trucks. And he thinks he's going to just waltz in and gobble up our water and get away scot free? I'm going to show him what we do with thieves!"

"We don't have proof it was Buster, Buck," Morgan replied sharply, and urged his own stallion to move in front of Ajax. Buck stopped his own horse and spat, "Get out of my way, Morgan! We let that sneaking scum get away with it this time, he'll just keep coming back, and then where will we be? Buster only understands one thing, and that's what he's going to get!"

He urged his horse forwards again, and it took off flying. Fury was so hot in him that the only relief he could imagine was ramming his fist into Buster's chin, and then kicking his fat bottom to the moon. He could hear Morgan riding after him and calling for him to stop, but he wasn't going to let anybody stop him.

If they had to call Eugene to come bail him out of jail, that was all right with him; but nobody was going to steal their water and get away with it while he was running the show.

Get ready Buster, he fumed to himself, *you thieving snake.*

I'm coming for you!

Chapter 7

"Look, Mommy, I'm riding a pony!"

Molly laughed and waved from atop a fat, docile pony as it slowly walked in a circle around a little outdoor ring. Molly looked cute as a button in her little pink riding helmet and pink tee shirt, and Kate felt a bloom of affection as she waved back.

"I see you, baby. You're doing great!"

Kate was leaning against the gate, and she glanced back over her shoulder and murmured, "Thank you for inviting us here, Carson. Molly's having such a good time."

Carson flashed a big, bright smile. "I'm glad you could come. Are you in the mood for a ride yourself after lunch? You can't really appreciate the Seven unless you see it on horseback."

Kate shaded her eyes and glanced out beyond him. She had to agree: it was hard to grasp just how big the Seven Ranch was until you saw it for yourself. Carson had brought them out to the pony ring, but it was only one corner of a huge complex of beautiful horse stables, riding and training rings, barns, and outbuildings. The area was lightly wooded, and trees and buildings partly blocked her view of the land beyond, but Carson had told her that the main ranch house was over a mile away, and she couldn't even see it.

He'd also told her that the horses were only a sideline for them. That their main business was cattle. She couldn't see any of them, either.

Kate gazed off into the horizon, far off to the west. Its farthest point was still part of the ranch; and she had to admit, she was beginning to understand Roxanne's awe a little better.

"That would be lovely," she smiled. "It's been over a year since I've been on a horse. I've missed riding."

"We'll have to get you back in the saddle, then," Carson smiled. "Are you hungry?"

Kate glanced away in embarrassment, because she was, but she didn't like to admit it. "I could eat something," she admitted.

"Well, why don't we let Molly ride her pony, and we can go up to the house for a bite of lunch. She should be finished by the time we get back, and then you and I can go for a ride. I'll show you the ranch."

"I'd like that." Kate turned to watch Molly urge the pony into a sluggish trot, then guide it up to the gate. She slid down off the pony's back, then clambered up onto the fence.

"I like riding horses," Molly informed her. "I'd like to come back and ride again!"

"Well, that settles that," Carson told her, mock-serious. "You have to sign Molly up for a class. We host a group that runs a program for children."

Kate glanced at him, then back at Molly's happy face. "Molly, would you like to learn how to ride horses?"

Molly nodded vigorously, and Kate laughed, "It's settled then." She reached up to pinch Molly's nose. "Would you like to ride the pony a little while longer, while Mamma and Carson talk for a while?"

Molly's face brightened. "Can I?"

"Just be careful," Kate warned, because Molly was already clambering down from the gate. "Keep your helmet on!"

Carson laughed and took her arm. "Come on, Mamma," he teased, with a twinkle in his eye. "Baby is going to be fine."

Kate sighed as Molly pulled herself up onto the pony. *She's growing so fast,* she thought wistfully. *She's getting to love the outdoors.*

Just like Kevin.

"Come on."

Kate turned back to Carson, smiled weakly, and followed him back to his car. A gleaming silver Jaguar was parked on the gravel drive outside the complex, and Carson opened the door for her.

Kate slid into the buttery soft leather seats and inhaled. Carson's Jag had that lovely, new-car smell, and the console was dark polished wood punctuated by blue electronic displays.

Carson slid into the driver's seat and cranked the car. The engine turned over with a barely perceptible purr, and he sent it scratching off across the gravel and back to the long, main drive to the main house.

Kate gazed out over the equestrian complex as the car turned onto the main drive. The neat, gabled, well-tended barns and stables reminded her of Kentucky, and she caught a glimpse of sleek, gleaming horses being led around a ring by handlers.

"I was told that you raise racehorses," she murmured as she watched them.

Carson nodded. "We do indeed. I'll show you when you come back. One of our horses won the Breeder's Cup last season."

Kate turned to smile at him. "Really?"

Carson nodded. "Beautiful chestnut we sold to a Kentucky racing family. Jazz Cat."

"Oh, I remember," Kate breathed.

Carson turned to her, and his beautiful eyes twinkled. "The horses are my line," he told her. "I run our racing stock. Most of my brothers work the ranch, but I got the glamor job. "

Kate's lips curled up. "Why am I not surprised, Carson?"

He grinned at her and switched gears with a flick of his wrist, and the Jaguar growled and found a new burst of speed. Kate watched as the low, rolling countryside sped past. Green meadows rolled off to the horizon, broken only by an occasional line of trees. The Seven Spades was a beautiful ranch, and Kate had to admit, if only to herself, that she was a bit awed at the scale of it. It was the biggest chunk of private property she'd ever seen in her life, and it boggled her mind to imagine how much money it probably took to maintain it.

When she turned her attention back to the road ahead, she noticed a huge building in the distance, what looked to her like a resort or a hotel; but Carson pointed toward it and murmured, "There it is. Home sweet home."

Kate had to press her lips together to keep her mouth from dropping open, because as they approached, its glittering glass facade and towering stone walls reared up almost to the sky. She'd seen smaller museums.

She turned to Carson in disbelief, and he grinned and shrugged. "Don't look at me," he teased. "Buck's wife was the one who ordered it."

Kate inhaled as sharply if she'd been slapped. She had no idea why, but she was just curious enough to ask, "Buck's wife?"

For once, the amused look faded from Carson's eyes. He sobered a bit and replied, "Yes. Delores died of cancer two years ago. She and Buck were very close. He hasn't been the same since."

"Oh." Kate turned her eyes back to the passenger window, because now she felt a tiny bit guilty about dumping beer into Buck's lap. In light of this new information, she couldn't help feeling sympathy for him, even though he'd been insufferable.

She knew what it was to lose someone dear.

She turned to Carson. "Pardon me for asking, but—has anyone suggested grief therapy?"

To her consternation, Carson threw his head back and laughed. She frowned as he sputtered, "I'm sorry, but you'd have to know Buck. He wouldn't go to therapy if he was dying."

"That's a shame," she replied evenly. "It helped me a great deal after my husband died."

Carson shot her a rueful look, then reached for the console. "How about some music?" he muttered, and flicked on the radio.

After a few minutes the Jaguar pulled up smoothly in the paved courtyard of the main house, but to Kate's surprise, there was another car parked in front of the door. It was a brand-new olive-green Hummer, and a very unhappy-looking man was standing in the open driver's side door.

Carson frowned as he pulled the Jaguar to a gentle stop. "Excuse me, Kate," he murmured. "I have to talk to this guy. I'll be back in a minute."

"Certainly."

She watched curiously as Carson stepped out of the car, closed the door behind him, and walked slowly toward the other man. She couldn't hear what was going on, but Carson's wary approach and stiff body language, and the other man's scowling expression, told her that it wasn't a friendly meeting. She struggled with her conscience for an instant, then bit her lip and pressed the passenger side window button. The window rolled down silently, and she heard Carson call out:

"You better get out of here while you can. If Buck catches you here you'll be sorry you stayed."

She frowned as the other man pushed off of his car door and came ambling up to Carson. He was middle-aged and balding, had an unremarkable face and was only average height. But he was dressed like a cowboy, and he was built as hard and compact and solid as a rock. His tilted jaw and narrowed eyes suggested that a fight might be coming, and Kate straightened up in alarm.

"I'm here because my hands are telling me that they're getting threatened by the Seven hands," he replied angrily. "You better tell your hired help to back off if you want to keep 'em!"

Carson crossed his arms. "Or what, Buster? Are you saying you're going to kill our hands, or just thrash them? Our lawyer likes things precisely defined."

"Laugh it off then," the other man replied softly. "You won't be laughing long, pretty boy." He turned away, then turned back suddenly and added:

"You tell that brother of yours that he ain't the king of the world," he spat, "and he better stop acting like it!"

Carson's eyes flicked to a point just beyond him. He leaned back and drawled: "Why don't you tell him yourself, Buster. Here he comes."

Kate followed his gaze. A man on horseback had just ridden up, and he was down off its back so fast that he was only a dark blur. The stranger barely had time to turn around to face him before the blur resolved into a furious Buck Spade, and he stomped up to the stranger with his fists clenched.

"Throw down, Buster, you thieving snake," he roared. "If you've got the guts to fight!"

Kate's eye snapped to a fourth man. He galloped up on horseback, threw himself down, and lunged for Buck. He clamped his arms around Buck's and held them down.

"Calm down, Buck!" he grunted. "This is what he wants. He's trying to make you do something crazy so he'll win his lawsuit!"

"Too late," Carson murmured, and rubbed his nose.

The stranger's face twisted, and he took a wild swing at Buck's jaw. Buck hooked his foot under the other man's boot, jerked it sharply, and sent him sprawling on the ground before the fourth man dragged Buck out of his reach.

"Buck, have you lost your mind?" he hissed fiercely; but Buck didn't seem to hear him. He jabbed a finger at his gasping adversary and yelled, "You get off this ranch if you don't want me to put my boot—"

"Buck!"

The other man clamped Buck's arms down again, and with a mighty heave, yanked him around and dragged him off to the house. Buck threw him off, and glanced back at Buster for one parting shot.

"You send any more cattle across our fence line, and we'll shoot 'em!"

The other man shoved Buck through the front door, and Kate could hear more shouting from inside the house. She rolled her eyes back to the stranger. His mouth was bleeding, and he wiped it with the back of his hand as she stared.

He pulled himself up to his full height, squared his shoulders, and shot Carson a bloody smile.

"See what that lawyer of yours tells you now," he gasped, and limped off to the Hummer. He climbed in, slammed the door shut, gunned the motor, and roared off in a cloud of exhaust.

Carson sighed, turned around, and came walking back to the car. Kate snapped back to herself and hurriedly rolled the window up just before he opened the door.

He leaned down and smiled at her apologetically. "Sorry about that," he murmured. "I hope it hasn't affected your appetite.

"Shall we go have some lunch?"

Chapter 8

"Thank you, Conchita."

Carson shook out a napkin and glanced up as a smiling older woman placed a massive platter of *huevos rancheros* down on the glass tabletop.

Kate glanced over her shoulder. They were sitting on a paved patio overlooking a massive pool. The water was a serene, Caribbean blue, and flecks of light danced off its tranquil surface as a slight breeze flowed in off the meadows beyond.

A trellis covered with trailing vines and flowers shielded them from the sun, and a cheerful bouquet of bluebonnets brightened the table. Kate took a sip of tea and murmured:

"I don't like to pry, but—what on earth did I just watch?"

Carson grinned and nodded. He glanced up at her with a mischievous gleam in his bright eyes.

"What you saw is the latest chapter in the running feud between the Seven and the Lazy H," he replied briskly, and made her a generous plate. He handed it to her with a smile and added, "The guy Buck almost slugged is Buster Hogan. He's the owner of the Lazy H."

Kate frowned at him. "So there's some kind of dispute between your two ranches?"

"You could call it that," Carson drawled. "Buster's stealing our water."

Kate shot him a startled look. "So…that's why your brother is so furious with him?"

Carson gave her a dry look. "Yes. That would do it," he replied. He took a bite of steak and shook his head. "Buster's suing us for the rights to our biggest source of water. If he wins, we'll go out of business. We won't be able to water our cattle."

Kate stared at him in dismay, but he grinned at her. "Lucky for us he forged his claim. Buster's a cheat and a born liar, and he and Buck have hated each other since they were kids."

"I see," she replied faintly. "Does he…come over here often?"

Carson sputtered. "Hardly. You saw what nearly happened to him this time." He shook his head. "No, this was strategy. Buster knows he doesn't have a case, so he came over here to pull Buck's nose. It almost worked. Buck has the temper of a wildcat, and he almost did what Buster hoped he'd do. If it had worked, poor Eugene would've had to come and bail Buck out of jail when Buster lodged an assault complaint." He chewed his food and stared past her.

Kate raised an eyebrow. "Is your brother in jail often?" she drawled, and Carson laughed again.

"Buck's doing a lot better," he replied, and took a sip of coffee. "Only two times this year."

Kate shot him a startled glance, but after what she'd seen that morning, she couldn't tell whether he was joking or not.

The conversation flagged for a few moments as they enjoyed their meal, and Kate allowed herself to relax and enjoy the shaded patio, the flower-scented breeze, and the glittering water. The huge wall of the house stretched out just behind Carson, down the western side of the pool, and beyond. It was solid glass, with a massive sliding glass door, and so she could see the interior clearly. There was a huge lounge room inside with a big stone fireplace, several long, low gray couches and red chairs. When she first glanced, it was empty, but when she looked up the second time, to her alarm, Buck was standing in it, and the other man followed him into the room.

She watched, her fork frozen halfway to her mouth, as Buck slid the big glass door aside and came striding out to the poolside. The other man called to him from inside the house.

"Take a dip, Buck. Cool off!"

Kate watched as Buck sighed, sauntered to the edge of the pool, and began to unbutton his white cotton shirt. She got a glimpse of his tanned chest, and she rolled her eyes to Carson's. They were screened by the trellis, and she was sure Buck couldn't see them sitting there.

Carson glanced at her, then at Buck. He blotted his lips with his napkin, then leaned back in his chair and called, "Hello, Buck! I have a guest. Don't put her eyes out."

Kate felt her face going red as Buck looked up, then came walking over with his shirt halfway open. She couldn't help noticing that his chest was broad and chiseled, and to her alarm, it gave her an awkward flutter that she prayed didn't show on her face.

Buck ducked under the fall of vines hanging over the end of the trellis and poked his head in. To Kate's surprise, his face brightened into a beautiful white smile at the sight of her.

"Afternoon, Mrs. Malone," he nodded. He stuck out his hand, and Kate put down her fork and shook it limply.

"Hello again," she said faintly.

He glanced down, as if he was embarrassed, then, his vivid blue eyes found hers again. "I owe you an apology, Mrs. Malone," he told her. "I haven't been fit for company the last few days."

Kate stared up at him in sympathy, remembering what Carson had said about Buck's wife.

"Yes, she knows all about Buster and our legal drama now," Carson observed wryly, and Buck glanced at him with a rueful expression.

Kate gave Buck's hand a reassuring squeeze before releasing it. "I wasn't exactly my best self when we first met, either," she told him. "And please—call me Kate."

Buck's smile deepened. "Kate." He glanced down at Carson, whose answering glare was a pointed, unspoken comment. "Well, I guess I'll let you two enjoy your meal," Buck coughed. "I hope you come back and see us again, Kate."

"I will. I signed my daughter up to take riding lessons here," Kate told him. "We're both looking forward to it."

Buck glanced down at Carson's dry expression, and cleared his throat. "Well. Bye."

"Bye," Carson echoed softly, and applied himself to his food.

Kate watched as Buck sauntered back to the sliding door, glanced at her once over his shoulder, and then disappeared into the house.

Chapter 9

Roxanne leaned against the loading dock wall at the back of the Stonehouse and took a long drag on her cigarette. She blew a quick plume of smoke into the air and turned to the other waitress taking her smoke break.

"Can you believe Kate hasn't been in town for a month, and already she's snagged one of the Spades?" Roxanne sighed wistfully. "It must be nice. Meanwhile, I'm up to my eyeballs in credit card bills and car note payments, and no rich boyfriend in sight."

"Which one of the Spades is Kate with?" the other waitress, Trina, retorted. "I saw her with Buck Spade last week. Then with Carson the other day at lunch."

"Oh, not with Buck," Roxanne assured her, and tapped ashes onto the concrete deck. "She hates him. I was surprised to see her with Carson, to be honest. But Kate's open minded."

"You think she's gonna reel him in?"

Roxanne tilted her head, considering. "She's got the looks for it. I wish I had her figure. And her hair."

"Think she colors it?"

Roxanne sputtered smoke into the air. "I hope so, because I'd like to know who does it."

The door to the kitchen opened behind them, and they both turned to see Sebastian's thin, frowning face in the opening. He planted his hands on his hips and called, "If you ladies are finished sucking on your cancer sticks, you might come in and get back to work. It's been twenty minutes, and you only get fifteen."

The door closed behind him with a *bang*, and Roxanne scowled as she threw her cigarette down and ground it with her shoe.

"I hope Kate fires him," she muttered. "Sebastian's a jerk. He acts like a bratty kid."

The other girl straightened up and stretched. "He's always lecturing me about eating animals," she grumbled. "He told me he's a vegan. Can you believe it? He cooks steak all day and doesn't even eat meat."

Roxanne glared at the closed kitchen door. "He used to work at some bougie vegan place in Austin, and he thinks that makes him more evolved than the rest of the world.

"But that's not the worst thing about him," she added in a low voice. She pinched her lips into a hard, straight line. "He's got a sneaky look to him. Shifty eyes. I'd bet a hundred dollars he's stealing from the till or the bar."

"I don't think he drinks," the other girl replied glumly. "He's a health nut."

"He's a royal pain," Roxanne grumbled, as she picked up her handbag and stuffed her pack of cigarettes back into it. "I'm going to start watching him. If I can catch him stealing, we can get rid of him."

"Good hunting, then," the other girl muttered as she opened the door, and they drifted back into the kitchen. Sebastian glared at them from behind the counter and snapped, "About time!"

The other girl shot Sebastian a resentful glance, but Roxanne didn't even look at him as she walked past, and she made a mental note to settle down and control her temper.

Sebastian was doing something he shouldn't around the place, and she wanted him to relax. To think that he was safe. Then, when he least expected it—*wham.*

By the time Roxanne's afternoon break rolled around, she'd given her goal enough thought to break it down into small, attainable steps. If she wanted to get rid of Sebastian, she had to get dirt on him; and he wasn't going to volunteer that information.

She was going to have to dig it up. And that would require a little industrial espionage.

Roxanne glanced through the window in the kitchen door. Sebastian usually took his own lunch at three o'clock, when the lunch rush was over and the dinner rush hadn't yet started. The relief cook took over for an hour, and then Sebastian came back at four.

His lunch and her break just happened to coincide.

Roxanne waited until she saw Sebastian walk out the back door. There was a little picnic area around the side of the building for the employees, and Sebastian ate there every day.

He packed his own lunch, and Roxanne wrinkled her nose to think of what he pulled out of that glossy black lunch box. Something disgusting, she was sure; and it suited him. But her mission that afternoon was to gather more important information about him.

Roxanne slipped through the main hall, past the kitchen door on one side, past the door to the main dining room on the other, and on to the back hall. It turned sharply left and ran just behind the kitchen, and the only doors off of it were the restrooms, the utility closet, and the employee locker room.

Roxanne moved all the way to the end of the little hall, up to the locker room door. She fished the key out of her jeans and slid it into the lock. The door opened with a soft click, and she glanced back over her shoulder, then slipped in.

The room was dark and empty, and Roxanne left the light off as she padded in. A row of big gray lockers lined one wall, each identified only with a number; but she knew which one was Sebastian's.

Roxanne glanced up at the ceiling. She was gambling that the room wasn't monitored with a security camera, but she saw no sign of one, and Kate struck her as the kind of employer who'd put her cameras on the outside doors of the building, not the inside rooms.

She was about to find out, anyway.

She reached up into her hair, pulled out a bobby pin, and pulled it out straight. She moved to Sebastian's locker, slid her improvised pick in, and began to rake the lock. Her pick didn't jiggle the lock open, and she was feeling for the pins when the sudden sound of women's voices in the hall outside made her yank the pick out and move away.

She waited, heart pounding; but the voices turned into the bathroom, and the door slowly closed behind them. Roxanne closed her eyes and sagged back against the lockers in relief, then scratched up her courage and tried again.

Come on, she thought grimly, and raked the lock again, harder and faster this time. The pins rippled under her pick, held, and then rippled again.

There was suddenly a soft *click*, and the lock turned.

Roxanne smiled and opened the locker at once. There was a jacket hanging in the locker, and she pushed it aside to riffle through the other things: a cell phone, a travel guide to Portland, a key ring. Roxanne picked up the travel guide and flipped through it. She raised an eyebrow to see a page turned down to mark the section listing pot shops, but there was nothing else interesting.

She took the jacket and searched the pockets, hoping to find a blunt or some other evidence of drug use, but there was nothing in them except a slip of paper. When she pulled it out, there was nothing on it but a penciled phone number. There wasn't even anything to show whose number it was.

I know that weasel is up to something, she fumed, but she didn't have time to search for more. She glanced at her watch. Her break was almost up, and she didn't want anybody to come looking for her.

Roxanne crammed the slip of paper back into the jacket pocket, closed the locker, and turned the lock. She took a deep breath, stuck the pin into her pocket, and turned for the door. A guilty adrenalin rush was swirling in her veins, her heart was pounding, but nobody had caught her.

Still, she'd come up empty; but she was just getting started. She was sure that if she kept snooping, sooner or later she'd catch Sebastian doing something he could be fired for.

Until then, she had to be patient—and careful. Roxanne pulled her mouth to one side as she moved to the door. There was no telling what Sebastian might do if he caught her spying on him.

She opened the door just a crack and scanned the hall outside. It was empty, and there was no sound or movement or voices; so she slipped out into the hall and turned to go back.

She'd taken two steps away from the door when lightning streaked through her head, followed by a flash of pain, and she felt herself fall on the carpeted floor. The world went gray, and she winked out for a few seconds.

She groaned and lay there, unable to move; and she was there for a long time before the sound of startled voices, and running feet, rushed up to greet her.

Chapter 10

"Are you sure you're alright?"

Kate frowned down at her injured waitress in concern, and she tried to press a wet napkin to her scalp. A small spot in Roxanne's black hair was matted with blood, and a big, ugly knot was forming on the crown on her head. Kate touched the wet compress to the spot as gently as she could, but Roxanne hissed in pain and pulled away.

"I'm sorry," Kate murmured, "I didn't mean to hurt you. But you've got a lump on the back of your head as big as an egg. A cool compress might reduce the swelling a bit."

"Here." Trina's freckled face clouded in concern, and she handed her friend a cup of water and an aspirin. Roxanne reached for them hungrily and downed the pill at one gulp.

"We found this on the floor beside you." Kate picked up an antique feed sign that had been hanging on the hall wall. It was made of metal, but didn't seem heavy enough to cause a lump like the one on Roxanne's head. "It must've worked loose from the wall when you opened the locker room door. I'm so sorry, Roxanne."

A flush of guilt made Kate go hot all over. Her head waitress had been knocked cold, even if only for a few moments, and she felt responsible for the accident. Roxanne's eyes still were a bit bleary and weak, but the more alert she became, the angrier she looked.

Kate was stabbed by the sudden fear that Roxanne might sue her for wrongful injury. She glanced down at the metal sign in her hands and suffered another jab of guilt. She could've sworn that the sign had been securely nailed to the wall, but it *had* fallen down.

They'd helped Roxanne into the kitchen, and she was sitting in a chair, but she suddenly sat up and glanced around the room hungrily. Kate followed her gaze, but she couldn't tell what Roxanne was looking for. The big kitchen was empty except for their startled-looking relief cook, Jose, and them.

"I want to go back to the locker room," Roxanne said abruptly. "I want to see where this sign was hanging."

Kate stared at her in pity and dismay. "Don't you think you should sit still for now?" she asked sympathetically. "You could have a concussion. We won't know until the ambulance arrives."

"I'm not going to the hospital," Roxanne announced, and stood up as quickly as she could.

"What!" Kate stared at her in dismay, then yelped, "Here, let me help you. You might pass out again!"

"I'm all right," Roxanne insisted and pulled out of her grasp. Kate watched in fear as her head waitress rushed out of the kitchen, then she turned to the other girl and hissed, "Go out to the parking lot, Trina. When the ambulance arrives, bring the paramedics through the back door. They can examine Roxanne in here."

Trina stared at her doubtfully. "You heard what she said," she objected, but Kate gave her shoulders a little push.

"Never mind what she said. She's babbling. Run on, now."

Kate turned on the words and hurried out after Roxanne. She found her in the side hall just outside the locker room door. Roxanne had one hand pressed to the back of her head, and she pointed up at the wall above the door with the other.

"Look!" she cried, "See the hole where the sign was hanging? The drywall's been ripped, and the nail isn't even in it any more."

Kate stared at Roxanne in baffled pity, then glanced reluctantly at the oblong hole in the wall where the sign had hung.

"Come back to the kitchen, Roxanne," she murmured in the same voice she used to soothe Molly to sleep. "You need to rest."

"Look at that hole in the drywall!" Roxanne cried angrily. "That sign didn't fall down, it was ripped out!"

"Okay," Kate replied softly. "It was ripped out, you're right. We'll take care of it. But right now, you need to come back to the kitchen."

Her waitress rolled dark, blazing eyes to hers. "Don't you get it?" she barked, and jabbed at the wall with a pointing finger. "This wasn't an accident. Somebody pulled that sign down and hit me over the head with it!"

Kate's mouth dropped open in astonishment, but the faint, distant wail of the ambulance siren made her close it again and take Roxanne gently by the shoulders. "Come on, Roxanne. Come with me."

"I'm telling you," Roxanne objected, but Kate only nodded and walked her down the hall as quickly as she dared. Roxanne was showing signs of delusion.

The poor girl must've been hurt even worse than she thought.

By the time they got back to the kitchen, the paramedics were standing in it, and Trina glanced up gratefully as they walked in. "There she is!"

Kate helped Roxanne to sit down, and the paramedics hurried over and pushed her to one side. Kate watched as they knelt down beside her and began their work.

"Can you tell me what happened?"

Kate looked up. One of the paramedics was holding a clipboard and he clicked a pen and began to write on it.

"Oh…this is my waitress, Roxanne Duchaine," she stammered. "A metal sign fell off the wall and hit her on the back of the head. She was knocked unconscious." She produced the sign, and the big man glanced at it, then scribbled on the clipboard.

Kate set the sign down and glanced over at Roxanne. The paramedics were shining a penlight into her eyes.

"Can you have her bill sent to me?" she whispered. "I'd like to take care of it."

The man's eyes flicked up to hers, then down again. "You'll have to work that out with the hospital, ma'am," he murmured.

Kate glanced back at Roxanne. Two paramedics were helping her to stand, and as she watched, they escorted her through the kitchen and out the back door.

A moment later Sebastian walked back in. He turned to Kate with a frown of confusion.

"What happened?"

"Roxanne had an accident," Kate sighed. "She was hit on the head."

Sebastian raised an eyebrow. "We're short a waitress, then."

Shock wiped a blank across Kate's face, and she pinched her lips into a tight line to restrain the reply that jumped to them. She reached for an apron and tied it around her waist just as Molly walked into the kitchen.

Molly stared up at her face, and worry knitted her smooth brow. "Does this mean I can't go to my riding class tomorrow?" she fretted aloud.

Kate reached out to caress her cheek and mustered a smile. "No, chickadee," she replied softly. "We'll go tomorrow, just like we planned. Upstairs, now. I don't want you running through the restaurant during the dinner rush."

Molly's face brightened, and she skipped out of the kitchen. Kate's own expression lightened as she watched the joy on her daughter's face; then she sighed and made her way out to the dining room for a busy night.

Chapter 11

"I can't do it. I've got plans tomorrow. You're the one who's been dealing with Eugene."

Buck hauled himself up out of the pool, shook water out of his hair, and reached for a towel. He glanced up at Carson. His brother was stretched out on a lounge chair with his long trouser legs crossed and a book in his hands.

"Eugene wants all those legal documents about the water rights, and you're the one who sits on all that stuff," Buck muttered, as he toweled his hair. "I told him you'd bring it to him."

Carson sighed and shook his head. "Without bothering to ask me," he clarified.

Buck glanced up at him. "Why, what have you got to do?" he demanded. "You just monkey around with those horses. They'll keep for a few days."

Carson lowered the book and stared at him over it. He looked as if he was coming up with a really crushing reply, but when he grinned, his brother sputtered and returned to his reading.

"I suppose I can go tomorrow morning," he grumbled at last.

Buck smiled and stood up. He dried off his arms, then rubbed the towel across his back. "Thanks, Carson."

"Mmm."

Buck crossed the patio, pulled the big glass sliding door aside, and walked barefoot through the house. A quick swim had relaxed his muscles and his mood.

He whistled to himself, swiped an apple off a bowl on a table, and munched it as he climbed the stairs to his own suite. He was trying hard not to think about Buster or their water problems for at least one afternoon, and so far he'd been successful.

His blood pressure needed the break.

He breezed into his own apartment, shut the door behind him, then flopped down onto a leather couch and stuck his feet up on a coffee table. It felt good to take a day off for a change. Lately he'd been so busy with their water problems, and meetings with vendors, and potential cattle buyers, and the cattlemen's association, and all the people who wanted a piece of him, that he'd kinda got bogged down in the nuts and bolts of running the ranch.

He needed to raise his head up now and then. Life wasn't all about work; and until Eugene had a chance to look at their documents, there wasn't anything more he could do about Buster's lawsuit anyway.

Buck felt himself getting mad again, and he steered his mind sharply away from that tempting subject. His thoughts drifted past it and on, idly, to this thing and that. Finally, for some reason, his thoughts returned to the pool a couple of days before. To the afternoon Carson had brought Kate Malone out to the house.

He had to admit, seeing her at the house had been kind of a shock. He was surprised Carson had asked her over, but when push came to shove, he wasn't really upset about it.

He'd been pretty rude to Kate when they first met, and it was a relief to get all that straightened out with her.

Buck shook his head and chuckled a bit. *Trust Carson*, he thought wryly. His brother always had a beautiful woman on his arm, so it made sense that when a new one came to town, he'd find her.

And he had to admit, this new woman *was* beautiful. Buck frowned as he munched his apple. Kate Malone had dark, lustrous red hair, pale, creamy skin, and big, clear green eyes.

She was as curvy as any model, and she had a soft, low voice.

Buck finished his apple and tossed it into a wastebasket with a flick of his wrist. Yeah, it stood to reason that Carson would like her. He was even sticking around to give Kate and her daughter horse riding lessons, and the thought of Carson babysitting a six-year-old was downright funny.

Carson wasn't usually the kid type; but maybe Kate was going to make him change his ways.

It's about time some woman roped him, Buck thought, and yawned. *Carson needs to settle down.*

Buck stretched out on the couch, crossed his ankles, and laced his fingers together across his chest. His swim had made him sleepy, and he closed his eyes, smacked his lips, and settled in for a nap.

His mind was still running vaguely on Kate Malone, and he thought, *It'd be nice to have a woman around the place again. The Seven is all roosters and no hens these days.*

Be nice to have a kid, too.

Buck frowned. Him and Delores had wanted kids, but they'd never had any. He adjusted one shoulder, settled more comfortably on the couch, and shut those memories out.

His nerves were shot already.

He cleared his mind to go to sleep, and had almost succeeded when a new thought intruded.

Hey—if Carson's going down to Dallas tomorrow to talk to Eugene, who's going to be here for his company?

Kate said that she signed her daughter up for that riding class. It'd be bad if she came out and there was nobody here to play the host. Carson did invite her, after all.

Buck turned over on the couch and settled in again. *I'm sure Carson'll take care of it, though,* he yawned. *He'll call her and tell her not to expect him.*

Buck sighed and curled up as well as a man his size could, and his mind went dark and blank for a good thirty seconds. *But still.*

Chapter 12

Buck crossed his arms against the metal gate and leaned into it as he watched six-year-old Molly Malone bounce around the ring on ponyback.

"That's the way," he called out. "Nice and easy, now."

The little girl looked up long enough to flash him a gap-toothed grin, and he laughed softly to himself. She was just old enough to start losing her baby teeth, and was cute as a button in her pink helmet, cowgirl jeans and matching pink sneakers.

Kate was standing beside him, and she glanced up at him with a smile. "It was nice of you to stand in for Carson on such short notice," she murmured. "I appreciate it, Buck. Molly's having such a good time."

"Oh, I was proud to do it," he told her easily. "I want you and Molly to enjoy the ranch." A thought occurred to him, and he turned to look down at her.

"Are you going to be doing any riding today?"

She looked surprised by the question. "I hadn't planned on it," she replied, and glanced down at her jeans and boots. "But I suppose I could."

"You ridden horses before?"

"I used to," she nodded. "It's been awhile."

Buck rubbed his jaw. "Well, I ask because the riding horses on this side of the ranch are retired racers," he explained. "Thoroughbreds can be a bit sensitive if you're new to riding."

Kate met his eye. "I'll be fine," she assured him evenly, and he let it go, because he'd seen that look in her eye before. It had happened just before she dumped his lap full of beer.

"Sure. I'll have Lester saddle up a couple of mounts, and I'll take you on a little tour of the ranch. Molly can ride along with us."

Kate glanced up at him again, and the faintly defiant look in her eyes melted into something almost like confusion. He had to say, though, Kate was pretty when she was confused. The afternoon sun made her auburn hair glow as red as a garnet, and her bafflement had painted her white cheeks a delicate peach-pink color.

"That's—really nice of you, Buck," she stammered. "Molly will love it, but I hope you're not putting yourself out for us."

"Not a bit," he smiled. "To tell you the truth, I'll probably enjoy it more than you do. It's nice to take a day off now and then." He glanced up through the leaves fluttering over them, and up at the sky beyond. "It's a pretty day for a ride, what's more."

Kate shot him another smile, but this smile looked genuinely pleased, and not just polite. "It is that," she dimpled, then turned to call out, "Molly, Buck says he's going to give us a tour of the ranch. We're going to ride our horses."

Molly's freckled face split into a grin as she turned the pony toward them. "Yay!"

They both laughed to see Molly send the pony trotting across the ring as fast as it would go; and Buck pushed off from the gate.

"I'll go find Lester," he promised. "He's around here somewhere. "I'll be back in two shakes."

He strode off across the gravel drive, past the pony stables, and on up the grassy hill behind to the main stable complex. Buck grimaced as he walked. He'd never been able to see keeping thoroughbreds. They were high-strung, fussy horses, they cost a ton of money to raise and to train, and if he had his way they'd sell 'em all and concentrate on good working quarter horses. But his brothers Carson and Jesse liked 'em, and since he didn't have to fool with them himself, he'd gone along.

But in his opinion, the Seven thoroughbreds were a hobby, not a real business; and they had Carson's brains and charm to thank for the fact that they managed to make any money at it.

But as Buck topped the rise and arrived at the exercise ring, he had to admit that he could see why people got sucked into buying them. He stopped momentarily to admire a gleaming, long-legged stallion as it danced along behind its handler. Its pale gray mane and tail floated in the breeze, and it tossed its head and snorted as it sashayed past.

Buck shook his head. Most people would only see a pretty horse, but he was seeing a million dollars prancing along; and it was up to Carson whether they'd get that money back or not.

He couldn't help thinking of all the ranching equipment they could buy for that money, but he knew it was useless to bring it up. Carson would argue, and Jesse would probably just take a swipe at him.

He skirted the ring and walked into the stables through the side door. A half-dozen sleek, intelligent horses turned to look at him from the stalls, and a half-dozen ears pricked up as he went looking for Lester, the head man at the stables.

He found him in his little office at the other end, with the phone to his ear. Lester was a small, wiry man with a sharp face and an irritable expression. He looked up, looked again, and hung up immediately.

"Well, hello Buck!" he yelped. "What can I do you for?"

"Hey Lester. I need two horses saddled," Buck told him, and rubbed his nose. "Make 'em the calmest ones we got. It's for company."

"Coming up," Lester told him, and hurried out of the office to fetch the horses.

Chapter 13

Kate looked up to see Buck leading two saddled horses down the hill beyond the pony stables. Her mouth dropped open slightly.

Molly turned to look, and she spoke the thought in both their minds. "Wow, Mamma," she gasped, "what pretty horses!"

Kate agreed silently, except that pretty was an understatement. She'd honestly never seen such beautiful horses. They were thoroughbreds, she could see that at a glance. They were vibrant, beautifully-groomed blacks with gleaming flanks and shining manes. Their ears were pricked up and alert, and their dark, intelligent eyes met hers as they approached.

"Buck, what gorgeous horses," she murmured, as he walked up. Even the saddles were beautiful: they were made of hand-tooled leather and adorned with silver studs.

Buck turned to pat the foremost horse on the neck with his hand, and it tossed its head and snorted. "Lester does a great job with them. Carson gets a lot of the credit, too. The thoroughbreds are his project." He tied them up to the fence rail and turned to smile at her.

"You ready to go?"

Kate glanced at the horses excitedly. "Ready when you are."

"All right then. Pick your horse."

Kate glanced at them. One of the horses was smaller than the other, and looked more manageable, and she reached for the reins. "I'll take this one," she decided.

"Good deal." Buck came over to help her mount up, and Kate glanced up at him gratefully as she reached for the saddle. He put a hand lightly on her waist, and gave her a quick boost up as she stepped into the stirrup. Kate landed solidly into the saddle and settled in with a sigh of relief.

Buck's brown face smiled up at her, and she got a vivid flash from his bright eyes. "All right! Let's go."

He turned and bounced up into the saddle athletically, turned his horse's head, and led the way out to the main road. Kate took the reins and turned to make sure that Molly was following along.

"Ready, Molly? Let's go." She let Molly bring her pony up behind Buck's horse, and then nudged her horse forward to bring up the rear.

Buck sent his horse across the road and down a shallow, grassy slope toward a green meadow. A little stream ran through it, and he blazed a trail along its banks as it ran under the shade of a long line of oak trees.

Kate glanced around her as they rode. The countryside was warm and sleepy under the afternoon sun. Leaves nodded over their heads as they moved along the creek, and it's cool, pleasant breath perfumed the air as they passed.

Molly turned her head to exclaim, "Mamma, look, a butterfly!"

Kate smiled and nodded as a big monarch flitted through the air between them and flapped off into the trees. She had to say, the Seven was a breathtaking ranch, not just for its imposing main house or its sprawling stable complex, but for the land itself. The ranch was nestled in the arms of a peaceful river valley, and she could see that river through the trees, glimmering far away. Miles of pasture stretched out in between, and she could see cattle dotted here and there, grazing lazily in the sun.

Buck turned in the saddle and looked back at her. "Where you ladies from?"

Molly perked up. "We're from Denver," she told him proudly.

Buck nodded. "That's a pretty town, all right. I was there last year for a cattleman's convention. I didn't have much time to get up into the mountains, but I'd like to go back sometime. Did you have a restaurant there?"

Kate smiled and shook her head. "Afraid not," she confessed. "I had a little art gallery in LoDo. Nothing important, just a hobby really, but it was a lot of fun."

His brows went up. "Art gallery, huh? I've never met an artist before."

Kate sputtered and shook her head. "Oh, I didn't paint," she confessed, "not really. I just liked to give other artists a platfo—"

As she was talking, a bird suddenly dived in front of her horse, as white and fast as a flash of lightning. The mare rolled its eyes, snorted, reared, and reared up again.

Whoa," Kate gasped."Whoa, whoa!" She fought to stay in the saddle and held onto the reins, but to her horror, instead of pulling up, the mare bucked, then bounded right across the stream and galloped away with her.

"Mamma!" Molly shrieked in panic, "Mamma!"

Kate could hear Buck shouting from somewhere behind her, but she couldn't hear what he was saying. She was bouncing in the saddle like a rodeo rider and her teeth felt like they were going to shake right out of her head. She grabbed the reins and tried to stop the horse, but the mare tossed her head, took the bit in her teeth, and began to turn in a circle, bucking as she went.

The world became a green, spinning blur, and Kate could feel herself sliding to the right as the mare jerked and turned. One more hard buck, and she was launched into the air.

Kate hit the ground hard, rolled, and came to a stop at the foot of a big oak tree. The horse bucked again and galloped away, and Kate groaned and closed her eyes. The fall had jarred every bone in her body, and her head was spinning so that she could hardly see.

She saw Buck come riding up, saw him throw himself down off his horse and kneel down over her. He put a hand on her brow and lifted one eyelid, then reached for her wrist.

She groaned and closed her eyes, and the next thing she knew, she was rising up. When she opened her eyes, Buck's big arms were under her and her feet were bobbing in the air as he carried her back to his horse.

"I can walk," she gasped. "Put me down!"

To her amazement, instead of putting her down, Buck Spade put one arm under her, shifted her weight to that side, reached for the saddle with his other arm, and mounted his horse carrying her. As bad as she felt, she still watched in wide-eyed disbelief as he settled in, cradled her in his lap, and turned the horse's head. Kate slumped there on his chest, light-headed, aching, burning up with embarrassment; and yet something made her turn her face into his shirt and grab his collar with one feeble hand.

Molly's panicked voice yanked her attention back to her daughter. "Is my Mamma all right?" Molly shrieked, and Buck called out, "I've got your Mamma, doodle bug. Here we come."

Kate raised her head just enough to muster a crooked smile. "I'm all right, baby," she mumbled, but her head was swimming, and she fell back weakly against Buck's broad chest. She felt him move his arm, and soon after heard him mumble: "Miss Ada, is that you? This is Buck. I need you to call Doc. —No, but I need him to meet us up at the house. I got a lady who just got bucked by a horse. That's right. Thanks, Miss Ada."

Kate swayed back and forth in Buck's arms as his horse ambled down to the little creek, then crossed it with a splash and slowly climbed up the shallow bank. She got a glimpse of Molly's worried face, then the grassy bank, and the oak trees; then she closed her eyes, and closed the fluttering green leaves out.

Chapter 14

Kate opened her eyes. Her whole body ached, and she had the impression that she was floating in the air. She was still swaying against Buck Spade's chest, but she was indoors now, in a big, open space. There was a massive chandelier hanging from a high ceiling ten feet to the right. She glanced back over Buck's shoulder and widened her eyes, because a massive marble staircase dropped steeply below them, and she closed her eyes again.

"Mrs. Malone."

Kate groaned, and her eyes fluttered open. She had dropped off, but now she was lying on something soft, and the ceiling was high above her and had molded swirls and curlicues. An elderly, bearded man was leaning over her. There was a stethoscope slung around his neck, and his brown eyes looked dark and concerned.

"Mrs. Malone, can you hear me?"

Kate frowned, then murmured, "Of course I can. Where's my daughter?"

Buck's face swam into view just behind the old man. A shining black curl was falling down over one eye, and his handsome face was drawn into a worried knot.

"Molly's downstairs eating lunch," he murmured. "She's okay."

Kate tried to struggle up on one elbow. "Where am I?"

A compassionate look flitted across Buck's eyes. "You're upstairs at the house, Kate," he told her softly. "I brought you in."

"Oh," she whispered, and leaned back into the pillow. "I remember now."

"How are you feeling?" the older man asked. Kate blinked at him, and Buck added, "This is Doc Billings. I called him in to look at you."

The gray-haired man pressed, "Do you have a headache? Dizziness? Numbness, weakness?"

Kate shook her head. "No, none of those things. My bones ache though," she admitted. "I hit the ground like a rock."

"Have you lost consciousness, even for a few seconds?"

"No. I closed my eyes, but I was awake."

The doctor's concerned brown eyes stared at her for a long moment. He sighed, then went on, "You don't have the classic signs of a concussion, Mrs. Malone," he murmured, "but you should go to the emergency room to have an x-ray and probably an MRI. You took a pretty hard fall, and it pays to err on the side of caution."

Kate frowned at him. "No, I don't want to go to the ER," she replied firmly. "I just fell down. It hurt, but I'm all right."

Buck's clear eyes clouded with worry. "You should take Doc's advice," he urged. "You got busted up pretty good. You don't want to have something come back on you in a week or two."

"I'm not going to the hospital," Kate told him simply, and turned her eyes from his dismayed face, to the older man's. The doctor raised his brows, sighed, and leaned back in his chair.

"In that case, my strong recommendation is that you lie still and rest here for a few days," he replied briskly. "If you won't go to the hospital, the best thing is to assume that you do have a concussion. You should rest quietly in bed for the next few days. It's important that you call me if you get a headache, particularly a bad one, or feel dizzy or numb."

"But I can't stay here for days on end," Kate objected in alarm. "I have a restaurant to run!"

The doctor turned to give her a serious look. "You look like a sensible woman," he told her solemnly. "And you have a little daughter. If you won't take common sense precautions for your own sake, you should take them for hers."

Kate drew herself up and glared at him. She wanted to snap, *Leave my daughter out of it,* but she couldn't deny the general justice of his words.

The doctor looked up at Buck. "Call me if anything changes."

"I will, Doc. Thanks for coming over."

"Yep." The older man stood up, and Buck followed him out of the room.

Kate stared after them indignantly. Neither man had asked her what she thought about those high-handed plans, and since they'd walked out of the room, she couldn't bless them out about it.

She glanced around. She'd been drowsy and weak when Buck brought her in, and had entered the room with her eyes closed. But now she saw that she was in a huge, luxurious bedroom that reminded her of nothing so much as the executive suite in a resort hotel. The far wall of the room was made of glass, and she could see the ranch pastures stretching out for miles below. The floor was some kind of marble tile and was mostly bare.

There were huge, contemporary paintings on the walls, mostly of men on horseback roping cattle, or riding broncs, with bold swipes of vivid color and movement. The furniture in the room was sparse and expensive-looking. There was an antique wooden table beside her bed, and a polished French armoire beyond with graceful, curving legs and a starburst pattern on the door in inlaid wood. There was what looked like a Louis XIV chair across the room, and a highly-polished antique chest of drawers.

Kate looked down. She was lying under a bright, silky coverlet in a vivid orange-red. She was surrounded by all kinds of exotic, brightly-colored pillows, and there was a remote of smooth white plastic at her elbow, but she couldn't see what it controlled.

The door opened suddenly and Buck came walking back in. He closed it softly behind him, stuck his hands in his jeans pockets, and ambled back over to her bedside.

Kate stared up at him with a flick of defiance in her eyes, but he looked down at his boots and rubbed the back of his neck.

"I'm real sorry about this, Kate," he mumbled. "If there's anything I can do to make you more comfortable, why, you just tell me."

Kate's defiance faded at the sheepish look on his face, but she replied promptly.

"I want to see Molly."

"Sure. I'll bring her right up. She's been having lunch downstairs. Do you want me to tell Conchita to bring you something?"

Kate glanced down and picked at the coverlet. "No, thank you, I'm not very hungry right now."

Buck gestured at a phone on the table. "Well, if you change your mind, you can call down to the kitchen until about eight. That's when Conchita goes home."

You mean your kitchen has its own extension? Kate thought in amazement, but clamped her lips together and nodded.

Buck rubbed his jaw and went on, "I want you and Molly to stay here as my guests this week. If there's anything you need, like clothes or something, just tell Miss Ada and she'll have somebody pick it up for you in town this afternoon. The bathroom's that door over there." He turned and pointed to a big double door on one wall. "It's all stocked, so you should be good."

Kate stared at him in mingled gratitude and dismay. "Thank you, Buck, that's very kind of you. But I can't stay here for a week," she sputtered. "I have a restaurant to run!"

Buck waved his big hand. "Aw, it'll be alright. It's only a few days, and you heard what the doc said. You need to lay low."

"But what about Molly?"

Buck kicked the foot of the bed lightly. "She's not in school yet, is she?"

"Well, no, but—"

"Then she'll be fine. She'll have the time of her life here. There's a lot to do. She'll love it."

Kate's gaze drifted from Buck's determined eyes to his stubborn jaw, and she thought, You *sure do like to have the last word, don't you?*

But at the moment, the only sensible thing to do was to follow doctor's orders, and so she nodded. "Thank you, Buck. I'm sure she will."

His brown face split into a beautiful white smile, and he nodded. "I'll go get her. You just relax. Watch some television, if you like."

He walked out, and Kate frowned after him. There was no sign of any television, and she reached for the remote in puzzlement. There was a small red button on the top, and she pushed it curiously.

To her flabbergasted astonishment, one of the paintings on the wall slid aside to reveal a huge flat screen television underneath; and Kate raised an eyebrow and pulled her mouth to one side.

She wasn't sure if she was impressed, or just a tiny bit disgusted.

Chapter 15

Buck closed the bedroom door softly behind him, but paused a few paces beyond and pulled his hands over his face. His heart was right down in his boots.

He'd been playing host, he'd been responsible for Kate and her little daughter, and now Kate was lying in bed all busted up. Maybe with a concussion.

He felt like a penny with a hole in it, and when Carson found out Kate had got hurt, his brother was going to kick him from one end of the house to the other.

He wouldn't blame him, either.

Buck sighed and slowly descended the stairs from the guest room. He'd just about had a heart attack when he saw that horse go over the creek with Kate. It was all his fault, he should've known better than to give her a thoroughbred to ride. Those horses were high strung and always looking for a boogeyman.

And as for Kate, she'd talked a brave game, but it turned out that she was a beginning rider. It hadn't been a good match.

He was responsible for her lying up there in bed.

Buck frowned as he walked down the stairs. Kate had looked so broken and still lying under that tree that his heart had almost stopped. There for an instant, he'd been scared that she might even be dead; and he'd been weak with relief when she'd looked up at him.

He stopped and put his hand on the stair rail. Her eyes had looked so pleading and helpless, he couldn't keep himself from scooping her up in his arms. Almost like she was a child.

Buck sighed and shook his head. Kate was all woman, she was beautiful, she'd been soft and warm and curvy in his arms; but in that moment, he'd felt as protective toward her as he had toward Molly.

She'd curled her fingers into his shirt like a little girl.

Buck sighed and moved down the stairs again. Maybe that was because she'd got the wind knocked out of her; but it had stirred something in him, and that worried him. Kate was going out with Carson, and he'd be wrong to interfere with that. To go where he didn't belong.

But he couldn't deny that he was thinking about it anyway.

He found Molly still sitting at the table in the little dining room off the kitchen. She was already staring at the doorway when he walked through it, and her worried voice piped: "How's my Mamma?"

Buck put reassurance into the smile he gave her. "Just fine. She wants to see you. You wanna come up?"

Molly slid down out of her chair and rushed over to put her hand in his. She pulled him along behind her as she hurried to the stairs.

Buck followed her up the marble staircase, then turned left at the top and down the hall to the guest room door. He stepped up and rapped on the door with two knuckles.

"Kate, you've got a visitor," he called, then turned to wink at Molly. "Can she come in?"

He could hear the smile in Kate's voice as she answered, and that was a good sign.

"She better come in."

Buck opened the door softly and peeked in. Kate was sitting up in bed, propped on a dozen pillows with the red coverlet pulled up to her waist. She held out her arms, and Molly rushed past him to jump up on the bed and crawl into them. Kate hugged Molly tight, pressed her cheek against her daughter's hair, and closed her eyes.

Molly looked up at her mother. "Mamma, are you all right now?"

Kate kissed her hair. "I'm fine," she whispered. "Just resting a bit, that's all."

Buck paused for an instant to enjoy a pretty picture. Kate's gleaming hair tumbled over her shoulders, her expression was tender and loving as she gazed down at her daughter, and her lips were still puckered in the shape of a kiss.

To Buck's alarm, his imagination suddenly projected him into that sweet scene, and he knew enough to duck out and close the door behind him before he enjoyed it too much.

The cell phone in his back pocket buzzed suddenly, and Buck reached for it. "Yeah?"

Carson's drawling voice came trickling out. "I'm down here with Eugene," he began abruptly, and his usually smooth voice was irritated. "We've run into a snag, and I'm going to be in Dallas for a few more days."

Buck frowned as he descended the stairs. "What's wrong?"

"Nothing, I hope. Eugene says there's a problem with the rights agreement. That it's not as cut and dried as we thought."

Buck's voice rose sharply. "What's that supposed to mean?"

Carson sighed heavily. "If you wanted a legal consultation, you should've come down here yourself. I'm just telling you what Eugene says about our documents."

Buck stopped short at the foot of the stairs. "What's the bottom line, Carson?"

"The bottom line is that if we want senior water rights to the Big Sandy, we're going to have to come up with documents that prove it. These don't."

"What do you mean our papers don't prove it?" Buck demanded angrily. "I've seen 'em. They say that Big Russ paid for the water rights in 1972. We've renewed those rights every five years!"

"Yes," Carson echoed. "But Buster isn't disputing the renewals, he's disputing the original claim, and I have no idea where the original document is."

Blunt-force shock temporarily robbed Buck of a reply. He recovered well enough to croak, "Let me talk to Eugene."

"He's not here. He's off on an errand."

Buck sputtered and fought the temptation to kick something. "Well what are we supposed to do now?" he fumed."Haggle with Buster?"

"It hasn't come to that yet," Carson sighed. "Eugene said that Buster's papers are almost certainly bogus, and that's good news. If he had ironclad proof he owned the water rights, he'd produce it."

"So the water rights are up for grabs?"

"That's what Eugene is going to check," Carson explained. "He says it won't take long. I'll let you know what he finds out." There was a short pause, and he added, "Tell Kate that I'll be back in a few days, will you?"

Buck bowed his head and stared at his boots. "Carson, ah—there's something I have to tell you."

"You can tell me when I get back," his brother answered briskly. "I have to go. See you."

"Carson—"

The line abruptly went dead, and Buck grumbled, then stuck it back into his jeans pocket. He hadn't got to tell Carson about Kate's accident, and he'd just got the worst possible news about that water rights lawsuit.

He hadn't seen that old agreement in years, and now that mistake had come back to bite him hard. He shouldn't have assumed Carson was keeping track of everything. He should've hunted that contract down.

But he hadn't, and now the ranch was in real danger of losing its water rights.

If they did, the Seven could go out of business.

Buck suddenly hauled off and kicked the banister in frustration. He felt trapped and desperate, like he was stuck in a locked room; but he wasn't going to stay stuck for long. He didn't know how, but he was going to find a way to nail down those water rights.

But in the meantime, he needed to blow off some steam or he'd go crazy. He stormed outside into the sunlight and fresh air to go find that runaway horse.

It would keep him from busting something up.

Chapter 16

The next afternoon Kate reached for the t.v. remote and flicked it off impatiently. It was a gorgeous, sunny day outside, with big, fluffy clouds marching past her window, but she couldn't go out and enjoy it. The doctor had told her to rest and to only get up when she had to.

But she was heartily sick of soap operas and silly talk shows, and she was feeling fine. The doctor wanted her to stay at the Seven for a week, but that wasn't going to happen. It couldn't.

Kate glanced over at Molly, who was curled up at the foot of her king-sized bed, reading a book. Molly seemed happy at the ranch, but she didn't want her daughter to be away from home for long. Molly was still grieving for her father. She'd been uprooted from their home in Denver and moved to a brand new place. She was having to deal with a lot of upheaval, and she was only six years old.

Kate's worried eyes scanned Molly's freckled face. She was trying to establish a predictable routine for Molly. To create a pleasant, stable home environment that would help her daughter feel secure.

But so far that goal had gotten thrown down and danced on.

Kate's cell phone trilled, and she reached for the bedside table. She dug the phone out of her bag and flicked it on.

"Hello."

To her surprise, Sebastian's voice greeted her from the other end.

"It's me, Kate. I hope it's okay to call. I assume that since you called us yesterday to tell us about your accident, you're feeling well enough to talk a bit today. I just wanted you to know that everything's going fine here," he assured her.

Kate nodded. Sebastian had just happened to pick up the line yesterday; and that meant that he'd grabbed for the phone during one of his breaks. She had to admit that she was touched.

"We're doing great," he assured her. "We were full last night, and we have a group of Shriners coming in this evening for the private room."

Kate raised an eyebrow. *Maybe I was unfair to Sebastian,* she mused. *I never expected him to step up like this. Looks like he might be a team player after all.*

"Have you heard anything about Roxanne?" she asked. "Has she called?"

Sebastian sighed gently. "No and no. But I took the liberty of having a friend of mine come in to sub for her. He did great. No one even noticed that Roxanne was gone."

"Let me know if she calls in," Kate murmured, and stirred uncomfortably. "And thank you for taking the initiative. Please tell your friend thanks for me. If he wants to, he can just keep working until Roxanne comes back. I'll settle with him then."

"I was just about to ask," Sebastian replied quickly. "And I'm sure he'll agree. Waiting tables is his side gig." He paused, then went on, "Where did you say you are again?"

Kate glanced over at Molly. "I'm at the Seven Spades Ranch. It's on the way to Salt Lick. I'll be here for a few more days."

"I hope you feel better soon."

"Thank you, Sebastian, I hope so, too. Just keep things on an even keel until I get back, and if you have any issues, call me at this number."

"Will do, *Ciao, bella.*"

Kate sputtered a bit. "*Ciao,* Sebastian." She hung up and tapped the blue screen on her phone. The phone was the best internet access she had, since her laptop was still back at the restaurant, but it had also been two weeks since she'd posted on the Stonehouse social media account.

It was a new account, but she already had several thousand followers who liked her recipes, coupons and news about local events at the Stonehouse. She kept her posts strictly about the restaurant, out of protectiveness toward Molly, but there was enough going on to keep interest high.

She was in the act of tapping out a post when there was a soft knock at the door. Kate looked up from her task.

"Yes?"

The door opened a crack, and to Kate's surprise, Buck's face peeked in. He called, "Is it all right for me to come in?"

Kate set her phone down. "Of course."

The door swung open wide and Buck walked in. He was wearing a simple white tee shirt that showed off his muscular arms, and plain jeans; but he was half-hidden behind a huge bouquet of red roses. Kate's mouth dropped open at the sight of them.

Molly's startled eyes were yanked away from her book. "Look, Mamma, what pretty roses!" she gasped.

Buck took a few awkward steps toward the bed. "Thought I'd bring you some get-well flowers," he mumbled, and scratched his head.

Kate's eyes moved over them in surprise. The roses were beautiful, perfectly shaped, and fresh. They were a dark, deep,velvety red, and their edges were a wine-black color.

"They're beautiful, Buck," she breathed. "Thank you! I've never seen such a deep red."

"They reminded me of your hair," he observed, and presented them to her. "They're kinda the same color."

Kate took the roses and bent down to inhale their fragrance. "They smell heavenly," she murmured in wonder and lifted her eyes to Buck's face. "This is so kind of you, Buck. Thank you."

Kate stared at him in wonder. She didn't want to presume, and it was more than likely that Buck was just being polite. He probably felt responsible for her bad luck, though he wasn't.

But she'd surprised a look in his eyes just then, a look that was warm and tender and just a touch…hungry. A look that was a whole world of things, *except* polite.

"There's a nice big vase on the table out by the pool," Buck mumbled, and rubbed his nose. "Would you and Molly like to come down and have lunch? It'd be a change of scenery, and it's not far."

Kate glanced over at Molly. The eager look on her face told the story.

"Maybe Molly would like to take a swim," Buck suggested, and Molly's eyes blazed with hope; but Kate murmured, "She doesn't have a swimsuit, though."

"Molly can swim in whatever she's got," Buck shrugged. "I don't care. Let her enjoy herself."

Kate's lips curled up. "Well…"

"Can I, Mamma?" Molly whined; and Kate gave her a rueful look. "Go put on your new top and the shorts. Don't forget to put on flipflops!" she called, as Molly bounded off the bed and went running off to the adjacent bedroom.

Kate sighed. Miss Ada, the iron-willed head maid, had sent one of her helpers into town to buy them pajamas and various articles of clothing for their stay; and she'd only snorted when Kate had asked her for the total.

Buck's voice diverted her attention. "I'll wait outside," he told her, and left the room.

Kate glanced at the fluffy white clouds floating outside, smiled, and threw off the covers.

* * * * *

"Mamma, watch me!"

There was a loud splash as Molly jumped into the clear blue pool, and Kate waved and laughed as she sank down into the chair at the patio table.

Buck pushed her chair in, then moved to sit down at the table opposite. He settled in, then lifted a pitcher full of tea and poured a glass for her.

Kate glanced up at the sky. "It's good to be outside again," she sighed, and took the glass that Buck handed her. "I'm an outdoor person. It's hard for me to be cooped up."

"I know how that feels," Buck commiserated, and poured himself a glass. "I broke my leg when I was a kid and got laid up for a month. I've never been more miserable in my life."

"How did you break your leg?" Kate asked, and took a forkful of chicken salad.

Buck glanced up at her, and she was pierced by a vivid flash of blue. "I went over the fence to our neighbor's pasture," he mumbled from a full mouth. "I don't even remember why I wanted to go. But as soon as I got over, I noticed that there was a bull on the other side. Big Longhorn. I looked at him and he looked at me, and then I turned around and jumped for that fence. But I must not have been fast enough, because he got under me with those horns and sent me flying. I landed on the other side of the fence, but my leg got broke." He shook his head and laughed.

"It hurt all right, but I was more scared of Big Russ," he mused. "When he found out I was okay, he told me that when I got well he was going to whale me with a stick for sneaking over on somebody else's land."

Kate's smile faded. "Your father struck you?" she stammered.

Buck nodded and laughed. "My grandfather. And oh yeah. He beat my butt. When Big Russ gave you a whooping, you knew it."

Kate stared at him in dismay, then glanced over at the pool, where Molly was splashing happily. She'd never once raised a hand to her daughter, and the very thought of it horrified her. Molly was an obedient, well-adjusted child precisely because she'd been raised in a peaceful, loving way.

Kate shuddered. She couldn't imagine using violence on a child as a teaching tool; and she glanced at Buck again, this time in bemusement.

Maybe that explains why Buck has such a fiery temper.

It runs in the family.

Buck reached over to grab a platter. "Have some dessert," he mumbled. "It's cream something. I can't pronounce it, but it's good."

"Thank you."

Kate glanced at him again. The afternoon sun, as it sifted down through the trellis overhead, made Buck's wavy hair gleam blue-black, and her lips curled up slowly in frank admiration.

Buck's temper aside, she could understand why Roxanne had lost her breath when she talked about him. Most women loved cowboys, and Buck was such a cowboy that he'd probably wear a Stetson over a tuxedo. Kate's eye flicked over him. She watched in fascination as he hunched over his food, noticed how he cupped his plate with his hands, followed the little muscle in his jaw as it moved.

Buck Spade was gorgeous. Their disastrous first meeting had kept her from admitting it, but now, in the mottled shade beside the pool, she had to confess it at last. His shoulders were as wide and square as a barn door, and his white tee shirt was doing a terrible job of hiding his muscular chest.

And the more she got to know Buck, the more it looked as if her first impression of him had been wrong. He might have a formidable temper, but he was also capable of surprising kindness. Even...tenderness. Her mind flicked back to the first seconds after her fall. She saw Buck's shadow looming over her, saw his eyes wide and dark with fear.

Kate's imagination showed her a split-second of Buck bending down to kiss her, and Kate immediately suffered a wave of heat and guilt. Kevin had only been gone two years, and even the thought of kissing another man was like a betrayal. Kate frowned into her tea.

Still, Buck had put that thought in her head for the first time since her husband died. Even Carson, for all his good looks and charm, hadn't managed it.

Kate lifted her eyes to Buck's face again, and he met her eye and grinned at her.

Chapter 17

"So you got hit on the head, Miss….Duchaine?"

Roxanne shot the emergency room doctor a resentful glare. It wasn't his fault that she'd had to spend the night in an ER bay lying on a brick-hard cot listening to a beeping machine, she knew that. But somebody at that place needed to step up their game.

"I'm Dr. Wilburson," the newcomer murmured, and Roxanne shook his offered hand limply.It was obvious that she'd been hit on the head, and she was mad enough to tell him so. But she wasn't mad enough to insult her doctor; so she just nodded.

He walked over to the exam table and gave her knot a preliminary inspection. "That's a big lump all right," he murmured. "But your CT scan didn't show anything suspicious. How are you feeling now? Are you still having any pains at the site, or any headaches?"

"I have a splitting headache," she drawled.

The doctor scribbled on his clipboard. "How did it happen?" he mumbled. "The notes here say a sign fell on you? What kind of sign?"

"It was made out of metal," Roxanne replied glumly, then glanced up at him sharply.

"Tell me," she added suddenly, "Would a falling metal sign be enough to raise a lump on my head?"

"That depends on how big and heavy it was," he mumbled, with his eyes still on the clipboard.

"It was made of tin," Roxanne told him, "and it was about as big as your clipboard."

He looked at her over his glasses. "I don't think so," he replied slowly. "A falling sign would probably make a cut in your scalp, like the one I saw. But it shouldn't be enough to raise a lump like yours."

Roxanne narrowed her eyes and nodded. *I knew it,* she fumed silently.

The doctor glanced up at her. "Maybe you struck your head on the floor when you fell."

Roxanne crossed her arms. "I fell down face forward," she retorted, but the doctor only handed her a piece of paper.

"I wrote you a prescription for pain," he murmured. "Avoid strenuous exercise for a few days, and if anything changes, or if your pain worsens, call your regular doctor."

Roxanne took the slip of paper, then slid off the exam table and abruptly abandoned the room. Resentment was bubbling up around her ears like hot lava, because the doctor had just confirmed what she already knew.

That sign hadn't fallen down all by itself. Somebody had hit her with it: and she knew who it was.

She didn't yet know how she was going to get even, but she was going to if it was the last thing she ever did. She shouldered through the crowded halls with a scowl, then burst out into the hospital parking lot.

She found her red jeep, climbed in, and cranked the motor. The engine snarled to life, and she backed it out with a jerk, then scratched off in a cloud of exhaust.

By the time she got back to the Stonehouse, it was the middle of the lunch rush. She pulled up into her usual parking spot with squealing tires and jumped out.

She was exhausted after a sleepless night in the ER, but she wanted to tell Kate that the lump on her head hadn't been an accident. That the doctor had confirmed that.

Then she was going to tell Kate who did it.

Roxanne took the front steps two at a time and yanked the big main door open. Trina was working as the greeter, and her face brightened as she came walking in.

"Roxanne, are you okay?" she yelped in surprise. "I didn't expect to see you back here so soon! Are you okay?"

Roxanne swept the hall behind her with hungry eyes. "Where's Kate?"

Trina's face clouded over. "She's not here. She took Molly out to the Seven Ranch for riding lessons, and she got thrown from her horse. The doctor told her she has to stay out there and rest."

Trina paused, and a wistful look flitted over her freckled face. "Some people have all the luck."

"Who's running the restaurant then?"

Trina shot her a disgusted look. "Sebastian," she drawled. "He thinks he owns the place. Or at least he acts like it." Her voice sank to a conspiratorial whisper. "You better watch your back, Roxanne," she hissed. "He's got a friend of his working your job, and you haven't even been gone a day!"

"What?"

Trina nodded earnestly. "He says we're short handed, but he sure didn't waste any time trying to replace you."

Roxanne recoiled as if she'd been slapped, then growled, "Who's the new guy?"

Trina glanced at the front door. There was no one new in it, and she tilted her head. "Come on, I'll show you."

She led the way down the hall to the dining room entrance. She paused in the doorway and nodded toward a young blonde man with a moustache and neatly-trimmed beard.

"That's him," she murmured. "He's good, too. If I was you I'd call Kate and tell her you're back now. Don't give this guy a chance to get comfortable here."

Roxanne watched the newcomer in scowling silence. She wanted to charge into the kitchen and tell Sebastian exactly what he was, and then to tie on an apron and work the rest of the shift; but her head was throbbing, and she was so tired she felt ready to fall down.

"I will call her," she growled. "And don't worry, I'm going to tell her I'm back. I'm going to tell her more than that. Where's Sebastian?"

"In the kitchen," Trina replied with a frown. "Don't fight with him, Roxanne. You're just back from the hospital!"

Roxanne ignored her and stormed back down the hall toward the kitchen. She burst through the swinging doors and entered the kitchen, fists clenched and ready to scream accusations; but Sebastian wasn't there. Three pots were still bubbling on the stove, and there was no one else in the room.

Roxanne pushed out the back kitchen door, onto the loading dock, and a few paces down the steps. The corner of the dock partially blocked her view, but as she moved, the back side of the building swam into view.

Roxanne looked up. There was a little private patio there, a kind of back yard for Kate that connected to her apartment, and a narrow metal stair descended from it down the side of the building.

She narrowed her eyes. A slow smile curled her lips as she stared at it; and Roxanne turned on her heel and skipped back up the steps, into the kitchen, and away.

She blew past Trina, and answered her questioning look by putting a finger to her lips. "Don't tell Sebastian I was here," she urged, and kept on moving.

"But—"

Roxanne ignored her friend, burst out through the front door, and hurried off to her car. She was going to go home, grab a bite to eat, and get the good night's rest her body was screaming for.

She had a plan, and she was going to carry it out; and when it was over, she wouldn't need to worry about anything.

Chapter 18

Buck stood at the window of his great room, gazing out to the blue smudge of the horizon. Storm clouds painted the distance a gunmetal gray, and as he watched, a white thread of lightning flicked far away.

He raised his glass to his lips. They desperately needed rain, and he was praying for it. He'd had breakfast with Morgan, out in a pasture about five miles from the house. They'd had hot coffee and bacon and eggs from a camp stove.

The eating had been good, but the news had been bad: ten more calves had died from dehydration in the sweltering heat, and they were having to supplement the nursing cows with extra water so they could keep on giving milk.

They needed good news, but he hadn't heard anything from either Carson or Eugene.

They couldn't lose their water rights to the Big Sandy.

Buck's face darkened as he remembered Buster's sneering face. Buster had a lot of guts to come barging up to their ranch house, bawling threats; but Buck could admit to himself now that his brothers had been right. Buster had been trying to get him to do something crazy, and he'd almost succeeded.

Buck grumbled into his drink as he took another sip. His urge to knock Buster's teeth out was like a nagging itch on his best day, and this bogus lawsuit made him want to scratch it.

Bad.

A white thread of lightning flicked on the horizon again. Buck watched it and wondered, for the thousandth time, what had happened to that water rights contract. Carson thought they didn't have it, but he knew he'd seen it, somewhere. He was the oldest, and he remembered more about their grandfather than his brothers.

Buck smiled as he gazed out across the rolling landscape. Big Russ had been a pistol, and he was grateful he'd been old enough to remember him well.

The rolling green hills faded away, and in their place, Buck saw a long, low, pine-green ranch house in the shadow of three huge oak trees. Big Russ and Miss Annie's house.

Their parents had died when he was about 13, and when they went to live with Big Russ and Miss Annie, it had been like going back to the fifties. Big Russ had been hard-core old school. His big ranch house had been mostly off grid and way out in the boonies. Buck sputtered and shook his head as he remembered it. They'd barely had electricity. The air conditioner had been a couple of big box fans in the windows, and they'd gotten their water out of a big well in the front yard. Buck rubbed his right arm, remembering how hard it had been to crank that bucket all the way up.

Carson had hated living that way.

He'd loved it.

Maybe because he'd looked up to Big Russ, wanted to be like him. Big Russ had been as independent as the side of a mountain, and he'd asked no one else to do for him and his.

Big Russ hadn't trusted anything but God: not government, not politicians, and especially not banks. Buck conjured his grandfather in his mind, saw his bright eyes in a brown weathered face, saw the plaid cowboy shirt he always wore. Big Russ' gravelly voice echoed in his memory.

Never trust a banker, boy. If you ain't holding that money, it ain't yours.

Buck sighed, and the rolling countryside gradually reappeared beyond his window. Big Russ had been old enough to remember the Depression, and he used to tell stories about people who lost their life savings when the banks shut down. Big Russ had kept his money in his mattress until he got too much of it to fit in there.

He kept his important papers close by, too. Never in a bank deposit box.

Buck raised his glass to his lips. Big Russ and Miss Annie had been gone for years, and their old ranch house hadn't been lived in since they died. It was at the farthest edge of the Seven, up in the northwestern corner of the ranch. He hadn't been out there in a long time.

Buck frowned. After Miss Annie passed, Carson had organized all the official documents he'd found in the old house. Most of them had been crammed into a big tin coffee can on a kitchen shelf.

Carson had taken those documents to Big Russ' country lawyer. And after he'd inspected those papers, and updated them, they'd all assumed that they were in good shape legally.

Of course that had been close to eleven years ago, now. Before they met Eugene.

That experience had taught them the wisdom of hiring the best lawyer they could find.

Thunder grumbled overhead, and Buck set his drink down and turned toward the door. He seemed to remember that Big Russ liked to stuff papers into books. Sometimes important papers, too; and they still had a lot of Russ' old books in the library.

Buck abandoned his own apartment and skipped down the stairs to the library. He didn't have much hope that he'd find what they needed in one of Big Russ' old fishing and hunting books, but it was worth a try.

He remembered more about their grandfather than most all of his brothers, so they probably wouldn't think to look there.

Buck rounded the corner of the staircase and headed down the first-floor hall behind it. There were lots of rooms off of the back hall: their big home theater room, the downstairs dining room, the pool table room, and the library at the far end.

Buck walked into the center of the room and stuck his hands on his hips. The library was one of the smaller rooms in the house, but all four walls were lined with books right up to the ceiling. He walked slowly from one end of the room to the other, searching for a handful of small, torn covers. He was just about to give up when he spied a small, beat-up looking book titled *Angling in North Texas.*

Buck reached for the book, and when he pulled it out, a few stray pages fluttered to the floor. It had been old when Russ had it, and now it was falling apart, but Buck smiled as he opened it. Russ had scribbled all over the pages in spidery blue ink; phone numbers, notes to himself about fishing, even a grocery list.

Buck riffled through the pages, but on inspection, there were no papers stuck into the book. He stuffed the stray pages back in and replaced the book on the shelf. He was about to resume his search when the sound of footsteps in the hall made him turn his head.

It was mid-morning, almost lunchtime, so he figured it was one of Miss Ada's helpers, getting ready for lunch. But a whisper of cologne drifted in from the hall, and it wasn't a woman's perfume.

Their maids didn't wear cologne, and Carson was in Dallas.

Buck walked out into the hall, slowed as he passed the dining room, then stopped and backed up. He put a hand up to the door jamb and frowned.

There was a stranger standing in their dining room. Or at least, the man was a stranger to him. Buck straightened up and advanced.

"Can I help you with something?"

The stranger was a tall, slim man with dark hair slicked back from a high forehead. He jumped slightly at the sound of Buck's voice, but recovered instantly.

"I suppose I'm lost," the young man smiled, and gestured toward a bouquet of daisies on the dining room table. "I understand that Kate Malone is staying here, and I just dropped by to say hello." He shrugged and gestured at the room around him.

"This is such a big place, it's easy to get turned around."

Buck crossed his arms. "It is that," he admitted, and nodded at the other man. "I'm Buck Spade."

The stranger extended his hand, and Buck reached out to take it. "I'm Sebastian, the chef at the Stonehouse. I heard that Kate had an accident, and I thought that some flowers might make her feel better."

Buck relaxed a bit. "Well, Kate is staying upstairs," he replied. "The doctor's put her on bed rest, but I'll be glad to go up and tell her you're here."

"Thank you."

Buck turned and walked out, but frowned as he ascended the stairs. He didn't like to meet people for the first time inside his house, but he was going to give the fellow the benefit of the doubt.

After Buster's full frontal attack, a random stranger wandering through the dining room wasn't going to throw him.

Chapter 19

"Really?"

Kate stared up at Buck in surprise. He was leaning against the door frame with his arms crossed.

"That's what he said. He says he's your cook. Wants to come up and visit."

Kate blinked in surprise. *Maybe I've misjudged Sebastian*, she thought with a jab of guilt. *Maybe he was just going through a bad patch before.*

Buck rubbed his nose. "You want me to tell him to come up?"

Kate's eyes flicked back to his. "Yes, thank you, Buck," she murmured, and moved to pull the covers up a bit. She was a little embarrassed to talk to Sebastian from her bed, but at least she was wearing a caftan, and not pajamas.

Buck disappeared, and her cell phone suddenly jumped to life. Kate glanced at her bag in irritation and decided to ignore it. Her phone had been ringing all morning, over and over again, but she didn't recognize the number, and she'd been busy with their payroll software.

After a few minutes there was a soft knock at the door.

"Come in."

To Kate's surprise, the first thing through the door was a beautiful bouquet of fresh daisies, followed by Sebastian's smiling face.

"Hello, Kate," he murmured, and walked over to present the flowers. Kate took them and glanced up at him with a smile.

"How thoughtful, Sebastian. Thank you." She nodded toward one of the chairs. "Please, sit down."

Sebastian quickly pulled up a chair and settled in. "How are you feeling? Better, I hope."

"Yes, thank you. It was the silliest thing. A bird flew in front of my horse, and it panicked and threw me," she laughed. "But I feel fine. We're just humoring the doctor."

Sebastian gave her a sympathetic look. "Well, I just wanted to let you know that we're holding down the fort," he nodded. "I'm so glad that my friend was able to step in when he did. He did a great job covering for Roxanne."

Kate's smile faded. "Has anyone heard from Roxanne?"

Sebastian tossed his head. "No, and I'm not surprised," he retorted. "And that brings me to something else. I'm afraid I have a little confession, Kate. I didn't come here just to visit. I wanted to talk to you about something."

Kate could feel a faint frown spreading across her face. "Is something wrong?"

Sebastian's look was now rueful. "I'm afraid there is. I hate to be the bearer of bad news, but—I think I know what Roxanne was doing in her locker the other night. She was filling it with loot.

"I'm afraid she's been stealing from you."

Amazement wiped a blank across Kate's face. "What!"

Sebastian sighed and nodded. "I didn't believe it either, but what can I say, when I found this in her work locker?" He reached into his pocket and pulled out a diamond necklace.

Kate gasped, "That's the necklace my husband gave me for our anniversary. It was in my bedroom!"

"It makes me so angry," Sebastian sighed. "When I think of how much you've done for Roxanne, only to have her stab you in the back like this!"

Kate clapped a hand to her trembling mouth as her glittering drop necklace dangled from Sebastian's fingers. She reached out for it, then stared down at it in disbelief.

"I found Roxanne's locker slightly open," Sebastian told her, as he examined his fingernails. "I think maybe someone was coming and she didn't have time to do more than slam it. She rushed out of the locker room, and she yanked the door open so hard that it brought that sign down on her." He sighed and folded his hands in his lap. "It was poetic justice, if you ask me."

"I can't believe it," Kate quavered. Her fingers closed over Kevin's gift, and a stinging sense of betrayal jabbed her heart.

I thought Roxanne and I were friends.

She raised her eyes to Sebastian's. His face looked slightly blurred.

"I can't believe it either," Sebastian shrugged. "But there's the proof. I also found my watch and a few other things that had gone missing around the restaurant. My watch is brand-new, and I put it on the counter last week to keep it from getting wet when I was cooking. I thought I'd lost it, but it turns out Roxanne just stole it from me when I took it off."

Kate reached for her bag and set it on her lap. She placed her precious diamond necklace in its zippered pocket, but it wasn't easy, because her hand was shaking.

I'm going to have to change the locks on my apartment, she realized with a slap of shock. *I had no idea they were so easy to pick!*

Kate thought of all the nights she'd locked her apartment doors, thinking that she and Molly were safe behind them. She pictured her little daughter, sleeping on her pillow, and her blood went cold.

As she was processing that mental image, her phone buzzed for the tenth time that day. Kate picked it up and murmured, "Excuse me, Sebastian. I have to take a call."

"Certainly. I'll run along now. I don't want to tire you."

She glanced up at him as he stood. "Thank you for the flowers, Sebastian. And...the information."

"Anytime, gorgeous. I'll see you."

Kate watched as her chef walked out of the room and closed the door behind him, and she glanced at the phone in annoyance.

Somebody wants to talk to me pretty bad, she thought, and wiped her eyes with her fingers. *I hope it's not any more terrible news!*

"Hello?"

Roxanne's anxious voice jumped out at her. "Oh Kate, thank heaven I got you! I've been trying to reach you all morning!"

Kate stiffened angrily. A tidal wave of rage jumped up in her, but Roxanne gabbled on before she could reply.

"Kate, I was released from the hospital this morning, and I went back to the restaurant," she explained. "I wanted to talk to Sebastian, but he wasn't in the kitchen. I went out on the back dock to look for him, but he wasn't there."

She paused and took a breath, then added, "He was coming down the stairs from your roof patio, Kate. I saw him with my own eyes!"

Kate sucked in air for the second time that day. Her first instinct was to tell Roxanne she was lying, that she was busted, and that she was fired. She closed her eyes. The memory of her anniversary necklace swaying from Sebastian's fingers made her mad enough to scream.

But she squeezed her eyes closed and fought her fury down. The matter at hand was a theft, an official crime, and she couldn't afford to indulge her feelings. Kate frowned down at her handbag.

"Kate, are you there?"

Kate bit her lips and replied, slowly and evenly. "I'm here."

"Kate, Sebastian's a thief, I know it in my bones. I've had his number from the first day he came to work, but now I have proof!"

Kate bit her lip again. "Are…are you saying you have something else?"

There was a short pause. "No," Roxanne confessed. "But I saw him, Kate, he was coming down—"

Kate took a deep breath. "Okay, Roxanne, I get it," she broke in. "Right now, I just need you to rest up and—I'll talk to you about it when you get back to work."

"That's another thing," Roxanne retorted. "Sebastian hired somebody to work my job, and I wasn't even gone two days!"

Kate opened her eyes in surprise. "Take a couple of days off to rest," she replied slowly. "I'll take care of it. We'll talk about your schedule going forward."

Roxanne's voice was an audible frown. "What do you mean, talk about my—"

"I have to go now, Roxanne," Kate went on. She was getting angry again. "I'm not feeling my best right now. Goodbye."

She pressed the red button on her phone before she had a chance to let her fury run wild. The sense of being betrayed, of her child's safety being violated, burned in her chest until she wanted to scream.

Kate dropped her bag on the floor and flung off the coverlet. Her caftan trailed behind her as she stalked off to the wardrobe. She pulled the clothes off the rack, stuffed them into a big plastic shopping bag, and tossed it onto the bed.

She turned on her heel and charged off to the door to her daughter's bedroom. "Molly!"

Her tone made the door pop open, and Molly's startled face appeared in the opening.

"Pack your things. We're going back home right away!"

Chapter 20

Buck polished off a fried chicken leg, then licked his fingers and mumbled, "*Mm-mm!* That was some good food, Conchita." He grabbed a buttered biscuit out of a bowl on the table and stuffed it into his mouth.

His cook, a short, stolid Mexican *abuela* with a long braid, shot him an indulgent look from her dark eyes. "Why you don't want to eat in the dining room like everybody else," she chided, in a tone usually reserved for badly-behaved children.

Buck washed the biscuit down with a long slug of tea. "It's too shiny in there. Who wants mirrored walls in a dining room?" he complained. "I don't like to be staring at myself when I eat. Makes me feel like I'm in a casino."

Conchita turned and walked back to the gleaming, industrial-grade stove. "I don't like nobody looking over my shoulder when I cook," she complained. "Why don't you go and find your lady friend. You and her like each other."

Buck's hand paused halfway to his mouth. He shot her a startled look and blotted his lips with a napkin.

"Kate and Molly are only staying here until Doc says she can leave," he informed her, but she just gave him a skeptical look.

"Uh-huh."

"She's Carson's friend," he replied, as much to himself as to her. "I'm just playing host until he gets back."

"Okay," she murmured, and busied herself with a pot on the stove.

Buck shot her a worried glance, then wiped his mouth with a napkin and pushed his chair back. "But it might be a good idea to go check in on her, at that," he mumbled. He hadn't much liked the looks of Kate's visitor, and she wasn't up to an extended visit.

It might be a good idea to give the guy a little push, if he was still up there.

"Thanks for the snack, Conchita," he mumbled, and leaned over to give her a peck on the cheek. She presented it, but waved him away. "Ay, get out of here," she told him. "You like a big kid."

"You know you love me," Buck told her over his shoulder, and grabbed another biscuit to munch on the way up to Kate's suite.

Buck took the stairs two at a time, then turned to march down the guest hall to Kate's door. He polished off the last of his biscuit, brushed the crumbs off his shirt, and knocked on the door.

"Kate? It's Buck."

There was no answer, and he straightened up and knocked again a little louder. "Kate?"

To his surprise, his rapping pushed the door slightly ajar, and the only answer was silence. *Maybe she's asleep,* he thought; but he poked his head in to look anyway.

To his dismay, the room was empty.

He pushed the door open and walked in. The bed was made, the room was neat as a pin, but Kate was gone, her clothes and her bag were gone, and there was no sound from next door. Buck walked over to the connecting door between the two suites and rapped on it.

"Molly, you in there?"

He pushed the door open, but the adjoining room was the same: neat, empty and silent.

Kate and Molly were gone.

Buck turned and blew out of the suite and down the stairs. Doc had told Kate to rest, and she'd seen the sense of it. Something must've happened to make her change her mind so fast, and without a word to anybody.

And by 'anybody,' he meant himself.

He strode out into the big great room downstairs and met Morgan just coming in from outside. His brother took off his hat and wiped his brow with his arm.

"Shoo! It must be ninety degrees out there today," he grumbled. "I'm gonna have to come in and cool down before I hit it again."

Buck's eyes moved past him. "Morgan, did you see Kate out there?"

Morgan's piercing blue eyes met his. "You mean that redheaded woman who's been staying here?"

"Yeah, Kate," Buck frowned. "I went up to her room to check on her, and she's gone."

Morgan walked past him. " I saw somebody's car in the courtyard a minute ago," he threw over his shoulder. "Didn't see who was in it."

Buck frowned and walked through the atrium to the front doors. As he watched, Kate's car dwindled into the distance down the long main drive. He planted his hands on his hips.

Wonder if it was something I said, he mused; but he couldn't think of anything he'd said or done to make Kate bolt like a skittish foal.

He remembered the guy he'd surprised in the dining room, and his frown deepened. He hadn't liked the stranger's looks, but he couldn't put his finger on just why.

But Kate had been okay before that guy came, and now she wasn't.

Buck turned back into the house and found Morgan with a glass of water in one hand and a piece of paper in the other. "I found this on the table over yonder," he mumbled, and handed it over. Buck took it and read:

Thank you all for everything. You've been so kind, but I have to leave. Somebody broke into my apartment.

Kate.

Buck exclaimed in outrage and hit the paper with his hand. "Somebody robbed her house," he marveled. "Lowlifes! Thank God they weren't there when it happened."

Morgan grumbled under his breath. "Sandy Creek ain't the same place it was twenty years ago," he mumbled.

Buck scowled at the paper. "I'm going over to Kate's place to make sure they're all right," he thought aloud.

Morgan's eyes followed him as he turned to go. "You might want to think about that thing," he rumbled. "Ain't she Carson's friend?" he warned, and Buck stopped, turned to glare at him, and stuck his fists on his hips.

"I never said she wasn't," he snapped. "I said I was going over there to check on her. You wanna make something out of it?"

Morgan held his eye. "No. But Carson will, if he finds out."

Buck scowled at him, then turned to stalk out to his truck, yank the door open, slide in, and crank the engine with a roar. He turned the truck around, then sent it zooming down the driveway. He was mad, but even he knew it was because Morgan was right.

Because his brother's warning had hit just a little bit too close to home.

Chapter 21

"Mamma, are you all right?"

Kate glanced over at her daughter as she drove past the 19th-century brick storefronts lining the main street of Sandy Creek. Molly's big blue eyes looked worried.

Kate pasted on a smile for her. "I'm fine, baby," she murmured.

"You don't look fine," Molly replied in a small voice, and then added: "I'm scared, Mamma."

Kate pulled up at a stop sign and turned to her daughter. "There's no need to be scared," she murmured, and reached out to caress Molly's cheek. "Mamma's going to have our locks changed. Everything's going to be alright."

"Why would somebody break into our house?" Molly whimpered. "Are they mad at us?"

Kate turned back to the wheel and stared resolutely at the street, because if she didn't, her fragile self-control was going to snap.

"No, chickadee," she said at last. "Somebody was just selfish and bad, that's all. It won't happen again. That's a promise."

To her relief, the puckered frown between Molly's eyes smoothed out, and Kate nudged the car down the street to the restaurant. She turned into the Stonehouse parking lot, but pulled around to the back of the old warehouse, to her own parking space.

She wasn't ready to face her employees and get embroiled in the drama between Sebastian and Roxanne. She was shaken, she was angry, and she needed to make sure their apartment never got burgled again.

She pulled up the parking brake and unlocked the doors. "We're going up the back way this time, Molly," she murmured, and climbed out of the car. She glanced up at the black metal stair. It drew a diagonal line across the brick wall and ran straight up to her rooftop patio.

She let Molly slide out of the car, then took her hand and led her up the stairs. "Be careful, now," she murmured, and followed her daughter up to the roof.

To Kate's relief, when they reached it, the patio looked untouched. The big potted plants were still there, their patio table and chairs were still in the same place, and the big green shade awning was still in place. She shouldered ahead of Molly and pulled her keys out of her bag, but when she went to unlock the door, she noticed that the lock was heavily scratched, and that the strike plate on the door frame was slightly bent.

Kate pinched her mouth into a hard, angry line and unlocked the door. As it swung open, to her horror, she saw that the living room was a shambles. Their lamps were thrown down on the floor, pillows were strewn everywhere, and every piece of furniture that could be knocked over was lying sideways.

"Oh, Mamma," Molly gasped, and the high-pitched whine that followed warned that she was going to cry. Kate reached out and took her daughter into her arms and kissed her hair.

"It's okay. It's just messy," she whispered. "We'll clean it up. It'll be alright."

"But it's *our house*," Molly insisted. "It's *ours*, not anybody else's!" She lifted her head and stared around the room with dark, frightened eyes.

"What if the bad people come back, Mamma?"

"They're not coming back," Kate reassured her. "Come on. I need you to pick up those pillows and put them back on the couch. I'm going to check our rooms. I'll be back."

She slapped Molly's seat to get her moving, and stood there until Molly began to reluctantly clean up the pillows; then she ventured to the back of the apartment and steeled herself for what she was going to see.

She opened Molly's bedroom door and had to stifle a gasp. Her daughter's room had been ransacked. Molly's lavender coverlet and pillows were on the floor and her stuffed toys were scattered everywhere. Even her little pink jewelry box was opened and overturned, and her plastic bracelets and rings were strewn over the nightstand.

Kate covered her mouth with a shaking hand. Nothing had been damaged, and there was nothing of great value in Molly's room; but the thought of a stranger pawing through Molly's jewelry box and searching her bed was like a knife twisting in Kate's ribs. Her eyes blurred with tears, and she quickly turned to shut the door behind her to keep Molly from walking in.

Kate wept as she hurried to pick up the quilt, the pillows, and the toys. She didn't want Molly to come walking in and be traumatized by the intrusion; but her grief quickly curdled into anger as she tossed the toys into the toy bin, pushed the pillows against the headboard, and threw the quilt back over the bed.

So help me, she vowed, *whoever did this is going to pay. I don't care who it is. When I find out, I'm going after them.*

I'm not going to stop until I see them in jail!

She bent over to pick her daughter's scattered jewelry off the floor. She lifted a little heart-shaped locket with Molly's name engraved on the front, and tears blurred her eyes again. It was a trifle, a spur of the moment gift from Kevin when they'd gone to the state fair a few years back; but Molly cherished it now.

Kate's mouth twisted as she returned it gently to the pink box. *This is never going to happen again, baby*, she thought grimly. *I don't care if I have to buy a gun. No one is ever going to break into our house again!*

A shrill scream made Kate drop the jewelry box and rush out into the hall. Molly's shriek clawed at the ceiling.

"Mamma, somebody's trying to open the *door*!"

Kate flew into the living room, yanked Molly behind her, and turned to face the patio door, heart pounding. She watched in horror as the doorknob turned, and she cast about her for something to defend them. Her fingers curled around a heavy terracotta pot, and she pulled her arm back.

Molly screamed as the door swung open, and Kate smoked the pot through the air like a fastball. The missile smashed against the far wall and shattered into smithereens, barely missing the tall shadow of a man as he stepped inside.

Kate snatched up another pot and brandished it like a weapon. "Get out of my house!" she screamed, and raised her arm to throw it; but the shadow rushed her and grabbed it away.

Molly shrieked in panic, and Kate was forced to drop the pot; but her adrenalin rush gave her the strength to curl her fingers around the intruder's big arm and scratch him like a cat.

The stranger yelled and broke free, and Kate pulled back and slugged him in the jaw as hard as she could. They both shouted in pain, and Kate danced back, clutching her throbbing hand. She looked over her shoulder and gasped, "Run, Molly!"

But to her panic, instead of running, Molly just stared at the intruder and tilted her head in confusion.

The shadowy intruder fell back against the far wall, panting. He lifted wide, baffled eyes.

"What is *wrong* with you, woman?" he demanded. "I think you brought blood!"

Molly raised a shaking hand and pointed at him. "Mamma, it's—it's only Buck," she announced in a tiny voice.

Kate stared at the intruder in frowning confusion. The tall, threatening shadow slowly resolved into a harassed-looking Buck Spade.

But instead of feeling regret, her pent-up anger and frustration exploded in a fountain of fire.

"What are you doing in my *house*?" she screamed, and to her own fury, her voice was on the edge of tears. "You nearly gave me a heart attack!"

Buck lifted startled blue eyes from his wounded arm to her face. "I just wanted to see if you were all right!" he exclaimed. "I didn't expect you to claw me like a wildcat!"

Kate glanced around her and her eyes fell on her daughter. Her maternal instincts roared up, and she pulled Molly tight to her chest. She closed her eyes and replied in a throbbing voice: "I didn't ask you to come here. And you're supposed to knock before you come barging into someone else's house!"

Buck spread his hands out in appeal. "The door was standing open," he explained, and Kate's eyes blazed.

"Because the *lock* is broken!"

Buck's bright eyes flicked over her trembling arms, and Molly's tear-stained face. His look of outrage faded, and he rubbed his arm.

"Sorry if I scared you, Kate." His glance moved beyond her to the overturned furniture, and his expression darkened. "Looks like somebody tossed your place pretty good. Have you called the sheriff?"

Kate glared at him. "I haven't had a chance to do anything!" she cried. "I just got here. Look at this place! Look at it!"

Her voice broke on a sob, and she shook her head angrily. "Just go," she told him. "I can't talk to you right now!"

"I can call the sher—"

Her voice jumped to a scream. "Get out, get out, *get out!*" she sobbed, and clamped Molly tighter to her chest.

Buck's voice was soft and resigned. "All right, Kate." She could hear the patio door creak open and his heavy footsteps receding across the patio and down the steps to the parking lot. A few moments later a truck motor cranked up, followed by the sound of it driving away.

Kate buried her face into Molly's silky hair and closed her eyes. Her heart was still galloping, and the adrenalin pumping through her veins made her feel as if her hair was crackling with electricity. She wanted to scream, she wanted to cry, and she wanted to beat somebody up.

But there was nobody there but Molly; and so she pressed a kiss into her daughter's hair and wept over her.

Chapter 22

"Next Wednesday? My apartment was broken into," Kate sputtered into her phone. "My door is compromised! I need the locks changed tonight!"

The voice on the other end drawled, "I'm sorry, ma'am, but I'm booked until next week. I can't get out to your place until next Wednesday."

Kate squeezed her eyes shut in frustration and stifled an angry retort. She reminded herself that the man wasn't to blame for being busy.

"I see. Thank you."

"You might try some of the other locksmiths," he mumbled. "Good luck."

Kate hung up and paced back and forth across her bedroom. She'd had to clean it up, too: her own jewelry box had been rifled, her bed had been stripped, and every drawer in the room had been pulled open.

The lock on her back door had been picked and damaged, and she and Molly weren't safe until it was changed; but she'd called a half-dozen locksmiths, and none were able to come out that night.

Kate closed her eyes and put a hand to her head, because it had begun to throb. She'd solved her immediate problem by jamming a chair back against the broken doorknob, but she wasn't going to get a wink of sleep as long as it was compromised.

She'd cooked up some spaghetti in her little kitchenette for Molly, but she was too upset to eat any of it. She'd tucked Molly into bed after, and had whispered reassurance until her little daughter drifted off to sleep.

Kate paced back and forth unhappily. It was a minor miracle that Molly had even been able to sleep after the drama of that afternoon. Anger whisked up in her again when she remembered Buck barging into their living room without so much as a knock on the door. Molly had been terrified, and so had she.

They'd been scared enough already.

Kate clasped her hands as she paced. Her anger at Buck lingered, but it was beginning to be tinged with regret. She was still charged up, still upset, but the initial shock had faded, and while her nerves were badly jangled, she'd regained control of them.

I slugged Buck Spade, she thought unhappily. *I clocked him across the jaw.*

True, I thought he was a home invader, and he didn't knock or tell me he was coming.

But still.

Kate hugged herself and turned to stalk back across her bedroom. *Buck was so kind to us after my fall,* she thought ruefully. *He probably thinks I'm a barbarian, now.*

Kate stopped pacing and rubbed the knuckles of her right hand. They still hurt, and it was a safe bet that Buck's jaw did, too.

I'm going to have to apologize to him, she fretted.

If he'll let me get near enough to do it.

She walked to her bedroom window and peeked through the blinds. It was past closing, the restaurant was closed and locked, and she scanned the parking lot below.

It was empty, but she was still on edge.

Kate turned and paced back toward her bedroom door. That the thief might be one of her employees was the most painful part of the ordeal. She was going to have to deal with that, too.

Her first impulse was to fire Roxanne, but she knew that would be unfair without solid proof of her guilt. And there were conflicting accusations. Sebastian and Roxanne were both accusing one another of theft.

Sebastian had been in possession of her stolen necklace, but he'd also been the one to return it to her.

Roxanne had been struck on the head, and she'd implied that someone else had done it. Also that Sebastian had been on her patio in her absence.

Kate narrowed her eyes. The memory of Molly's jumbled bedclothes lying on the floor was something she'd never forget and that she couldn't forgive.

Whoever had done that—and she was going to find out—was going to regret ever having dared.

A little clock on the wall wound up and chimed one in the morning, and Kate rubbed her arms. She was wearing her peignoir, and the night was getting cool.

She turned and paced back to the window. She lifted one of the blinds and glanced out again. The parking lot was still empty.

Kate released it. At one o' clock in the morning, the whole world felt dark and dangerous; and until she could get the door repaired, their apartment wasn't safe.

She shuddered, remembering the horror she'd felt when that door had swung open and she'd had nothing to defend them but a pot. If it had been a real intruder, she and Molly would've been helpless.

She'd lasted all of ten seconds fighting with Buck.

Kate's lips drooped unhappily. *I've never been concerned about my safety in my life,* she thought. *But I'm going to have to think about it now, no matter how much I hate the idea.*

This can't happen again.

Her thoughts returned to Buck, to his comical blue eyes and O-shaped mouth when she'd punched him. He'd looked as shocked as a cat-clawed puppy. She pressed her fingers against her lips and giggled a bit. He'd looked gobsmacked, all right.

Kate's smile faded, and she sighed wistfully. *It isn't really funny. I hope I didn't hurt him badly,* she fretted; but she had to say, his jaw had been as hard as a rock.

It had even been hard to make an impression on his arm with her nails.

Kate hunched her shoulders and set her regret aside. She couldn't do anything to mend it that night. She reached for her flowing housecoat, shouldered into it, and abandoned her bedroom for the living room.

She was going to have to stand guard until morning; so she might as well go make herself a strong pot of coffee.

Chapter 23

The sound of heavy knocking on her front door woke Kate from a sound sleep. She straightened in alarm and looked around. Morning light was pouring through the windows.

She'd fallen asleep.

Her eyes flicked to the patio door, but to her relief, the chair was still jammed tight against the broken knob. Kate pushed a tendril of red hair out of her eyes and stood up sleepily.

The sound of knocking came again, followed by a man's voice. "Mrs. Malone? Are you home?"

Kate tightened her flowing silk housecoat around her waist. She walked to the door and called, "Who is it?"

"I'm the locksmith, Mrs. Malone. I came by to fix your door."

Kate frowned and opened the door a crack. She peeped out, and sure enough, a handyman was standing in the hall outside with a toolbox in his hands.

"I thought you said you weren't able to come by until Wednesday," she murmured. "But I'm glad you're here. Give me a minute to get dressed."

"Yes ma'am."

Kate closed the door and hurried off to her bedroom. She rapped on Molly's bedroom door as she passed. "Molly, get up and dress! It's"—she glanced at the hall clock— "almost eight o'clock!"

Molly mumbled sleepily from inside, and Kate hurried on to change clothes. She saw her new cotton kaftan thrown over a chair, and she quickly changed into it and slid her bare feet into a pair of flat scuffs.

She blew back into the living room, pushed her hair back from her face, and opened the door. The man standing outside nodded to her.

"Come in," Kate murmured, and stood aside to let the man pass. "Did you have a cancellation?"

The man walked into the room, then turned to face her with a wry expression. "You could say that," he told her sheepishly. "I got a call from the Seven Ranch. That sends you to the head of the line, ma'am."

Shock wiped a blank across Kate's face, and she stared at him in open-mouthed surprise before gathering her scattered wits. Her first impulse was to tell him that she didn't want to cut in line, but the prospect of another night behind a compromised door made her bite her lip. "Let me—let me show you the broken lock," she stammered. "I want the best security lock you have on both exterior doors, plus serious deadbolts."

"Yes, ma'am."

Kate showed him the patio door and watched as he pulled her chair back, turned it around, and sat in it. He set his toolbox down on the floor and pulled the door open to inspect the scratched lock.

"Yeah, somebody picked this," he mumbled, and turned the knob. "See these scratches?" He pointed to some scuff marks with a long brown finger.

Anger danced in Kate's heart again. "I see them," she growled. "Was the lock easy to pick open?"

The man shook his head as he leaned down to open his tool box. "Afraid so. Someone who knows how to do it can rake the lock with a jiggler and get it open pretty fast. If you'd had a deadbolt on the inside, they would've had to do something noisier to get it open. They'd have to kick it in."

Kate stared at him. That unwelcome mental image was playing in her imagination, and she turned away to shut it out. "What would I have to do to keep *that* from happening?"

The man ran a hand up the door jamb. "You'd have to get three-inch screws to anchor the lock deep into the door frame. Even then they could kick it in, if they wanted. It'd just take longer."

"Anchor the lock, then," Kate growled, and then bit her lip and closed her eyes to get control of her temper. *I can't get mad at this fellow*, she told herself. *It isn't his fault.*

"It'll take me awhile," he mumbled. "I'm going to have to go to the hardware store to get the locks you want."

"That's fine."

A distant jingle from the back of the apartment made Kate turn on her heel and walk to her bedroom. She found her handbag and pulled her phone out of it.

"Hello?"

Buck's voice mumbled to her from the other end. "Are you okay?" he began.

Kate closed her eyes and exhaled in embarrassment. "I am now." She bit her lip and forged on, "Buck, I'm so sorry. I was so upset yesterday. I didn't even know that it was you until Molly told me. I thought you were a prowler breaking into our house!" She paused and added, "I hope I didn't hurt you too…badly."

"Oh law, no," Buck replied easily. "I'm fine. I was just calling to make sure that you and Molly were, too."

Kate pulled her hair back from her brow. "I'm better. I think Molly's okay. The locksmith is here working on the door." She smiled a bit and added, "He told me that I have you to thank for that. It was very kind of you."

"Aw, I just wanted to make sure it got fixed."

His voice was gruff, but Kate's heart melted at Buck's generosity. She played with a little tendril of hair and murmured, "You know, I haven't cooked a nice meal in a while. Why don't you come over tonight and have dinner with us?"

She could hear a smile in Buck's voice. "That'd be real nice," he rumbled.

Kate was a little surprised by how pleased she was. "Good. I'll make my famous trout in brown butter with creamed corn grits."

"Come again?"

Kate laughed and twirled her hair in her fingers. "You need to be a little adventurous," she told him. "Have something beside beef for one night."

"I'm looking forward to it."

Kate twisted around toward the bedroom door. She could hear the handyman tinkering with the door.

"The locksmith is going to take awhile, but he should be finished by five, I'd think," she thought aloud. "Drop by at six. I'll have dinner ready."

"I'll be there."

"I'll be here. See you then, Buck."

Kate smiled and pressed the red button on the phone. She felt so much better that she had to admit that she was beginning to like Buck Spade.

She felt guilty about it, but she hadn't been nearly as pleased about spending time with Carson. And she hadn't heard from Carson in over a week in any case.

Kate smiled to herself and walked to her closet to throw open the door. She had to get dressed to run out to the market for the ingredients she needed. She was going to get the freshest she could find, because she had a sudden desire to blow Buck Spade's mind; and she was just the girl to do it.

Chapter 24

Buck adjusted his collar, gave himself a last critical glance in the mirror, and walked out of his bathroom suite. He was wearing his best Sunday go to meeting dress shirt, and it was so starched and ironed that the collar practically creased his neck. He was wearing a black string tie, a leather belt with a silver concho buckle, and his best dress slacks.

He reached for his best gray Stetson as he walked out his front door, and he set it on his head as he trotted down the stairs.

Morgan was sitting in the big common room beyond the stairs. His long, jean-clad legs were crossed underneath a newspaper, and he lowered it to follow Buck with his dark blue eyes as he passed. "You're gonna get your can kicked."

"I don't want to hear it."

Morgan drawled, "I could swear I'm smelling cologne." He turned the page of the paper and scanned an article. "Yep. Eau de Swamp Bottom."

"Stay out of it," Buck tossed over his shoulder, and blew on through the atrium.

Buck pushed through the big wooden front doors and out of the house. He paused on the front steps, planted his hands on his hips, and looked up at the sky.

It was a cool, peaceful twilit evening. The sky overhead was a pale, empty lavender except for the North Star. It burned high and white above the far horizon, and the air smelled sweetly of dried hay and clover.

Buck paused for a moment to enjoy it, then turned to climb into his truck to drive into town. He was surprised to find that his heart was beating a little quicker as he cranked the truck and sent it cruising down the drive. He rolled the windows down to enjoy the soft evening air as he drove, and he whistled a bit.

He hadn't gone out on a date in years, and he'd forgotten how pleasant it was to have dinner with a beautiful woman. Beautiful place, too.

He'd only got a glimpse of Kate's loft, but what he'd seen was stylish. Her place had an artsy, relaxed feel, and he liked it. He was looking forward to a nice meal, too. He liked trout, though he didn't have an idea in the world what grits were.

But if a gorgeous redhead like Kate offered it to him, he was gonna eat it.

He pulled the truck into the Sandy Creek city limits just as the street lights were beginning to come on. The main drag was about five blocks long and its highest building was the Sandy Creek Baptist Church, and that was only because of its steeple. Most of the shops were red brick storefronts that were pretty much unchanged from the 1800s.

He loved that about it.

The Stonehouse was in full swing, and its big warehouse windows were blazing with light. Buck pulled in and circled the building to the back. He parked beside the stairway to Kate's rooftop patio, and as he glanced to the right he was startled to see the same man who'd visited her at the Seven.

The tall, slim man was wearing a white apron and was leaning against the wall of the loading dock. He lifted a bottle of something to his lips and glared out across the parking lot. He didn't look happy.

Buck pulled the keys out of the ignition and slid out of the truck. He walked to the stairs and trotted up to the patio, but he could feel the cook's eyes on his back all the way up. The feeling was so strong that he stopped at the head of the stairs and turned to return the stare; but when he looked, the man was gone.

Buck set his mouth and turned back to the patio. There were potted plants everywhere, and tiki torches and little white lights were strung all around the fenced space. A nice big glass table was already set for dinner, and a mouthwatering aroma of grilled fish floated on the evening air.

As he stood there, the patio door opened and Kate came walking through it carrying a big platter. She smiled as she saw him, and Buck took off his hat.

"Hi, Buck. You hungry?"

Buck's eyes followed the platter as Kate set it carefully on the table. Fragrant mist trailed in the evening air behind the plate, and his stomach rumbled.

Kate licked her thumb and glanced at it. "I made plenty," she murmured. "I'm kind of hungry tonight."

His glance lingered on her. Kate's wavy auburn hair was tumbling over her shoulders, and the soft light of the torches painted her skin gold and flickered in her eyes. Buck stared at her. He'd seen a movie once about medieval Ireland, and Kate reminded him of the female star.

The woman who'd played the young queen.

She was dressed in a soft, off-the-shoulder crocheted top with bell sleeves over a long, flowing cotton skirt in a delicate yellow print. She looked beautiful and feminine and romantic, and he blinked when she turned to smile at him.

"Thanks for inviting me over," he murmured, hat in hand. "Can I help you?"

"You're my guest tonight, Buck," she told him softly. "You can sit down and get comfortable. I only have to bring out the sides and the pitchers. I'll be right back."

She disappeared through the door again, and Buck pulled out a chair and sat down. It was a beautiful night, just getting dark, and the rooftop patio was tall enough to catch the cool evening breeze. There was a new moon in the sky overhead, and the faint sound of people laughing and talking wafted to him from the front parking lot.

His eyes returned to the platter. He pulled his chair up to the table and leaned over to inspect the main dish. The platter was ringed with parsley and red potatoes and arrayed with perfectly browned trout fillets. The fillets were hot out of the oven, they gleamed with a faint sheen of butter, and they were sprinkled with slivered, toasted almonds.

Molly came walking out with a salad bowl in her hands, and her face brightened as she saw him sitting there. "Hello Buck. I'm glad you came over to our house."

Buck turned to smile at her. "I'm glad, too, doodlebug. Are you helping your Mamma cook?" he teased.

Molly nodded as she set the bowl down on the table. "I picked out the dishes," she announced proudly. "I picked the yellow ones."

"Well, they're real pretty," Buck assured her, with a nod. "You've got a good eye."

"We've got new doorknobs too," Molly told him proudly as she climbed up into a chair. "Mamma says that now we're safe."

Buck's smile faded. Molly's sunny confidence made him cough and muster a smile for her. "That's right. You're locked up like Fort Knox."

Kate reappeared carrying a pitcher of tea and a bread basket. She set them both down on the table and pulled up a chair. "Well, are you two ready to eat?"

"I am," Buck told her with a smile. "I've been sitting here looking at this food. I'm ready."

Kate shook out a napkin and beamed at him. "All right then. Why don't you say grace tonight, Buck?"

He nodded, bowed his head, and took a breath before praying, "Lord, we're real grateful for this food, and for this pretty night, and for the pleasure of good company. Please bless this food to the nourishment of our bodies, and our bodies to your service. Amen."

"Amen," Molly echoed, and Kate reached out for the platter. "Hand me your plate, Buck," she commanded.

"Yes ma'am."

Kate took it and lifted a big, beautiful trout off the platter with a server. "How many fillets would you like?"

"Two big ones," Buck answered instantly, and stuffed his napkin into his collar. "Some of those potatoes, too."

Kate smiled and heaped his plate. Buck took it from her with a hopeful smile. He loved good food, and the perfect, crispy-brown fillets and tender potatoes made his mouth water. He waited until Kate had served Molly and herself, then took an eager forkful of trout.

To his delight, the fish was flaky and tender and the butter glaze added a faint nutty aftertaste. The slivered almonds provided a light, satisfying crunch after the fish itself melted in his mouth, and he shook his head in wordless appreciation as he took another bite.

"This is really good, Kate," Buck mumbled through a mouthful of potatoes. He didn't know why he was surprised, but he was. He didn't know many knockout women who could cook better than his grandmother, but then again, maybe that was why Kate was in the restaurant business.

Kate shot him a pleased glance. Her skin glowed like pearl in the yellow torchlight, and her eyes were big black pupils, ringed with aquamarine blue. She tucked a red curl behind her ear and smiled.

"Thank you, Buck. It was nice to try my hand again. I love to entertain, but it's been awhile since I've had someone over."

Buck's eyes lingered on her. Kate had the redhead's blessing, all right; pale, flawless skin, delicate, peach-pink lips, and the face of a woman in her twenties.

She was the real dish at that table; and he was caring less and less about what Carson would think about him spending time with her. If it was all right with Kate, it was all right with him. Buck shot her another glance as she turned to murmur to Molly.

She was the one who'd decide in the end, anyway.

They made pleasant small talk as they ate, and when Buck blotted his lips with his napkin at the end of the meal, he had to say, it had been the best dinner he'd had in a long time. It was a cool, breezy night, the air smelled of the rose bushes at the side of the building, and the meal made him want to moan like he'd just had one of Miss Annie's sausage biscuits.

Kate turned to her daughter. "Molly, I want you to go brush your teeth and change into your jammies. I'll come and tuck you in after a little bit."

"All right, Mamma."

Kate watched indulgently as Molly slid down from her chair and ran inside; then she turned back to him.

"That was a fine meal, Kate," he told her with a smile. "Best I've had since I can't remember."

"Why don't you come inside," she invited, and rose. "Would you like an after-dinner glass of wine?"

Buck rubbed his nose. He hated wine, but he smiled big and bright just the same. "That'd be great."

"I'll go get some," Kate murmured, and paused in the doorway with her hand on the jamb. She stood there for an instant, a silhouette against the golden light beyond.

"Come on in."

Yes ma'am, Buck thought to himself, but only nodded and followed her.

He stepped inside, and now that he had the leisure to look around, he approved of Kate's place. The brick warehouse walls had been left untouched, but there were big potted plants everywhere, a couple of big splashy paintings on the walls, and some bright, simple furniture that looked like it'd come from a sixties sitcom.

Kate's voice drifted back to him from the kitchen. "Do you like red or white, Buck?"

Buck stifled a grimace, but called out: "Red, thank you ma'am."

Kate turned and smiled at him over the bar. "Oh, don't call me ma'am," she laughed, and disappeared.

Buck pulled his slacks up, sat down on the low couch, and stretched an arm over the back. Kate came padding back with two wine glasses in her hand. She took a sip from one and gave him the other.

"Mamma?"

Molly's querulous voice came faintly from the back hall, and Kate set her drink down on the side table. "I'll be right back," she told him, and hurried off. Buck noticed that Kate was barefoot, and for some reason, the sight of her manicured toes made his scalp tingle.

It wasn't like he'd never seen feet before; but it messed him up, and he took a slug of the wine to distract himself.

The wine tasted just like he remembered, and he set the glass down on the sofa arm and sighed as he waited.

Kate came padding back after a few minutes and settled in on the couch beside him. She pulled her feet up under her like a child and took the wine glass.

She took a sip, and her laughing eyes met his over the rim. Buck turned toward her, and his brown fingers tapped the back of the couch.

"Are you sure you're alright?" he asked quietly. Kate nodded and set her glass down. She gave him a rueful look.

"I'm fine," she smiled, and looked down at the couch. "It's just that I have"—she sighed and pulled her hair back from her brow— "*anger* issues. I'm sure you've noticed," she sputtered.

Buck listened as she went on, "When I came home to this ransacked house, I was mad as fire. And when you showed up in that doorway I thought you were the burglar, returning to the scene of the crime. I wanted to kill something, and—there you were."

"I'll have to be careful then," he replied softly. "Don't want to get scratched again."

Her brows rushed together in dismay. "Buck, I'm so sorry about that—"

He leaned in slightly and took her chin in his hand. "It's all right," he chuckled. "I don't even think about that. But I am thinking about something else.

"Miss Kate, I've been wanting to kiss you for awhile now," he whispered. "Can I?"

Her eyes searched his, and a smile slowly curved one end of her mouth. "Only one way to find out, cowboy."

Buck smiled and was leaning down when Molly's voice murmured from the hall.

"Mamma?"

Both of them froze. Buck rolled his eyes toward the sound. Molly was standing in the doorway in her pink nightgown.

"You didn't hear my prayers."

Kate pulled away from him and replied,"Okay. I'll come and hear your night prayers."

Molly dimpled and turned back for her bedroom, and Kate smiled up at him apologetically. "I'm sorry, Buck," she murmured, and rose to follow her daughter.

Buck watched her go, then exhaled silently. He was still all wound up, ready to kiss Kate, and his heart was bumping in his chest.

But the longer Kate stayed gone, the more he thought about what Morgan had been telling him. He hated to admit it, but maybe Morgan was right. Maybe it wasn't good for him to be there. Maybe he should hold off until Carson got back from Dallas. Let him and Kate decide what they wanted to do.

Then if they parted ways, he could visit Kate with a clear conscience.

He stood up slowly as Kate slipped back into the room a few minutes later. She smiled and murmured, "She won't go to sleep if I don't hear her prayers."

She walked in close and smiled up into his eyes. The look in those big green eyes was warm and inviting and all but saying *kiss me* right out loud.

Buck bit his lip. He wanted to kiss her, he was seeing himself kissing her, and he wasn't going to kiss her.

"Listen Kate, I think I better head out," he mumbled, and looked down at his boots. "I don't want to keep you up too late." He glanced at her face and smiled. "You and Molly have had a scare, and a long day, and you need your rest. Especially after this big meal you cooked up." He shook his head and sighed, remembering it.

"It was sure enough delicious."

A disappointed look flicked across Kate's eyes, but it was gone so fast that he wasn't sure he'd really seen it. She smiled and nodded.

"I was glad to do it, Buck," she replied softly, and searched his eyes. What she saw there brought a smile back to her lips.

"I hope you and Molly come back to the Seven and keep on with her lessons," he murmured. "Be a shame if she quit."

"Oh we'll be there," Kate assured him. "We're not quitters. I may even take my chances again." She arched an eyebrow and smiled, and Buck laughed and turned for the door.

"Be sure and call me when you come out," he rumbled.

"I will, Buck. Good night."

He paused in the doorway and turned to look down at her. He leaned down, gave her a peck on her smooth brow, and walked out.

He picked his hat up off a chair in passing and walked down the steps to his truck. It was late now, getting toward midnight, and the restaurant was closed and dark.

Buck paused at the door of his truck and looked back up at the patio. Kate was standing there at the head of the stairs, backlit by the glimmering torches, a shadow rimmed in gold.

Buck raised a hand and climbed into his truck, but his smile faded as he cranked the engine and pulled out of the parking space.

He was willing to wait for Carson, but not for long; and as he nudged the truck out into the street Buck didn't know whether to hope that Carson would come back quick, or stay gone.

Chapter 25

The next morning, Kate took a deep breath and announced: "I called the two of you here because I want to tell you what I've decided."

She turned around to face the table where Sebastian and Roxanne were sitting. They were all in her little office, and her two employees were glaring at one another across the table. Unspoken accusations were heavy in the air.

Kate clasped her hands together and forged on. "The two of you have given me conflicting reports on the break in that happened while I was gone," she went on evenly. "And since I'm not a detective, I've decided to let the professionals handle it."

Roxanne frowned at her. "What do you mean?"

Kate lifted her chin and marched over to the door. She opened it to admit a uniformed police officer. Both of her employees straightened up in alarm, and she went on, "This is Officer Jenkins. I want each of you to tell him what you told me. It'll be part of the report he's filing on the break in."

Sebastian leaned back in his chair and sputtered, "I hardly thought you'd take things this far, Kate. Not that I blame you," he added quickly, as Roxanne turned to scowl at him.

Kate met his eyes coolly. "I intend to find out who broke into my apartment," she informed him. "And when I do, I'll prosecute him or her to the fullest extent of the law."

She turned to Roxanne. "Roxanne, you can talk to Officer Jenkins first, and then you, Sebastian. Please don't leave out anything."

Roxanne crossed her arms defensively. "I still don't know my schedule," she complained. "Am I working here, or not?"

Kate met her eyes. "Yes. But we're changing the schedule," she drawled, and swept out of the room. She could hear Roxanne's outraged voice calling behind her, "You surely don't think that I—"

Kate made her way to the greeter's lectern in the restaurant lobby and set up for the lunch opening. She was tempted to fire Roxanne outright, but that would be unfair until she knew for sure what had happened. She'd already decided to keep the replacement Sebastian had hired, at least until she knew the truth.

Either Sebastian or Roxanne had broken into her apartment; and her plan was to keep both of them close, so she could watch them. She was pretty good at reading people, and she believed that the thief would slip up eventually.

Of course, she was going to have to endure complaints and infighting until then.

Kate fired up the computer console at the greeter station and entered the scheduling program. She was going to have to arrange the work schedule to keep Roxanne and Sebastian as far apart as possible. She tapped on the keyboard quickly.

She was going to put Roxanne on greeter duty. It was slightly awkward, but it was necessary. If Roxanne and Sebastian got close enough to talk to one another, there was going to be a fight. Maybe even a physical one. Roxanne had all but accused Sebastian of hitting her from behind with the metal sign, and she'd already vowed to get even.

Anger stirred in Kate again, and she frowned and rubbed her brow. *I'm going to send one of them to jail,* she vowed. *They shouldn't be worried about one another.*

They should be worried about me.

Molly came running up with a bouquet of flowers in her hand. "I put the daisies in all the little vases, Mamma," she announced, and Kate reached out and caressed her cheek.

"Thank you, baby," she smiled. "We can't open up without flowers on the table. You're a big help." Kate sighed as she gazed down at Molly's cheerful face. She'd had to find something for Molly to do while the police were upstairs in their apartment.

Kate stifled a sigh. The detective had told her that they were going to inspect the apartment, but he didn't give her much hope that they'd find a smoking gun after other people had been in and out. Still, the inspection was part of the burglary report, and Kate was determined to do whatever she had to.

"Mamma, when can I go back upstairs?"

Kate stroked her hair. "We have to let the police finish looking at our apartment," she smiled. "We have to give them a good long chance. But you won't be bored," she promised, and reached down to lift Molly in her arms. She propped Molly on her hip and groaned, "Oof! You're getting too big for Mamma to lift you." She smiled into her daughter's eyes and added, "We're going to go get ice cream as soon as they're finished. Then you can go back up to the apartment and play games until Mamma comes home."

"Goody!"

A furious voice called out from the direction of the conference room, and Kate turned, still holding Molly. An aggravated-looking Roxanne came stomping up and stuck her hands on her hips.

"I don't need this job so bad that I'm willing to be treated like a thief," she growled. "I told you what I saw, and if you don't believe it you can—"

Kate turned and set Molly down on the ground. "Run along, baby," she smiled. "Go and put the rest of the flowers in the restroom vases."

"Yes, Mamma."

Kate watched as Molly ran off, and as soon as she was gone, she rounded on her waitress with hard, narrowed eyes.

"Maybe you aren't aware of this, Roxanne," she began, "but Sebastian has accused you of breaking into my apartment and stealing a diamond necklace from my bedroom."

Roxanne's face was wiped blank by shock; then it twisted in fury.

"It's a lie!"

Kate nodded grimly. "He gave me back my necklace, and he said he found it in your work locker the night you fell."

Roxanne's mouth dropped open. "I don't know how he got into my locker," she sputtered, "but I saw him sneaking down from your patio the day after I was attacked. Yeah, I was *attacked*," she added angrily, and jabbed the air with her forefinger, "even the ER doctor told me a falling sign couldn't have raised up such a big lump on my head! It was Sebastian, it had to be," she hissed. "He hates me and he knows I'm watching him. I knew he was a thief the first time I met him. He stole your necklace and blamed it on me!"

Kate took a deep, calming breath. "All right," she replied evenly. "We'll let the police do their investigation, and see what they say. In the meantime, I want you to work the greeter station."

Roxanne's brows rushed together. "Why can't that friend of Sebastian's do it? I'm back now. I can work my own job!"

Kate shot her such a green, narrow glance that Roxanne took one look and closed her mouth. She hunched a shoulder, looked away and muttered, "Fine. But you're going to find out I was telling you the truth all along. I hope you can live with yourself!"

Kate clenched her hands and struggled sharply with her temper. She needed to be smart, and she bit back the first reply that jumped to her lips. "I'll let you take over here," she murmured and walked away; but she could feel Roxanne's indignant eyes on her all the way down the hall.

She met the police officer as he came walking out of the conference room. The man was looking down at his clipboard, and he looked up as she approached.

"All done?"

He nodded. "Yes ma'am. I got statements from your employees, and they just finished going over your apartment upstairs. You can go back now."

Kat raised her head just a bit and tried to read the papers, but he sighed and stuck the clipboard under his arm.

"What odds do you give me of finding out who did this?" she asked in a low voice. The big man looked up at the ceiling and sighed.

"Well, we dusted for fingerprints, but that's probably going to be useless because we got there after the knob had been smudged by other hands," he sighed. "Right now we're not seeing anything conclusive, but if we find something, we'll let you know."

Kate bit her lip. "Thank you, officer."

He touched his hat. "You're welcome, ma'am. You'll be hearing from us if we have any news."

Kate sighed and went to look for Molly. She found her in the women's bathroom, standing on tiptoe in front of the sink. She was just setting a spray of daisies into a glass vase.

"Come on, chickadee," she called. "Time for some ice cream. Mamma could use a break, too."

Molly slipped her small hand into Kate's and curled her fingers tight. Her hopeful blue eyes looked up at her mother's face.

"Can I get some chocolate mint ice cream? It's my favorite."

"Of course you can. We'll go down to Firehouse Freddy's and order a double banana split blowout and make the waiters come over and sing to us."

Molly giggled and skipped along at her side as they walked out of the main doors of the restaurant. It was a bright, hot day outside, and Kate slipped on a pair of sunglasses as she led the way to her car.

Kate opened the door and helped Molly climb into the shiny red convertible. She closed the door and walked around to the driver's side to slide inside.

She sighed as she cranked the car. The convertible had been Kevin's pride and joy, and she'd teased him mercilessly about it being his midlife crisis car; but it comforted her to use it. It was a way of feeling close to him.

She pulled it out of the restaurant parking lot and out onto the main street. Firehouse Freddy's was only two blocks down, an old red brick building sandwiched between two other red brick buildings. It was an over-the-top ice cream emporium filled with old-timey stained glass lamps, ads from the 1900s, and waiters dressed in straw hats, white shirts, armbands, and suspenders. It catered especially to children, and Kate was resigned to being serenaded by the waiters when they ordered the banana split blowout.

She pulled up into the little parking lot and smiled down at Molly's excited face. "You ready, Mollykins?"

Molly nodded vigorously, and Kate laughed and opened the door. "Come on, then."

Kate opened the frosted front door and let Molly scamper in, then followed her to the big wooden counter. The interior was modeled after an old-timey Victorian parlor with its polished wooden booths, stained glass lamps, and checkerboard floor.

Kate led the way to a corner booth next to the front window and they settled in. The menus were on permanent display beneath a layer of tabletop glass, and they had a moment or two to search them before a smiling waiter appeared dressed like a member of a barbershop quartet.

"Hello ladies," he smiled, and winked at Molly. "What would you like this afternoon?"

Molly surprised her by answering, "Lemonade and mint chocolate chip ice cream!"

"Coming right up, young lady." The waiter turned to Kate, and she murmured, "Mango ice with a glass of tea, half sweet and half unsweet."

"Yes, ma'am," he replied, and scribbled on an order pad. Kate watched wistfully as the pleasant young man scuttled off, and thought wryly:

I wish you'd shown up when I put out my own help wanted ads.

Kate sighed and glanced around the parlor. There were the usual vintage ice cream ads and mirrored signs, and the atmosphere was bright and cheerful. But fun outings with Molly always reminded Kate that they were one family member short, and she rubbed her arms.

She was suddenly stabbed by the guilty realization that it was the first time she'd thought about Kevin in more than a week.

Maybe that was because she'd been so involved with Buck Spade. Kate sighed and pictured him as he'd looked when he stepped onto the patio the night before, all slicked up like a proper cowboy in his gray Stetson hat, immaculate dress shirt, and string tie.

Buck's black hair had been neatly combed back from his brow, his brown face had been scrubbed shiny, and his smile had been big and warm. Kate closed her eyes. He'd been fragrant of some heavenly cologne that she didn't recognize, something that smelled old-fashioned and faintly spicy, though it was probably so high-end that only somebody like Buck Spade could afford it.

But as handsome and well-dressed as he'd been, Buck had been totally down to earth. Kate smiled and hugged her elbows, remembering how Buck had woofed those trout down. She liked a man with a big appetite. It was good manners to show zest for a fine meal, and the sincerest compliment a guest could give to the chef. She never failed to notice; and it pleased her that Buck had enjoyed her cooking.

"You look happy, Mamma."

Kate came back to herself. Molly was looking up at her with a little smile on her face. She leaned down and pressed her nose to her daughter's.

"I am, chickadee. Are you?"

Molly nodded, and Kate paused for a beat and added, "Wasn't it fun when Buck came by to have dinner with us last night?"

She searched Molly's eyes, and was gratified when her little daughter nodded again. "Buck likes to eat," Molly replied artlessly.

Kate burst out laughing. "Yes, he does," she agreed with a giggle. "I do, too."

She turned her head at the approach of the waiter. He was carrying a tray and Kate turned to Molly to enjoy the excitement on her face. "Here comes your ice cream," she whispered, and soaked up the happy glow in Molly's blue eyes.

Regret suddenly stabbed Kate again, and her smile faded. *Kevin, I wish you could see this,* she thought wistfully.

I miss you so.

But as much as she missed her husband, he'd been gone for two long years. She was still a woman, and she had to acknowledge, if only to herself, that she was lonely. To Kate's dismay, as the waiter set her ice cream down on the table, she couldn't keep her mind from drifting back to Buck, and the look in his eyes when he'd taken her chin in his hand and murmured:

I've wanted to kiss you for a while now.

She closed her eyes and relived the lovely anticipation of that moment; and she only opened them when Molly prodded her in the ribs and urged, "Eat your ice cream, Mamma. It's starting to melt!"

Chapter 26

That evening, Kate turned off her bedroom light, shouldered out of her satin housecoat, and drifted to her window. It was well past midnight, and the big warehouse below them was silent and empty. Molly's soft breathing from down the hall was the only sound.

Kate opened the blinds and stared outside. The parking lot was uninspiring, flat pavement washed white by the glare of her security lights, and the street beyond was empty. A pale, thin moon was riding high in the night sky, and the fields across the road were empty and dark.

She glanced up at the moon, then let the blinds fall back into place again. She walked back to her bed, threw the covers aside, and climbed in.

She turned toward the window and slipped a hand under her pillow. The moon painted ghostly white stripes across her bedroom floor, and the whole world was still.

Kate closed her eyes and a solitary tear blazed a cold path down her cheek. She sighed and turned her face into her pillow. Slowly her mind drifted, and then went blank.

When she opened her eyes again, she was back in her art gallery in Denver. It was a gutted two-story loft, a red brick box with high walls covered top to bottom with paintings: glowing Rocky Mountain sunsets, wild, colorful abstracts, neon screenprints of Bob Marley and Marilyn Monroe, homages to Picasso and Dali, and the Lichtenstein that Kevin had given her one year for her birthday. It was displayed proudly in the front window, and she skimmed it lightly with her fingers as she walked past.

Being in that gallery always gave her the feeling of being embraced by loving arms. She was surrounded by the passion of art, by wild revelations, by the love of beauty, by the spirit of discovery and adventure. Kevin had always said that art was her happy place, and he was right.

When she looked up, Kevin's warm brown eyes smiled at her, and he held out his hand. She took it, and together they walked through the gallery, painting to painting.

They gazed up at an electric-blue mountain snowscape. The massive sides of the mountain were expressed in bold swipes of white and aqua and charcoal gray.

"I miss you."

She turned to look at him, and he gave her hand a gentle squeeze. "I know it."

Guilt and longing tangled up in her chest suddenly, and she released his hand. "I almost feel like I've been unfaithful to you since you've been gone," she whispered, and looked down at the floor. "If only in my mind. Can you understand that?"

"You're in the land of the living, Kate. You're young and you're beautiful."

Her brows twitched together, because it wasn't Kevin's voice that had replied; and when she looked up, Buck Spade was smiling down at her.

"I've been wanting to kiss you for a while now," he rumbled. "Can I do that?"

Please, she told him, but didn't breathe a word; and he reached out and took her in his big arms. She felt herself melting into him, and his kisses made the colors on the wall begin to spin until they exploded right off the wall and flew away.

Kate woke with a gasp and sat up. Her heart was pounding, and she swallowed as her eyes moved around her moonlit bedroom. Then she turned her face into her pillow, and her shoulders shook with silent tears.

Oh Kevin, she wept. *It still doesn't feel real that you're gone. I can't move on when I still dream of you!*

She was instantly back at the ski lodge on that terrible weekend, nursing her twisted ankle and a steaming cup of caramel coffee. Kevin was beside her in a leather chair in front of the fire, but his eyes kept moving to the window.

"We came here to go skiing," she told him with a smile. "Go on. I know that you're dying to."

He'd given her an innocent look. "No, I'm not," he lied, and took a sip of coffee; but his eyes moved to the window again.

"This is your first vacation in years. You've earned it. Go enjoy yourself. I'll be fine."

His eyes moved to hers. "Are you sure? I don't like to leave you here alone."

"I'll be fine. Shoo. Go ski."

She'd almost laughed to see how eager he was, and how hard he was trying to hide it. He coughed a bit, and adjusted his shoulder.

"Well…if you're sure."

"Go already."

She watched him with amused affection as he stood up slowly, set his coffee down, and leaned over to give her a peck on the cheek. "I might go up for a few runs," he shrugged. "It's a nice clear day."

"Enjoy yourself, darling. I'll be here."

He'd smiled at her almost like a little boy and had hurried off to their hotel room to change and get his skis. She'd laughed a bit to herself and turned the page of the book she'd been reading.

Two hours later, she was almost through her book, and was beginning to think about getting lunch at the lodge cafe, when the door opened and a group of grim-faced men had come walking in. Some of them were lodge security.

The foremost had come walking up to her. "Mrs. Malone, can we speak to you for a moment?"

She'd put her book down and frowned. There was something about the look on their faces that made an alarm go off in her heart.

"Certainly."

The man sank down into the chair that Kevin had vacated. He gave her a solemn look.

"Mrs. Malone, I'm afraid we have bad news."

By this time her heart was in her throat. "What kind of bad news?"

The man's voice was soft and sad. "Mrs. Malone, your husband skied one of our black diamond runs."

She sat up straight in her chair. "Where is he?"

The man looked down at his hands, and her panicked eyes moved from him to the other men. None of them met her gaze.

"Mrs. Malone, your husband had an accident. For some reason he veered off the trail, and he lost control and struck a tree.

"He passed away. I'm very sorry."

The alarm clock on the bedside table suddenly buzzed, and Kate buried her face in the pillow and let it go.

Oh God, she prayed, *I can't move on. I've been in that ski lodge for the last two years.*

The alarm buzzed on, and Molly's sleepy voice called from the other room. "Mamma, make the ringing stop."

Kate pulled a hand across her eyes and dragged herself up on her elbows. She reached out and pressed the button on the alarm clock, and the buzzing stopped; but it was seven, and she had to get up.

Kate pulled herself up to a sitting position, pushed her hair out of her eyes, and wiped her eyes again. She glanced up at the ceiling in a silent appeal to heaven, then tossed back the covers.

She put her bare feet to the floor, padded over to the window and pulled back the blinds. Dawn always lifted her spirits, and the sun was just rising. Its fresh rays painted the trees at the edge of the parking lot and bathed the fields beyond.

It's a new day, Kate told herself resolutely, and put her hands against the pane. *I'm in the land of the living.*

Chapter 27

"The man at the pony ring told me that I could have the same pony this time," Molly announced excitedly, and bounced in the car seat. "Her name is Buttercup, and she has big brown eyes and long pretty lashes."

"That'll be fun," Kate murmured as she pulled the convertible into the gravel parking lot of the Seven Ranch pony compound. She was bringing Molly back for her pony lessons, and as she parked the car under the shade of a tree, she wasn't surprised to see Buck Spade leaning against the ring fence.

He was wearing a big cowboy hat, and his face was shaded under it. She could only see the tip of his nose and his chin as he turned to glance at them; but she knew that he was smiling.

She smiled herself as she pulled the keys out of the ignition. *Buck is such a gentleman,* she thought to herself. *Always such a gracious host.*

Molly burst out of the passenger side and went pelting across the lot to meet Buck, and Kate called after her, but it was too late. Molly went running to Buck with her arms stretched out, and to Kate's astonishment, Buck caught Molly up in his arms, lifted her high above his head, and swung her around in the air as she shrieked with laughter.

Kate scrabbled at the seat belt and came rushing out of the car in alarm; but by the time she got out, it was all over. Molly was sitting atop the fence next to Buck's shoulder, and both of them were waiting serenely as the ponies were led out of the stalls.

Kate stopped dead in the lot, huffed a bit, straightened her blouse and her composure, and walked toward them at a more normal pace. She shot Buck an exasperated look. She wasn't sure she liked having her daughter grabbed up and slung around without her permission, but since Molly seemed to be enjoying herself, she decided not to say anything.

Buck was a good man, and she knew he meant only the best, but it didn't take much to make her mama bear instincts kick in. And if he tried to sling Molly around again, he might just find it out.

Buck turned his head as she approached, then turned and flashed a row of beautiful white teeth.

"Well, it's good to see that you're still game after getting bucked off that horse," he nodded.

Kate shot him a startled look. "I didn't say that," she corrected, and walked up to the gate beside him. "Molly's the cowgirl here."

Buck turned to Molly. "Are you a cowgirl, doodle bug?" he teased, and grinned when she nodded.

"There, you see?" he told Kate with a grin, and she sputtered in spite of herself.

"I don't think I'm going to be climbing on a horse any time soon," she informed him. "I've had enough excitement with that burglary to last me for a while."

Buck's expression sobered. "What did the police say when they came over?"

Kate sighed. "They dusted for fingerprints, but the officer didn't give me too much hope that they'd find proof of who broke in. Maybe the thief was wearing gloves, I don't know. I'm just glad that Molly and I were gone when it happened," she shuddered.

Buck stared at her in silence, then nodded. "I am, too," he replied softly, then straightened up and clapped his hands.

"Well, what say you ladies decide which you want," he asked, with a look at Molly's eager face. "You can ride ponies today, or you can come with me on a helicopter ride."

His eyes moved to Kate's. "You never did get to see the whole ranch, and it's a lot smoother ride," he smiled.

Kate stared at him, and then at Molly. Her little daughter's open mouth and awed expression told her the answer beyond all doubt.

"Can we?" Molly gasped, with her eyes glued to his. "Can we go up in the helicopter with Buck, Mamma?"

Kate crossed her arms and gave him a grim stare. "Can Buck fly a helicopter?" she demanded, and he grinned and looked down at the ground.

"Yes ma'am," he promised. "I've had my pilot's license for years. You ladies will be safe as bugs in a rug."

Molly tugged at her shirt hem. "Can we, Mamma?" she wheedled, and Kate searched Buck's face. He returned her gaze serenely.

"Well…"

"Please, Mamma?" Molly whined, and trained pleading blue eyes on her mother's face.

Kate sighed and gave in. "Oh, all right," she sighed, "but you'll have to—"

"Whee!" Molly cried, and jumped up and down, "We're going up in a helicopter, we're going to fly!"

Buck laughed and pinched her nose. "That's the spirit," he nodded, and shot her a twinkling look. "Ride 'em, cowgirl!"

Kate snorted and looked away, and Buck laughed and took her hand. She let him do it, but bit her lip into a worried line as he led the way to a big red truck parked in the lot.

"Come on, doodle bug," he called to Molly, and she skipped along at his heels as he walked to the truck.

Buck opened the door and hoisted Molly up to the high side runner, then helped her into the back seat. He turned and offered his big hand, and Kate took it and climbed up into the truck. She settled into the seat and glanced back at Molly's happy face, then the dashboard. The dash was of polished wood and the radio was digital state of the art, but there was a pine tree air freshener dangling from the rear view mirror and a pair of muddy leather boots crammed into the passenger floorboard. She moved her feet over to the side as Buck opened the driver's side door and climbed in. He saw her staring at the boots, leaned over, and leaned back to put them in the seat next to Molly.

"Everybody in?" he smiled, and closed the door. "Let's go over to the helipad and see the country."

Helipad, Kate thought in shock, and shot Buck a boggled glance as she pulled the truck out onto the main drive and sent it back toward the main house. The broad landscape flowed past the windows until the huge complex loomed up ahead, but to Kate's surprise, Buck skirted the main house to the right on a secondary driveway. She watched as they passed the east side of the house, the pool, and a northern wing of the house not visible from the front.

Kate half-turned in her seat to stare at the back side of the house, thinking, *How big is this place,* as the truck began to ascend a tall green hill beyond. When she turned back around, she could see it directly ahead. The drive ran to the top from the lower pastureland all around. There was a big helicopter sitting on the crest, and Molly began to slap her little hands on the back of the seat in glee as the truck topped the rise and came to gentle stop a stone's throw away.

Buck turned to her with a smile. "Well, here we are," he announced. Molly bounced on the seat, but Kate stared at the helicopter in doubt. It was a gleaming silver craft, with black rotors and a sleek teardrop body; but she hadn't been in a helicopter since she was Molly's age.

Buck climbed out of the truck and walked around to open the passenger door. "Come on, Miss Molly," he called, and Molly practically fell out of the truck in her eagerness to get down. Buck lifted her up and set her down on the ground, then held his hand out.

Kate stared down uncertainly, but gave Buck her hand as she climbed down. It was a long way down from the cab, and her foot slipped sideways on the runner. Kate gasped and tumbled right onto Buck's chest. For the second time in as many weeks, Kate found herself gripping Buck's collar, and his arms went around her instantly.

"Steady there," he murmured, and Kate looked up into his eyes. They were ice-clear blue, but the look in them was warm, and Kate stared into them as if hypnotized. She found herself snared by those aquamarine eyes; and even when Molly called for her, she was unwilling to move out of Buck's arms.

"Come on, Mamma!" Molly called, and Kate looked down at Buck's chest. His arms slowly released her, and he cleared his throat and replied, "Here we come, Miss Molly! Come on, Kate," he added softly, and extended his hand. Kate took it, and they walked hand in hand to the side of the helicopter.

Buck opened the cockpit door, and they climbed in. Kate twisted around to help Molly strap in, and Buck leaned over to place a headset on her head. He adjusted it on her head, then asked, "Can you hear me, Molly?"

She shook her head, and he smiled and patted her head before turning to Kate. "Here's your headset, Miss Kate," he told her. "Go ahead and put it on, and we'll go see the sights."

Kate slipped the headset over her head, and Buck climbed in and pulled a headset on. He plugged it into a console, then reached back to plug Molly's headset in, and then Kate's. He pulled the mic arm down and asked, "Can you hear me? Thumbs up."

Molly gave Buck two thumbs up, and Kate nodded, and he smiled and cranked the helicopter. Immediately a massive, but muffled roar filled the air, and the ponderous rotors slowly began to turn. Buck let the copter sit as the rotors gradually began to spin, and the whole cockpit began to tremble as the roar intensified as they spun faster and faster.

Buck popped on a pair of sunglasses and grinned at Kate. "We ready?"

Kate gave him a sickly smile, and he laughed and turned up the juice. To Kate's dismay, and Molly's gasp of glee, they suddenly lifted right off the ground and floated up over the top of the hill. Instantly the house below, the pool, the courtyard and the driveway swam into view. The green countryside slowly stretched out before them, until they could see the black roofs of the stable complex, the big training rings, the pony stables, and the miles of pasture beyond, all the way out to the tiny main road, miles and miles away.

Buck turned the nose of the helicopter toward the house, and they floated high over it, to Molly's delight. They could see the rows of black solar panels on the roof, the blue ripples in the pool beside the house, and then another, even larger lap pool on the west side of the house, right next door to a red clay tennis court.

A bank dropped off steeply from the tennis court to pastures below, and a few football fields west, they saw a massive red horse barn that rivaled the main house in size and splendor. Kate glanced back at Molly, and was amused to see that her eyes were big as saucers as she gazed down at it. Tiny horses tossed their heads and pranced around huge corrals on either side, and as they watched, an equally tiny forklift puttered into the barn with a load of hay.

Buck nodded toward it. "That's our quarter horse barn," he told them in a crackling voice. "That's where we keep our working stock."

He pulled the copter up suddenly, and they zoomed sharply higher. Kate felt as if she'd left her stomach behind her, and her hands and feet tingled, but Buck reached over and patted her arm.

"Look there," he mumbled, and nodded toward the western horizon.

Kate looked, and the earth stretched out before them all the way to the distant blue horizon. And snaking across it, curving lazily from side to side, from directly beneath them all the way to the horizon, was a broad, muddy river lined by massive oak trees.

"That's the Big Sandy," Buck's voice crackled. "That's where we get water for our cattle."

Kate stared at it in wonder. Small flocks of water fowl vaulted from the river into the sky, their brown wings flashing far below. And below and on every side, the rolling earth was spattered with small T-shaped dots: thousands of massive Longhorn cattle, as far as the eye could see.

"It's amazing, Buck," she murmured, and meant it from the bottom of her heart. She'd thought she'd seen the Seven Ranch, but she'd only seen a corner of it. The Seven Ranch was vast in a way that could only truly be appreciated from the air.

Buck dipped the nose of the copter, and they zoomed down toward the rolling pastures. Molly squealed with glee as they rushed toward the ground, and Kate rolled her eyes to Buck's face and gripped the seat as the earth hurtled toward them. He leveled out just above the tree line, and sent them zooming over miles of pasture, running whole herds of Longhorns beneath them. Kate glanced down and couldn't help giggling as the big cattle loped away left and right.

They turned sharply south, and the helicopter zoomed across the countryside toward town. Kate could see it in the distance, a faint, concentrated smudge of color and motion. It grew bigger and closer every second, and they followed the two-lane road in town, watching as cars and trucks zipped along the road beneath them.

"Look, Molly," Kate smiled, and pointed to a biplane, flying on the other side of town trailing a long banner.

"What does it say?" Molly asked, and Buck answered, "It says, 'Vote for Leon Hardy.' He's the county commissioner. I don't care for him, but Carson says Leon is a better marketer than he is. I expect he's right."

Kate giggled as Buck slowed them down. They floated high over the main drag of Sandy Creek, watching cars and people pass under them, and Molly perked up.

"Look, Mamma!" she cried. "There's our house!"

Kate looked down. Sure enough, she could see the big white air units on the roof of the warehouse, and her own roof patio at the back of the building. The parking lot was full, and she was gratified to see that they were doing great lunch business.

Buck shot her a mischievous smile and sent the copter down the street and right over the restaurant. As they looked down, he began to slowly spin the copter around and around as the astonished customers in the parking lot looked up.

"Buck, what are you doing?" Kate laughed.

He nodded down at the smiling spectators. "Having a little fun," he chuckled. "It'll give folks in town something to talk about, and it'll be good publicity for the restaurant. Maybe not as good as a trailing banner, but I didn't have time to plan."

"Buck, you nut," Kate sputtered, but she couldn't help laughing. The people below were pointing at them, and Buck suddenly pulled the copter up and away.

Kate glanced at his smiling profile as they turned back for the ranch and thought: *If you keep this up, Buck Spade, I'm going to forget I was ever mad at you.*

I'm going to forget everything.

Chapter 28

"Come on in. I'll have Conchita send something up for us. What do you feel like this afternoon?"

Kate stepped into the huge great room of Buck's private apartments and gazed around. The living room was as big as most people's houses, the entire southern wall was made of glass, and the decor looked like something from *House Beautiful.*

It was so far outside her own experience that she felt almost like a trespasser, but she drew herself up and did her best not to let that feeling show on her face.

Molly padded in behind her and suggested, "I'd like a hot dog with french fries."

Buck beckoned to them from the center of the big room. "Come on, then. We'll go out to my patio, and I'll grill us up some hot dogs and hamburgers. Come on, Kate."

Molly ran across the marble-tiled floor to Buck's side, and he led the way to the opposite wall. He slid aside a glass door and both of them disappeared outside. Kate followed, but took her time on the way to drink in the massive leather furniture, the cowhide rug on the floor, and the huge map of the countryside on one wall.

She was hoping Buck's house would tell her more about him. She wanted to know more about him. *Needed* to know more about him, if she was honest with herself. Because she couldn't deny any more that she was attracted to him; but she didn't have the luxury of following a romantic whim.

She was the mother of a small child, and she was going to have to know and understand any man she admitted into Molly's life.

Kate stepped out onto the patio and was instantly surrounded by the massive panorama of the house's western overlook. The ranch pastures rolled away forever, just like she'd seen from the air. The massive stone terrace had a sleek metal railing on three sides, but on the western side it fell away, and an infinity pool gave the impression that there was no barrier between them and the far horizon.

Kate shook her head in wonder. She rolled her eyes to Buck, but he was preoccupied with the grill and didn't seem to appreciate her awe.

This is nothing new to him, she thought in amazement. *I can't imagine waking up to this view every day!*

Buck glanced up at her and asked, "How do you like your burger, Kate?"

"Medium rare," Kate murmured, her eyes still on the horizon.

"Conchita's going to send us some meat and trimmings from the kitchen," he mumbled, as he fiddled with the propane connection. "You two ladies make yourself comfortable, and we'll have some hot dogs and double cheeseburgers."

"Single," Kate murmured reflexively, "no cheese." She felt Buck's eyes on her, and she added, "I'm on a diet."

Buck looked surprised. He shook his head and mumbled, "I don't see why. I'd say you're perfect just like you are."

Kate glanced quickly at him and shut her mouth, because it had dropped open. She felt her face going hot, and it made her feel ridiculous to react like a schoolgirl getting her first compliment.

"You're very kind."

Buck smiled and glanced at her again. "I mean it."

Soon the elegant patio was filled with the mouthwatering scents and sounds of beef sizzling over mesquite wood. Buck hunched over the grill like a pianist playing a sonata, and with the same intensity. Kate watched him in amusement from a plush recliner near the pool.

"You must enjoy grilling out," she observed, as he deftly flipped the burgers.

"Nothing better than a good cookout," Buck replied, and licked his thumb. "Except maybe a fish fry."

Molly rose from the poolside, where she'd been splashing her bare feet, and skipped to the recliner beside Kate's. She plopped down, then stretched out with a sigh as the patio door slid aside and Conchita appeared with a rolling cart filled with pitchers, platters, and dinnerware. Buck looked up and grinned.

"Come on out, Conchita! You want a burger?"

The older woman snorted as she rolled the cart out. "Like I got time to sit down and eat! I brought you some lemonade for the little girl, and tea, and your favorite beer, and daiquiris."

"Thanks, Conchita. You're a brick," Buck told her with a grin.

"Eh," she muttered, and waved a brown hand as she walked out again.

Buck picked up a platter and walked over to a glass-topped table. "Well, who's ready for hamburgers and hot dogs?" he called, and Molly bounded off the lounge chair.

"Me, me!"

Kate followed her with her eyes. "Molly, mind your manners!" she chided, but Buck only laughed as Molly clambered up into one of the chairs.

"There's nothing wrong with a healthy appetite," he observed mildly, and went to fetch the buns. "Growing kids need to eat hearty."

Kate sighed. Buck clearly had a freewheeling attitude toward food, and she didn't like to let Molly go hog wild; but it *was* fun to indulge once in a while, and she had to admit, the scent of the grilled burgers was mouthwatering.

"Come on over, Kate, and get you a burger," Buck invited, and Kate smiled and abandoned the lounge chair.

She walked over to the cart Conchita had brought in. There were platters full of buns, lettuce, tomatoes, onions and cheese, squeeze bottles of ketchup and mustard, a bowl of chili, and a container of coleslaw.

"It's been years since I've had a slaw dog," Kate thought aloud, and Buck grinned and nodded. "Coming up, then." He took a fork and filled a plate full of grilled hot dogs and handed them to her. They were still sizzling, and the aroma made her stomach growl.

A few hours later, after they'd all eaten, and Molly had taken a swim in the shallow end of the pool, the three of them retired to the lounge chairs. They'd enjoyed a satisfying meal, and by that time the drowsy golden hour had come and gone. Twilight had turned the sky a soft lavender, and night was coming.

A pleasant breath of air eddied up from the pastures far below, fragrant of clover and freshly-mown grass. Crickets hummed faintly in the purple twilight, fireflies rose in the air like golden lanterns, and a horse nickered somewhere in the distance. Kate rolled her head back onto the cushion of her lounge recliner and looked straight up. The first tiny stars were beginning to wink in the high dome of the sky.

She took a sip of her drink. It was cold and sweet and slightly tangy, and its refreshing tangerine kiss was perfect in that moment. She was cool and comfortable and rested, and it had been a lovely day.

The soft pool lights suddenly flicked on and danced on the surface of the blue water. Kate turned her head and saw that Molly had dropped off to sleep. She was lying on her recliner with her eyes closed and her mouth slightly open.

"Sweet dreams," Kate murmured, and Buck turned his head. She smiled and shrugged one shoulder. "I always tell her that before she goes to sleep."

Buck's expression softened. He reached out, and Kate hesitated only an instant before she slipped her hand into his. They lay there side by side in peaceful silence, gazing out over the countryside as night slowly shifted down from the sky.

That tranquil silence was unbroken for a long time, as meadow birds purred their last, low songs of the dying day. Kate turned her head lazily to watch Buck's craggy profile.

"Have you always lived here?" she murmured.

Buck took a drink and stared out into the distance. "Most of my life," he nodded. "Our parents died in a plane crash when I was thirteen and we came to live with Big Russ and Miss Annie. Our grandparents."

Kate stared at him in dismay. "I'm so sorry," she stammered, but he only sighed and turned to point into the northwestern distance. "Their ranch house was way off yonder, and the Seven was a lot smaller back then. About a thousand acres." A wistful look colored his eyes.

"It was like living in the pioneer days," he went on softly. "Big Russ didn't own a television. We hunted and fished together, and we all sat around on the porch of an evening and listened to stories." He shook his head.

Kate searched his face. "It sounds wonderful."

He nodded. "It was. Or at least, I thought so. Carson spent his time plotting how to get away," he sputtered. He fell silent for a long time, then turned his piercing eyes on her.

"Kate, how do you feel about Carson?" he asked softly. "I know it's none of my business, but I'd like to know. It'll make a difference to what I do next."

A little frisson of anticipation skittered up Kate's spine, and she averted her eyes. "I like your brother," she replied softly. "He's a charming man. But we're not involved, if that's what you're asking. I haven't known him nearly long enough for that.

"Then, too, Carson's not exactly my type." Kate smiled and tilted her head to watch Buck through her lashes. "Your brother's very polished.

"But I prefer a diamond in the rough."

Buck's keen eyes found hers. "I'm glad to hear it." His hand slipped out of hers and slid up her arm to clasp her elbow. Buck gently pulled her to him, and Kate closed her eyes, lifted her chin, and yielded up to a slow, hot, hungry kiss.

Kate's brows shot up. The touch of Buck's lips shocked her like a live wire, and sent electricity swirling through every nerve in her body. Kate was amazed to feel the hair on her neck prickling in a way that even Kevin had never achieved, and before she knew what she was doing, she was leaning against Buck's chest with both arms twined around his neck. Kate felt herself going limp against Buck's chest, marveling at how his slow deliberation, the touch of his warm, rough hand on her cheek, the way his lips wandered from her mouth to her neck, could feel so maddening and new.

She gasped as Buck's lips moved to the tender spot just under her ear, and panic began to build in her. *Oh Lord,* she prayed as her eyes rolled up again, *I can't let this go on. We'll end up in…*

A soft yawn and a sleepy murmur made both of them freeze. Kate pulled back from Buck's chest and glanced over her shoulder.

Molly stretched and yawned again, and her dimples peeped out. "Mamma, it's dark. Are we going to spend the night here?"

Kate slipped back into her own recliner, glanced apologetically at Buck, and smoothed her mussed hair. She scrambled to gather her scattered wits and mumbled, "Um…no, baby. Buck has been a very gracious host, but we have to go home." She glanced at Buck again, and was comforted to see an understanding look in his eyes.

"You don't have to rush off," he said softly, and she bit her lip. The look in his eyes made her want to stay, but her skin was still tingling from his kisses, and she knew better than to give in.

"I think I'd better," she murmured ruefully, and turned to Molly. "What do we say to Buck, Molly?"

"Thank you," Molly murmured sleepily.

"You're welcome, doodle bug," Buck told her with a wink, and his eyes moved back to Kate's. "You and your Momma will have to come back again."

Kate smiled at him a bit wistfully. "I'd like that," she whispered, then inhaled sharply and turned back to her daughter. "Come on, Molly," she murmured, as she rose from the lounge chair. "Time to go home."

"I'll walk you out to your car," Buck muttered, as he stood up.

Kate held out her hand, and Molly took it. They followed Buck slowly and reluctantly as he led the way back inside. The golden lamps in his sprawling house were burning low, and it gave the space a homey, sleepy look. Kate glanced at the huge glass wall as they passed. The world beyond was a dark indigo blue, but she could see the lights of Sandy Creek burning small and faint to the southeast, and a couple of planes with their blinking lights, high and far away.

Buck opened the big front door and held it open as they passed through and out into the hall beyond. From that high point, they could see the massive atrium and the whole common room below. Kate tightened her grip on Molly's fingers as they walked down the huge staircase, and Buck put a hand lightly on her back as they descended.

The big open common room was empty as they passed through, and Buck opened the huge main door as they walked out into the soft summer night.

Kate pressed the green button on her keychain to unlock her car, and Molly skipped across the courtyard to open the door and climb in. She was about to follow when the courtyard lights dimmed, and Buck pulled her back into the shadows around the front steps.

Kate slid into his arms and curled her fingers into his hair as they kissed again; but this was a soft, sweet, goodbye kiss. Buck pushed a tendril of hair back from her brow and whispered, "I'd like to see you again sometime this week."

Kate swallowed and nodded. For some reason, she didn't trust her voice.

"I'll call you." Buck turned his head and kissed her ear, and she slid out of his arms as easily as she'd gone in.

"Mamma?"

Kate bit her lip and turned back toward the car. "Coming, baby."

They walked to the car with their fingers barely intertwined, then Buck leaned over to open the door for her. Kate slid in and looked up at him as he closed it.

"Thank you, Buck. We had such a good time."

He glanced at Molly, then nodded and backed away. "Drive careful, now."

Kate turned the key and the motor growled to life. She smiled at Buck, waved, and sent the convertible around the courtyard and down the dark drive.

But as they pulled away, Kate's eyes went to the rearview mirror. Buck's tall, broad-shouldered shadow was still standing under the entryway lights as they drove away.

Chapter 29

Buck stood on the front steps and watched as the red tail lights of Kate's convertible slowly faded into the distance. Kate's kisses still tingled on his lips, and he licked them wistfully. They still tasted faintly of a tangerine daiquiri, and a whisper of sweet cologne still clung to his collar.

He smiled and was just turning to go back into the house when something hard rammed his jaw and sent him spinning into the cobbled pavement.

"Oof!"

Buck rolled down to the foot of the steps and landed hard. He blinked the stars out of his head, peeled his cheek off the pavement, and looked up through his hair just in time to see Carson shake his right hand out, then clench it into a fist again.

"Get up, Buck," he growled.

Buck blinked at him. "You're back," he mumbled in surprise.

"And not a minute too soon!" Carson fumed. "I come back to find my brother making out with my date!"

Buck glanced over to see Carson's Jag parked in a dark corner of the courtyard, and he pulled a hand across his jaw. The taste of tangerine daiquiri in his mouth was now tinged with a little blood. He dragged himself up to his feet, backed away a pace, and put his hands up in a calming gesture.

"All right, Carson," he muttered, "I deserve a slug, and I'll take one. But it's not like you think."

"Now I know why you wanted me in Dallas," Carson replied in a throbbing voice. "To get me out of here so you could move in on Kate!"

"That's not true," Buck objected, then threw up an arm to block another right cross. He shoved his brother away, and Carson stumbled backwards across the courtyard.

"I asked Kate about you and her," Buck explained. "She told me y'all weren't serious!"

Carson swung at him again, and Buck turned sideways to avoid the blow, grabbed the seat of Carson's designer slacks as he passed, and threw him into the bushes. His brother landed face-first in the shrubbery with a yell.

Buck straightened up and rubbed his aching jaw. "You need to calm down, Carson," he panted, as his brother pulled himself out of a row of boxwoods.

Carson raised a resentful face. "I'd never have hit on any woman you brought home," he growled, and picked leaves out of his shirt as he stood up.

"I didn't hit on her," Buck told him. "She and her little daughter came here for pony rides, and I was just trying to be a good host."

"Good *host!*"

Carson charged him again, and this time Buck nailed his brother with one lightning-fast jab to the jaw. Carson yelled, clapped a hand to his cheek, wobbled, and fell back squarely on his seat.

Carson spat onto the ground. "I think you broke my tooth!"

Buck stared down at him in pity. "You never were any good in a fistfight, Carson," he sighed, and leaned down to extend a big hand.

Carson glared at him, but finally took it, and Buck pulled him back up to his feet. Carson swiped leaves from his trousers and shot him a fulminating glance.

"You played me a dirty trick, Buck," he growled. "I'm not going to forget it."

Buck stared at him in concern. "I didn't have any idea of getting between you and Kate, Carson. It just—happened. If you don't believe me, ask her," he mumbled. "She'll tell you the same thing. "

Carson sputtered in outrage and shouldered past him on his way back to the house. He stopped halfway to the door, turned, and pulled a sheaf of papers out of his pocket. He threw them into the air, and Buck watched as they fluttered to the pavement.

"There's Eugene's report," he spat. "If you were ever really interested in it."

He turned on the words and stomped back into the house, and Buck watched him go with a worried frown. He sighed deeply, pulled a brown hand over his jaw, and then walked over to pick up the papers before following his brother back into the house.

It was well after midnight by that time, and the house was mostly silent and empty except for the distant sound of Carson's feet on the upper level as he returned to his apartment.

Buck shook his head, drifted into the big kitchen, and flicked on the lights. He walked over to the cabinet refrigerator and pulled a handful of ice out of the freezer, wrapped it up in a paper towel, then pressed it to his sore jaw.

A sound from the doorway made him turn his head. Morgan was barefoot and wearing a black housecoat, and he walked in with two empty plates in his hands. He ambled over to the sink and washed them out as Buck looked on.

Morgan glanced at his bruised jaw. "I see Carson's back."

Buck mumbled, "He wasn't too happy with me, that's for sure." He nodded toward the plates and asked, "Your dishwasher out?"

Morgan nodded. "Kit chucked a handful of cereal down the drain and it jammed the works. I'm gonna have to fix it tomorrow."

Buck grunted an unintelligible reply and winced as the ice numbed his face.

Morgan nodded toward his free hand. "What are those papers you got?"

Buck glanced down at his hand. He was still clutching the papers Carson had thrown down, and he slapped them on the counter.

"Aw, Carson brought 'em back. He said it's Eugene's report about the lawsuit."

Morgan wiped his hands on his housecoat and picked them up. He flipped through the pages, skimming them as he went.

"What's the verdict?" Buck grunted.

Morgan shook his head. "Well, according to Eugene, we're sunk." He tossed the papers back onto the counter and clapped Buck on the back as he passed. "Night, Buck. Don't let it worry you. We'll hit it again tomorrow morning."

Buck glanced at him glumly. "Night, Morgan." He watched as his tall brother ambled out; then he sighed deeply and stared down at the papers. He was tempted to leave them lying there, but he gathered them up and stuck them into the waistband of his jeans before turning to go.

What with Carson, and Eugene's gloomy report, he knew his mind should be thinking of ways to smooth his brother down and some way to outflank Buster.

But as he slowly climbed the stairs to his own door, all Buck could think of was Kate Malone's mesmerizing eyes staring up at him, and the sleepy desire glimmering in their emerald green depths.

Chapter 30

Roxanne slipped out through the back door of the Stonehouse kitchen and out onto the loading dock. She leaned against the brick wall, lit a cigarette, and blew a plume of smoke into the air.

She glanced back over her shoulder. Sebastian was in the middle of the dinner rush and was up to his eyeballs in orders. He wasn't going to be coming out that door anytime soon; but occasionally he leaned over to check that she was still there.

Scumbag, she thought resentfully. She still hadn't recovered from the shock of being called a thief; but her anger at Kate had faded. Sebastian had turned Kate against her, and she was going to get even with him for that, and for the lump on her head, if it was the last thing she ever did.

She was going to prove to Kate, and to everybody else, that she wasn't a thief.

She sent another cloud of cigarette smoke spiraling into the night air, because she could see Sebastian's suspicious face out of the corner of her eye. He was still checking, still alert; but she could afford to wait him out.

He was just too busy to keep that up.

Roxanne cocked an ear toward the door as Trina's harassed voice called out, "Two more ribeyes, a filet mignon, and three porterhouse steaks!"

There was a short, sharp *bang* from the vicinity of the stove, and Roxanne sputtered smoke into the air in amusement; then she shot a quick glance through the doorway. Sure enough, Sebastian was scrambling for another skillet as a second waitress came through the door with another batch of orders.

Roxanne flicked the cigarette down and ground it out with her heel, then hurried down the steps and around the corner of the building. The employee parking spaces were just beyond, and Sebastian's blue Mini Cooper was right there. She only had a few precious minutes, but the Mini Cooper was convenient, low hanging fruit.

She glanced around her, and seeing no one, Roxanne tried the driver's side door handle. To her joy, it opened easily, and she slid in at once and scanned the seats. Sebastian's cell phone was lying right out in the open, and she grabbed it and flicked it on immediately.

The little blue screen flashed on, but she was confronted by the command: 'Draw unlock pattern.'

Roxanne grumbled under her breath and drew a number seven with her finger. It was wrong.

She glanced up at the building, then hurriedly drew a Z. It was wrong, too.

She bit her lip, and then drew an hourglass shape. To her grim satisfaction, the phone instantly opened up for her.

A shout from nearby made her heart jump up into her throat, but when she looked, it was only some drunk guy reeling off to his car. She hunched over the phone and hurriedly opened Sebastian's messages.

Her eye flicked down through the spam to pick out anything important.

Sebastian, make $500 a day with stock derivatives.

Big sale at Al's Furniture Barn in Dallas.

Surprise your girlfriend with these sexy secrets.

Roxanne grumbled in annoyance as she scrolled through the messages, then opened an untitled one. It read:

I expect you to show up when I call you. Flake again and you'll be sorry.

Roxanne's heart thrummed in her neck with excitement, but there was no signature, and the message had been sent from a private number.

A loud *bang* from the direction of the loading dock made her spit out an exclamation and jam her thumb on the off button. She ducked down in the seat, heart pounding, as Sebastian's furious voice called, "Get back in here, you lazy cow! I'm going to ask Kate to fire you!"

The door banged again, and Roxanne lay flat on the seat for a moment more before scraping up the nerve to raise her head. Sebastian was gone.

She tossed the phone back on the seat and slipped out of the car, crouching as she went to keep from being seen. She softly closed the car door, then poked her head up just far enough to scan the building and lot.

There was no one out there.

She crouched around the car to the shadows around the building, then hurriedly slipped around the corner and up the steps. She was barely through the door when Sebastian's angry voice snapped, "It's about time! Why Kate still lets you work here I don't know!"

Roxanne flipped him off as she passed, then blew out of the kitchen and on into the dining room; but the rude gesture was mostly a way of hiding her glee.

Sebastian was meeting somebody who didn't sign their name to their messages, and who was threatening him.

I always knew he was a perp, she thought in grim relish, as she reached for her order pad and put on her apron. *Sounds like home boy's stood up his fence. I wish I could catch him stealing!*

She bit her lip as she hurried off to the dining room. Sebastian was swiping something from the restaurant, or from Kate, or both; but what? He'd broken into her apartment and stolen her necklace to cover up what he was really doing; and he had to be doing something bad to justify that kind of risk.

Sooner or later, Roxanne thought grimly. *Sooner or later I'll catch him. I'll find out what he's stealing, and who he's selling it to.*

She walked up to a pair of young men seated at a table and pasted on a smile. "Good evening," she told them. "I'm Roxanne, and I'll be your server tonight."

She'd interrupted their conversation, and one of them kept talking on for a bit. The boy shook his head and complained, "Man, she's a psycho. I've never had a crazier girlfriend. I found a tracker underneath my car, dude!"

The other boy cleared his throat, and they both glanced up at her. Roxanne smiled again, but her mind was suddenly racing with a new and exciting thought.

Hey—why didn't I think of that?

Chapter 31

"The officers searched your apartment thoroughly, Mrs. Malone," the voice on the other end of the phone mumbled. "They dusted for fingerprints, but found none that were clearly strange to your home. There were your own and your daughter's prints, of course, and prints belonging to the locksmith you hired to repair your door." The officer on the other end paused and coughed. "Also, the prints of the, ah— guest you told us had been at your home.

"The intruder, whoever it was, must have been wearing gloves."

Kate paced back and forth in her living room with her cell phone to her ear. "Wasn't there any other evidence--fibers, hairs, anything?"

She detected a tinge of regret in the other voice. "Not so far, Mrs. Malone. We did determine that the lock had been snapped with a screwdriver. Of course, everyone has access to one of those, so…"

Kate stifled a sigh. "No prints on it, either, I suppose?"

"No, ma'am."

Kate ran a hand through her tousled hair and paced back across the living room. "Is there anything to show if the intruder was a man or a woman?"

There was a long pause. The officer finally admitted, "We didn't see any footprints, since the stairs up to your patio are metal and the patio floor is concrete. It would be harder for a woman to snap a door lock with a screwdriver, but it's not impossible. We see female burglars almost as much as male ones these days. If they have some experience, they're inside a house just about as fast as the men."

Great, Kate thought unhappily. She sighed, "Well, if you have anything else, please call me, officer. I'm anxious to find out who broke into my house. I mean to press charges if I can only find out who did it."

"Oh, of course, Mrs. Malone. If there's any new development we'll be in touch. In the meantime, keep your doors locked, especially when you're away. It's always a good idea to have a security alarm as well."

Kate closed her eyes in frustration. "Thank you, officer."

"Yes ma'am."

Kate clicked off, hugged herself unhappily, and rolled her eyes to the ceiling. She hadn't felt safe since the break in, in spite of the new locks on the doors; and the thought that there was somebody out there laughing at her made her blood boil.

The thought that it might be one of her employees made her mad enough to throw something.

Maybe a security system's a good idea, Kate mused. She'd never felt the need for one before, even though she and Kevin had lived in downtown Denver for years. They'd known all their neighbors, and even though they'd been a bohemian lot, they'd been warm and supportive and had never given her a moment of worry.

She'd always believed that understanding and support for the misguided was a better crime policy than police and legal charges; but since the break in, she was rethinking her opinion.

Kate put the phone down on a table and abandoned the living room to walk out onto the sunny patio. It was just past noon, and the green canopy provided a pleasant refuge from the blazing sun.

She glanced around her peaceful patio in discouragement. The police hadn't found any traces of the thief, and she hadn't helped by putting on that dinner for Buck. If there had been clues, she'd probably trampled them or swept them away.

There have to be some traces left, she frowned. *Surely a person couldn't climb up here and break a doorknob without leaving something behind!*

Still, when she walked over to the patio door and scanned the threshold, there was nothing to suggest that a break in had ever happened there. The concrete patio floor was bare and spotless, the potted plants were innocent of even a scrap of trash, and the doormat had been dusted by the police and come up clean. The only trace of the crime was the barely-perceptible scratches on the door jamb.

Kate tilted her head as she looked at it. The knob and the scratches were on the right side of the door.

That meant that the intruder was probably right-handed.

She thought back to all the times she'd seen Sebastian shake a pan over the stove. He was right-handed. And when Roxanne scribbled on her order pad, she always did it with her right hand.

Kate pulled her mouth slightly to one side. *So much for that clue,* she thought in discouragement.

I'm never going to find out who did this!

The sound of her phone buzzing from inside the house pulled her back inside again. Kate walked to the couch and leaned down to answer the phone.

"Hello?"

Buck's voice on the other end was as warm and soft as a cup of morning coffee.

"I thought I'd call you to see how you're doing," he said, without preamble.

Kate smiled in spite of herself and tucked a sprig of hair behind one ear. It had only been a day since she'd visited Buck's house, but she wasn't complaining.

"Fine," she murmured, then admitted, "Well, I'm a little frustrated, to be honest."

"What's wrong?"

Kate pulled her hair back from her brow. "Oh, the police called, and they don't have a clue who broke into my house," she sighed. "No prints, no marks, no evidence. It's maddening."

"Huh," he muttered. "You figure it was somebody who works for you?"

Kate turned and stared at the kitchen. "Probably," she answered unhappily. "I've got two employees that are accusing one another."

"Is one of 'em the skinny fellow who came to visit when you were over here?"

"He's one of them, yes. The other is a waitress. They hate each other."

"Well, that would figure," Buck muttered.

Kate frowned and hunched her shoulders. "I don't like to think about it. I can't stand to imagine either one of them breaking into my house. It's bad enough to do it to me, but to terrify Molly..."

There was a long silence on the other end, and Buck finally rumbled, "Well, it'll sort itself out in the end, I expect. But if you get to feeling spooky, you can call me. I'd be happy to come over and spend the night."

Kate raised an eyebrow, and Buck coughed and added, "Just to make sure everything's okay. Nobody'd mess with you with me there."

Kate relaxed and smiled. Buck's offer might sound risque, but she was sure that he meant it in the plainest sense: he just wanted to protect them.

It melted her heart.

"That's very sweet of you, Buck," she replied softly, "but I can take care of us all right. I know more than one way to use a skillet."

A knock on the door made her raise her head, but before she could answer a male voice called out from the other side.

"Kate, it's me. Carson."

Kate put her hand to the phone and murmured, "I have to go, Buck. Your brother's here."

"Huh? Wait, Ka—"

"I'll talk to you later." Kate hung up regretfully, tossed the phone onto the couch, and went over to open the door. She put a hand on the knob, paused, took a deep breath, and opened the door. She was instantly confronted by a bouquet of peach-colored roses.

"Why, Carson," she gasped, "how beautiful!"

Carson's smiling face appeared behind the flowers. "Can I come in?"

Kate's eyes moved from the roses to him. Carson looked very handsome, as always, in a loose white dress shirt open at the neck and a pair of gray linen slacks. His dark hair was swept back from his brow and he smelled faintly and pleasantly of cologne.

"Of course," Kate stammered, "and thank you for these. I've never seen such a beautiful color. I'll just go put them in a vase." She nodded toward the couch. "Please sit down. Would you like something to drink?"

"Love it," Carson smiled, and sauntered in. He closed the door behind him and settled down on the couch.

"Tea, coffee?"

Carson rubbed his nose and shot her a rueful look over the back of the couch. "Ah…"

Kate caught the look on his face and added dryly, "I think I have a beer in the fridge somewhere from last…"

Kate's voice trailed off. She didn't drink beer, and the one can she had left was left over from when she'd been hosting Buck.

"A beer would be great, thank you."

Kate found an indigo vase and arranged the peach-colored roses in them with a sigh of admiration. The colors set each other off beautifully, and Carson's gift had been a sweet gesture; but her pleasure was tinged with a tiny bit of guilt. She had to admit, at least to herself, that she was firmly involved with Buck now, and that made her friendship with Carson awkward.

Their relationship was very casual and new, but she was fairly sure that Carson had more than friendship in mind.

"I hear there's been some mischief going on while I was away," Carson teased, and Kate glanced at him. He took a sip of beer and shot her a comical look over the rim; but she glimpsed something deeper beneath the twinkle in his eye.

"Do I need to worry?"

Kate glanced away and smoothed her hair. The question was uncomfortably direct, but she had no problem with giving him a direct answer.

"If you mean Buck, we've been spending some time together, yes," she smiled. "I like him. I took Molly over to the ranch for her riding lessons, and he took us on a trail ride. I fell off my horse and bumped my head," she added with a sputter of laughter. "Molly and I spent almost a week at your house while I convalesced. Buck made sure we had everything we needed. It was very kind of him." She took a drink and hoped that the long pause would be the nudge Carson needed to drop the subject. To her relief, he seemed to take the hint.

"I didn't know about that," Carson muttered. "I'm glad you're all right now, but maybe falling off your horse is a sign you need a new trail guide," he quipped. "How about I take you to Molly's riding lessons?"

Kate gave him a helpless glance and smiled weakly. It was impossible to refuse such a gracious invitation, and so she murmured, "That's very nice of you, Carson."

But she made up her mind that when the time was right, she was going to tell him plainly that she wasn't interested in a romance. It wouldn't be fair to string Carson along when she was dreaming of his brother.

And she *had* been dreaming of his big, gruff, handsome brother.

Carson's voice snapped her out of her reverie, and his face wore a faintly worried look. "Well, that's settled then."

Kate poured the beer out into a glass, then walked out to hand it to him. Carson took it with a smile, then lifted it up in a salute. "Happy days."

Kate gave him a rueful look and took another sip of her drink. *They'll certainly be interesting,* she thought dryly.

Chapter 32

"What, you mean you're not going out with me on Saturday, because you have a date with *Carson*?"

Buck's baffled voice rumbled through the phone, and Kate put a hand to her hair in dismay as she paced back and forth in her bedroom.

"I didn't say that," she sputtered. "And it's not a *date*. I said that he offered to help Molly and me with her riding lesson this Saturday. I thanked him. What else could I say?"

"You could tell him you're coming out with me!" Buck retorted indignantly. "I thought we were going to the river this weekend!"

Kate bit her lip. "I do want to go to the river with you, Buck," she murmured. "But Carson asked first, and it would be rude of me to flake on that to go out with you. Of course he'd find out about it!"

"Now look here," Buck replied grimly. "You need to decide whether you're going with Carson, or if you're going with me. I won't play second fiddle to my own brother!"

Kate crossed her arms in irritation. "I don't have to *answer* to you, Buck," she warned him with a flash of temper. "And I was seeing Carson before I went out with you!"

"Well, I don't want you going out with my brother," Buck objected. "That's not 'answering' to me, it's just making up your mind!"

Kate paced across her bedroom. "He's certainly not as stubborn as you are," she retorted. "And he doesn't issue ultimatums!"

"All right, go out with Carson then, if you like him so much!" Buck snapped, and there was an angry edge to his voice. "But I'm not going to *compete* with him, Kate."

Kate's own temper flared up like a shower of sparks. "I didn't ask you to!" she cried.

"Well, I guess I know where I stand now," he replied in a huffy tone.

"Oh, for crying out loud, Buck," Kate sputtered in exasperation. "It's just Molly's riding lesson. What's wrong with you?"

"I'll tell you what's wrong with me," he retorted. "I expect any woman I'm seeing not to be going out with my brother at the same time!"

"I'm going to hang up now, Buck," Kate told him. "I can't talk to you when you're like this." She jabbed the red button on her phone, huffed, and hugged herself as she paced back and forth across her carpet.

She'd known there was going to be drama if Buck found out she was spending time with Carson, but she'd told him anyway. She didn't want Buck to think she was playing him, but it looked like he was going to think it anyway.

Buck's stubborn, she told herself. *Totally bullheaded! What did he want me to do, be rude to his brother?*

And just because I kissed Buck a few times, it doesn't mean he owns me. I don't have to check with him before I decide to go out with someone else!

It made her so angry that she snatched a pillow off the bed and kicked it across the room in a flash of frustration. Molly's puzzled eyes moved to the gray faux-fur pillow when she opened the door an instant later.

She looked a question. "You dropped your pillow, Mamma," she murmured, and picked it up.

Kate sobered instantly and reached out for it. "Thank you, baby," she murmured, and bit her lip as she took it back. She didn't want Molly to read anger off her face, and she averted her eyes in an attempt to hide it. But fire still simmered in her bones, and she pinched her lips into a thin line as she tossed the pillow back onto the bed.

"I can't wait to go see Buttercup on Saturday," Molly piped up, and she skipped around the bedroom. "I learned how to turn her right, and left, and how to say whoa. Next I'm going to make her run fast!"

Kate was momentarily startled out of her anger. "No you aren't," she corrected, with a worried frown. "You're going to ride Buttercup nice and slow, or not at all!"

Molly stopped skipping and stuck her hands on her hips. "But Mamma!"

"No buts," Kate told her. "And you need to think about poor Buttercup. She probably doesn't want to go fast at all. She wants to take it nice and easy."

Molly's freckled face scrunched into a puzzled frown. "She does?"

"I'm sure of it," Kate insisted. "So you need to be nice to her, and let her take things at her own pace."

Molly pulled her mouth to one side and crossed her arms. "Well…okay," she grumbled in a disappointed voice and kicked at the carpet. "I want to be nice to Buttercup."

Kate's heart melted as she looked down at Molly's face. "You really love Buttercup, don't you, baby?"

Molly's face lightened. "I sure do, Mamma," she replied in a small voice. "Buttercup is sweet and pretty and she likes me."

Kate smiled indulgently. *Maybe I should ask Carson if I can buy that pony for Molly,* she thought. *Her time with Buttercup has been so good for her. She's not nearly as sad now as she was when we first came here.*

Molly looked up at her and confided, "I can't wait till Saturday when I get to see Buttercup again."

Kate straightened up and pressed her lips together. "Carson is coming with us on Saturday," she replied carefully, and watched Molly's face. "It's very nice of him."

Molly tilted her head to one side. "Not Buck?"

Kate felt her face going hot and looked away. "Not this time, chickadee. We're friends with Carson, too."

"I like Buck better," Molly confided. "He showed me how to spit watermelon seeds. I spit one three feet. We measured it!"

Kate's mouth dropped open in dismay. "I don't want you spitting anything, young lady!" she objected, but Molly had already darted out of the room.

Kate squeezed her eyes together and struggled with a wave of frustration. *I'm really going to enjoy being with Carson this weekend,* she thought angrily. *He may not be my exact type, but he's reasonable and civilized and he has beautiful manners.*

At least he doesn't spit!

Chapter 33

"Mamma, Mamma, watch me!" Molly called out excitedly, and nudged her fat brown pony into a slow walk. Kate watched in smiling indulgence as Molly turned the pony to the left and sent it trotting across the ring.

Carson nodded toward Molly as she bounced along on the pony's back. "I think it's love between those two," he quipped, and Kate laughed softly.

"I think you're right," she sighed and shot him an admiring glance. Carson always looked more like Las Vegas than Sandy Creek, and especially that afternoon in his sunglasses, loose white shirt, and linen slacks.

"Carson, would you be willing to sell that pony? I'd love to buy it for Molly. She's become so attached to it."

"I don't see why not," Carson smiled, and lifted a cigarette to his lips. He inhaled and exhaled gently, and smoke swirled into the air. "But I wouldn't think of taking money for it. My treat."

Kate's mouth dropped open in dismay. "That's so sweet of you, Carson," she stammered, "but I'm paying, I insist."

Carson shrugged and grinned. "Well, I never argue with a lady," he conceded. "Have it your way, Kate."

Kate smiled at him, then glanced at her watch and called out to Molly as she nudged the pony around the ring. "Your hour's up, chickadee. Time to say goodbye to Buttercup until next time."

"Goodbye, Buttercup." Molly petted the pony's neck sadly, then slid down off of its back and walked over to them with a sigh.

"Don't look so sad, baby," Kate told her softly. "We'll come back and see her again next weekend."

Carson threw the cigarette down and crushed it out with the toe of his Italian loafer. "It's too pretty a day to kick around here. Why don't we drive down to Dallas this afternoon. I know a rooftop restaurant there with a breathtaking view of downtown."

Kate bit her lip. "That sounds lovely, Carson, but—"

"It's only a little over an hour's drive," Carson went on easily, and took her elbow. Kate bit her lip as she let him guide her to the Jaguar parked in the gravel lot. He walked over to open the door for her, and Kate slid into the car without objection, though she told herself that it was probably a mistake to encourage Carson.

I'm not attracted to him, Kate thought as he leaned down to flash her a white smile through the window.

Am I?

Carson opened the back door for Molly, and she tumbled into the back seat. Carson walked around the car, slid into the driver's seat, and closed the door with a soft *snick.*

He smiled at her, then back at Molly. "Are we all in?" he smiled. "Let's go down to Dallas and have lunch on top of a skyscraper."

Kate smiled in anticipation. She couldn't deny that it sounded like fun, and she'd welcome a break after all the burglar drama at the restaurant.

"Here we go." Carson turned the key in the ignition, but instead of the smooth sound of the motor growling to life, there was a loud *bang,* then a puff of black smoke from the front of the car.

"What in the—" Carson sputtered, and popped the hood. He climbed out of the car, lifted the hood, and bent down to peer into the engine.

Molly's worried voice murmured from the back seat. "Is something wrong with Carson's car, Mamma?" she asked.

Kate bit her lip as Carson grumbled from under the hood. "Hush, baby," she murmured. "I'm sure Carson will take care of it."

They sat in silence for a few minutes as Carson tinkered with the engine, and Molly finally whined, "It's getting hot back here, Mamma. Can I get out of the car?"

Kate weighed her answer. It *was* getting hot. It was only a little past noon, and the Texas sun was beating down on the metal roof. She turned her head and replied, "You can open the door if you like, but don't bother Carson. He's busy."

Molly opened the back door, and Kate cracked her own door, then opened her bag to pull out a couple of cardboard flyers from the restaurant. She leaned back to hand one to Molly.

"Fan yourself with this, baby."

The driver's side door opened and Carson stuck his head in. His expression was one of chagrin, but his voice was as pleasant as ever as he murmured, "I'm sorry, ladies, it looks like the Jag's developed a hiccup. If you'll just be patient a few more minutes, I'm sure I'll have it back up and running."

Kate smiled reassurance. "We're fine," she told him, and was rewarded by a beautiful white smile before Carson disappeared again to wrestle with the problem.

But as soon as he was gone, Kate fanned herself with the flyer and blew a tendril of hair out of her eyes.

"Mamma, it isn't helping," Molly whined, and Kate half-turned to soothe her.

"Just be patient, baby. Carson will have it fixed soon."

They sat in the car with doors open, waiting, as the sounds of clinking and clanking and muffled exclamations seeped from under the hood of the Jag. Kate's bored eyes wandered to the empty pony ring, to the stables, and even to the driveway beyond the lot.

As she watched, to her surprise, a pair of riders slowly walked their horses down the driveway toward the distant house. She recognized the first one as one of the Spade brothers, the man with the black cowboy hat and the beard. He swayed gently in the saddle as he rode past on the back of a beautiful black stallion, and Molly scrambled across the back seat to press her hands against the window.

"Mamma, what a pretty horse," Molly gasped, and Kate smiled at her dazzled expression.

"Yes, it is, isn't it, chickadee?"

Kate turned to watch, and to her surprise, the second rider was a big man on the back of a gleaming bay. He was wearing a cowboy hat too, and half of his face was in shadow, but it was Buck, she recognized him instantly.

Kate felt her face going hot. She was still mad at Buck, but when her eyes flicked over him, she suffered an infuriating swirl of excitement. It was a hot day, and he was only wearing a white tee shirt and a pair of jeans. They showed off his muscular arms and legs far too well for her composure.

Kate bit her lip and fanned herself faster; but to her annoyance, Buck looked over and seemed to see them. He turned his horse's head and sent it trotting over the parking lot toward them.

"Need a hand, Carson?" he called, and Carson's head popped up from underneath the car hood. His tone was sharp with annoyance.

"No, I got it."

"Okay, bud." Buck tilted his head and added, "Is that you, doodlebug? Kate?"

Molly laughed and rolled out of the car. "Hi, Buck!"

Buck threw a leg over the saddle and slipped down to the ground. He walked over to meet Molly and ruffled her hair with one big hand. "You come over to ride the range, cowgirl?"

"I came over to ride Buttercup," Molly announced proudly.

Kate felt herself going red in embarrassment as Buck leaned down and grinned at her. "Well, hello, Kate!"

Kate glanced away and crossed her arms. "Hello, Buck."

Carson's head popped up again over the hood. "I thought you were supposed to be working the ranch today, Buck," he said with a pointed glance at the horse.

"Well, I was," Buck replied affably, and winked at Molly. "But we decided to take a break and go inside for lunch." He put a hand on the car roof and leaned down a bit to glance at Kate.

"Maybe Kate and Molly would like to go, too. It's a lot cooler in the house than out here."

Molly came running over to Kate's open door. "Mamma, can we go with Buck?" she wheedled. "It's so hot out here!"

Kate reached out and adjusted Molly's collar. "Hush, baby," she hissed, with a stricken glance in Carson's direction; but Buck answered, "Sure, come on! Ajax can carry you easy. You ladies are light as a couple of feathers. We'll be there in two shakes."

Kate bit her lip and glanced toward Carson again. "Well, I—"

"Please, Mamma?" Molly whined, and Kate's eyes moved to her daughter's pleading face. Her skin was glowing pink, and little beads of sweat were forming at her hairline.

Kate reached up to pull herself out of the car. She curled her fingers around the top of the passenger door and faced Carson.

"Carson, I think I need to take Molly to the house," she smiled, and tried to make her tone soft and polite. "It is a bit…warm out here."

Carson had loosened his collar and rolled his sleeves up to his elbows, and he looked up at her ruefully. "Of course," he smiled. "I'm sorry for the inconvenience, Kate."

"Oh, no need to apologize," she assured him. "It happens to us all." She gave him a sympathetic glance. "Are you coming with us?"

Buck stuck his hands on his hips and looked down at the ground. "Oh, I don't think I could fit four people on Ajax," he mumbled, and rubbed his nose. "I'll send somebody back for you, Carson."

Carson stood up straight and threw a rag down into the engine. He jerked a thumb back toward the stables. "I'll just grab a horse and go with you," he replied in a suspicious tone; but Buck pushed his hat back on his head.

"Oh—they're at the vet, Carson," he mumbled. "It's check up day. You must've forgotten that."

Carson's face darkened. "This isn't checkup—"

"Let's go now," Buck called. He walked over to his horse, mounted it with one smooth motion, and leaned down to extend his hand to Kate.

She took it, and he pulled her up effortlessly. She threw a leg over the horse and settled in behind him; but she leaned close enough to murmur, "Don't look so smug. I still think you're a stubborn—"

Buck looked back over his shoulder and touched his hat. "Yes, ma'am," he murmured, and clapped his hands. "Let's go, doodle bug!"

Molly came running up, and Kate leaned down to pull her up. Molly flopped over the horse's back like a fish, but quickly righted herself and twined her little arms around Kate's waist.

Buck nodded toward his brother as he turned the horse's head. "See you at the house, Carson."

Kate shot Carson a stricken look from behind Buck as the big horse trotted away. Carson was standing there with his fist balled on his hips, and he was frowning.

Kate's eyes rolled back to Buck's broad back. He glanced over his shoulder and murmured, "Hold on tight, Kate. You can put your arms around my waist. You don't want to fall off again."

"I won't fall off," Kate told him in a suspicious tone; but after a minute or two she sent her arms around him anyway, and she felt, rather than saw Buck smile as they went jouncing down the long driveway to the house.

Chapter 34

Thirty minutes later, when Kate was lying cross-legged on a lounge chair beside the second pool, she had to admit that her pique at Buck had faded. A pleasant breeze swayed the tree branches stretching over the blue water, and the big red horse barn was visible in the far distance.

Kate sipped her drink as Molly shrieked and jumped into the pool with a splash, clothes and all. Molly was quickly followed by another child, a little boy of about four with dark, curly hair and big, beautiful brown eyes. He pulled his knees into his chest and cannon-balled into the water with a yell.

Kate smiled and shook her head. Buck had told her that the boy's name was Kit, and that he was Morgan's son. Morgan wasn't there, but Buck's big, bare feet waved back and forth on the recliner next to hers.

"Look at 'em go," Buck mumbled, and sipped a beer from a glass mug. "We should keep a swimsuit here for Molly. She'd be more comfortable."

"She's cool now, and that's the important thing," Kate sighed, and watched Molly's sleek head as it popped up in the water. "I was a little worried back there in the car."

Buck glanced at her over his glass, and she caught a vivid flash of blue as his eyes quizzed her.

"You feeling okay, Kate?"

She met his gaze in surprise. "Me? I'm fine." She paused, then swallowed her pride and added, "Thank you for bringing us in from the heat, Buck."

Buck's brown face creased into a beautiful smile. "You're welcome, Kate," he murmured. "You sure you're cooled down now?"

Kate raised her eyes to his and frowned. "Yes," she murmured in a worried tone, then shrieked as Buck suddenly snatched her up in his arms. He walked to the edge of the pool, as her bare feet dangled in the air, and swung her back and forth over the water.

"One...."

"Put me down right now, Buck Spa—"

"Two..."

"*Buucck!*"

"Three!"

The next thing Kate knew, she hit the water, lost her drink, thrashed briefly, and came up again, sputtering and gasping.

"Mamma, you jumped in!" Molly giggled, as she swam nearby.

Kate rolled outraged eyes to Buck's laughing face, and she struck out swimming for the ledge.

"Momma didn't jump in," she growled. "She was *thrown!*"

Buck put his hands up in a calming gesture and backed away from the ledge. "Now Kate, don't flare up," he soothed as she hauled herself up out of the water, drenched and dripping.

"You big donkey, I'm going to slap that smirk right off your face," she fumed as Buck scrambled away through the lounge chairs.

"Now calm down, Kate," he laughed, as he backed away.

"Calm down!"

Kate charged him, and Buck knocked over the lounge chairs as he skipped out of her reach. She was about to charge him again when she happened to glance down and catch sight of herself.

To her horror, her thin cotton blouse and slacks were plastered to her body, and her bra and undies were clearly visible beneath them.

"Oh!"

She gasped and fled through the open sliding door and into the privacy of the house. She passed the dark man with the beard as she escaped. His brows shot up in surprise, and he turned to stare at her as she retreated; but to her intense relief, he said not a word.

Kate dove into a bathroom just beyond the living room and slammed the door shut behind her. She peeled off her wet clothes, snatched a towel off the rack, and began drying her face and hair.

After a little while, there came a soft knock at the door.

"What!" she snarled, and Buck's soft voice wheedled: "I got some dry clothes you can put on."

"Go away!"

"If you'll open the door, I'll hand 'em to you."

"I don't trust you," she grumbled, but glanced at the door just the same. She hurriedly wound the towel around herself, then opened the door just a crack. Something was dangling from Buck's big hand, and when she took it, she realized that it was a swimsuit.

"Come out and swim, Kate," he wheedled, from the other side of the door.

Kate's outraged eyes moved from the silky white spandex to the cracked door. "You *planned* this!" she gasped.

Buck swallowed a bubble of laughter and sputtered, "That sounds like a conspiracy theory."

Kate frowned and demanded, "Buck Spade, did you *do* something to Carson's Jaguar?"

"Now what would I do to Carson's toy?" Buck's voice objected. "It's been trying to die ever since he started tinkering with the engine."

"You *did* do something, admit it!"

"I'm as innocent as the child unborn," Buck vowed solemnly, then his voice softened. "Come on out and swim, Kate. Everybody else is."

"Except Carson!" she retorted.

"Aw, Carson'll be alright. This ain't the first time he's had to walk. Come on."

Kate pinched her lips into a thin line. "My hair and clothes are drenched!" she complained.

Buck's voice softened again. "Bet you're not too hot any more, though," he murmured, and an angry retort died on Kate's lips. Buck's tone had changed from laughing and mischievous, to serious.

She had to admit that the dip in the pool had cooled her off. And maybe Buck really was worried about her. He'd acted on his concern in the most shocking possible way, but she'd learned enough about Buck to give him the benefit of the doubt.

"Well…" she grumbled, and Buck's tone switched again. His voice was cheerful as he replied, "Great! I'll be waiting for you out by the pool. I'll have Miss Ada dry your clothes out so they'll be ready once you're done."

Kate grumbled again as she closed the cracked door and shook out the bathing suit. It was an elegant, one-piece, strapless white bathing suit that reminded her of something a '50s starlet would wear.

It was beautiful.

Still, Kate mumbled under her breath as she slipped it on. She was mad at Buck for throwing her into the pool, but if she was honest with herself, the cool water had felt good.

And there was more to that good feeling than just relief from the heat. Kate straightened up and stared into the mirror for a long time, but she wasn't seeing her reflection.

Instead, she was face to face with her recent past. There in the privacy of that little bathroom, she was suddenly visited by the ghost of her own self, that pale, pinched-looking, harassed woman who never had a minute for herself. She'd had to cope with Kevin's sudden death, had to wrap up his practice and sell her studio and move to Texas and start a restaurant and be mother and father to Molly. In spite of the ache in her chest, she had to be the boss, the parent, the strong one.

It felt like ages since anyone had *played* with her. Since someone had tickled her, played a practical joke, teased her, made her laugh in spite of herself.

She hadn't played for a long time, until just now, and it felt good.

Kate adjusted the top of the bathing suit across her chest, then questioned her own reflection in the bathroom mirror.

Maybe Buck had played a trick on Carson, and maybe that wasn't fair. But now that she really thought about it, even if Buck was guilty, it just meant that he wanted to be with her enough to make the effort.

To plan out a mischievous scheme and pull it off.

Kate felt her serious mood melting away, and she gave herself permission to let it go. She sputtered a bit, controlled herself, then sputtered again as she saw Buck's goofy expression in her mind. His eyes had been wide with fear as he'd stumbled over the lounge chairs, as if he'd been scared to death of her.

She giggled a bit to herself, then shook her head in amusement. Buck might be stubborn and a bit possessive, but the more she considered why Buck did what he did, the better she liked him.

Maybe she could forgive him for tossing her into the water like a teenager.

It might be fun to feel like a teenager again for a little while.

Kate glanced at her reflection again, then turned the water on in the sink, cupped the water in her hands, and smoothed her tousled hair down. She stared at her reflection an instant longer, then pinched her cheeks until they flushed up, and bit her lips pink, before walking out to join Buck at the pool.

"Here she comes!"

Molly's happy voice called out to greet her as she walked through the sliding doors and out onto the patio. Kate tried not to feel self-conscious in the new bathing suit. It fit her like a glove, but she hadn't worn one in years.

Buck looked up, then looked again, and the smile faded off his face. Kate glanced down nervously, wondering if her wardrobe had malfunctioned, but Buck stood up slowly and stared at her with an odd, serious look.

He was wearing a goofy swimsuit, a big, baggy pair of navy trunks that reached almost to his knees. But Buck's athletic chest was a work of art, and it always made Kate suffer a flick of confusion. She stared at him for a stunned split-second, then her eyes moved reluctantly to the other man on the patio. The bearded man with the dark, shoulder-length hair who was sitting on a nearby lounge chair.

Buck coughed into one hand. "Kate, I don't think you've met my brother Morgan."

The dark man stood up slowly. "Ma'am."

Kate nodded to him and tried not to let her chagrin show on her face as she remembered how she'd run past him in her sodden clothes.

"Hello, Morgan."

Buck gave his brother a hard look, and Morgan coughed and called out, "Kit, come on out now, buddy. It's time to go back upstairs."

The little boy swam instantly to the side of the pool and clambered out of the water. His little tanned feet painted puddles across the concrete as he scampered to his father's big knee, and Morgan took a towel and rubbed him dry, starting with his tousled head.

Kate sank into a lounge chair and watched as Morgan finally stood up, ran a hand through his hair, and took his little boy by the hand. He nodded to her as he passed.

"Nice to meet you, Kate."

"And you," she murmured.

When the two of them had disappeared inside the house, Kate turned to Buck. "What a cutie," she smiled.

Buck planted his hands on his hips and teased, "Morgan or Kit?"

"Kit, of course."

Buck scratched his nose. "Yeah, he's a cute kid, all right. He looks a lot like Morgan when he was that age. Kit's a lot nicer, though. Morgan was mean as a snake when he was a kid."

Kate turned to stare at him. "It must run in the family," she drawled.

Buck looked up at the sky and smiled, "Aw, now, let's not dwell on the past," he teased.

"Fifteen minutes ago is not the past."

Molly swam up to the side of the pool with a splash and called, "Come and swim, Buck!"

Buck turned his head to smile down at Molly's upturned face. "Get back, then," he warned. "I'm gonna cannonball!"

Molly shrieked and jumped away, and as soon as she was clear Buck vaulted into the air like a six year old, grabbed his knees, and hit the water with a thunderous *splash*. A column of water jumped into the air and splattered Kate from three feet away.

Buck's head popped up from the water, and he grinned at Molly as she shrieked with laughter. "Come on in, Kate!" he waved.

"I've already been in, remember?" she replied.

"Come and swim with us, Mamma!" Molly called, and Buck beckoned to her.

Kate remembered her reflection in the bathroom mirror and bit her lip. She stood up slowly, adjusted her swimsuit, and took a few steps back from the edge.

"Cannonball!"

She got a split second glimpse of Molly's amazed, upturned face, and Buck's triumphant whoop was the last sound she heard before she splashed in, and the water closed over her head.

Chapter 35

Buck stood on the front steps, raised his hand, and watched as Kate's red convertible drove away. As he watched, Carson's small silhouette appeared in the distance as he trudged up the driveway toward the house. Buck frowned as Kate's red car drove toward Carson, slowed down, then stopped as he walked over to talk to her.

The car paused there as Buck planted his hands on his hips; but then the tail lights flicked on, and the convertible moved on.

A slow smile dawned across Buck's face, then he sighed and crossed his arms as Carson's silhouette slowly inched forward.

"He's gonna be mad as fire," Buck sighed to himself; but he figured that Carson had the rest of his life to get happy.

Carson was all wrong for Kate, and he wouldn't know what to do with Molly. Buck shook his head as he watched his brother trudge along. Carson was a pretty good guy at heart, but he'd never been domestic. He'd never even come close to getting married, and he wasn't especially good with kids.

Buck crossed his arms and narrowed his eyes as he watched his brother's tiny, slumped shoulders and dragging walk. Kate's beauty was what had drawn Carson, and that was fair enough; but he knew his brother well enough to know that Carson wasn't husband and father material. He would be one day; but he wasn't yet.

Buck rubbed his nose. Then there was the fact that he was interested in Kate himself. *Interested* was the way he described it to himself, but it was way more than that.

He was beginning to see himself at the heart of Kate's little family.

He was seeing himself waking up to Kate's smiling eyes in the morning, imagining himself teaching Molly how to fish, saw himself bringing them into his home.

He closed his eyes. The sight of Kate in that white swimsuit had hit him like a hammer, and he was still seeing her in his mind. Kate was a bombshell redhead and she'd blown him away, all right; but if that had been all there was to it, she wouldn't have captured him.

He lowered his head and stuck his hands in his jeans pockets as he walked back to the house. Kate was more than beautiful. She wasn't afraid to tell him to take a flying leap, she was smart enough to run a successful business, and she didn't ask anyone else for help. She had grit, and he respected that.

But what had really gotten him was the look he saw in her eyes sometimes. That soft, tender glow of love when she was looking at Molly; and lately, he even thought he'd seen it in Kate's eyes when she was looking at *him.*

He was ready to fight for that look in Kate's eyes, because he believed it belonged to him and to nobody else. He glanced back over his shoulder at Carson's distant figure, then walked back into the house.

Buck walked up the stairs on the way to his own suite and a nice hot shower after his swim. He'd barely reached the top floor when his phone trilled, and he dug it out of his pocket with one hand and opened the door with the other.

"Yello."

Eugene's voice barked from the other end. "Have you read the report I sent back with Carson?" he demanded.

Buck closed the door behind him, rubbed his brow, and forced his mind to switch from love to business.

"I scanned it. Give me the bottom line, Eugene."

Eugene's voice was curt. "The bottom line is that if you don't come up with the original contract, the Seven could lose senior water rights to the Big Sandy," he retorted. "You're sure that your grandparents had that document?"

Buck flopped down into a leather chair. "I'm sure. Big Russ took care of business. We just have to find those papers."

"My advice is to find them fast," Eugene drawled. "Buster's lawsuit may be a farce, but if you can't prove your own claim he may get those water rights in spite of it."

"Aw, I know Judge Collins. He 's a sharp one. He's not going to let Buster turn his courtroom into a circus."

"Don't count on it," Eugene warned. "Look Buck, I think it would be a good idea to call a meeting and let everybody sit down and hear about it. You need to start thinking about what you're going to do if you can't come up with that contract. Maybe have a vote. Why not have your brothers meet me at that restaurant we were in last time. The steak house, I can't remember the name."

"The Stonehouse," Buck murmured, but he bit his lip into a straight line."What odds do you give us if we lose first dibs, Eugene?"

"You know the answer," Eugene replied grimly. "You'll have to be happy with what's left after Buster's herd gobbles it up, which is another way of saying you're out of business. That might be his real goal, come to think of it. He might not even need the water."

"Oh, he needs the water," Buck retorted. "I don't know how things are in Dallas, but we're baking here and have been for months. Look, Eugene, I'll talk to everybody and see what we can line up. I'll call you."

"Don't take too long," Eugene warned him, and the line went dead.

Buck stared down at the phone, then tossed it onto a table with a sigh. He rubbed his brow, sighed, and glanced out through the big window, but he wasn't thinking about the problem of the missing contract, and he wasn't seeing the rolling countryside stretching out to the horizon.

He was still seeing Kate's green eyes, glimmering up at him with that soft, sweet look that took his breath away. He closed his eyes and enjoyed that pleasant mental image for all of five minutes before there came a soft knock at his door.

Buck hauled himself up out of his chair and walked to the door. When he opened it, to his surprise, Carson was standing there.

Buck's brows shot up in surprise. His usually-dapper brother looked as if he'd just run a marathon. Carson's starched collar had been pulled open and had wilted onto his shirt, his hair was damp and mussed, and two unsightly sweat stains were peeking out from under the arms of his dress shirt. Buck was stabbed by the fear that Carson might actually pass out, and he swung the door open wide.

"Come on in," he yelped, and followed his younger brother with worried eyes as he limped in. "Are you all right?"

"I should murder you," Carson mumbled, and collapsed into a chair with a groan. He rolled his head back and closed his eyes in exhaustion.

Buck walked to the sideboard, poured his brother a glass of ice water, and handed it to him with a frown. Carson took the glass in his hands and sat there in silence, as if he didn't feel well enough to drink it.

"Do you know how far it is from the stables to the house?" Carson mumbled, and lifted the glass to his lips at last. Buck planted his hands on his hips and shook his head.

"Four thousand two hundred and sixty-three steps," Carson muttered. "At least, that was when I stopped counting."

Buck bit his lip to stifle the chuckle that was building up behind them. He would've asked why Carson hadn't just taken a horse, except that he'd made sure they were all at the vet, so there weren't any to take.

Buck looked down and rubbed his nose. "Yeah, well, that's a long way, all right," he agreed.

Carson's beautiful eyes rolled to his over the rim of his glass, and for an instant they flashed; but then the angry look faded. Carson sighed and put the empty glass on a table at his elbow.

"Uncle," he muttered.

Buck tilted his head to one side. "Come again?"

Carson looked up at him again. "Uncle. You remember, that was what I always said when you twisted me into a pretzel as a kid."

Buck frowned and crossed his arms. "I still don't follow."

Carson slumped back into his chair. "Yes, you do. I give up. I'm not going to fight you for Kate. If this was the old days, we might've fought a duel or something, but when a woman abandons me to ride off on my brother's horse, I don't see the use."

Buck nodded and raised an eyebrow. "Well, you've got a point there," he agreed. "You always did have a good head on your shoulders, Carson."

"Shut up," his brother replied listlessly. "Some day soon I'll think of some way to pay you back for nearly killing me, but for now, pour me another glass of water."

He held out the glass, and Buck took it without a word of complaint, filled it up, and handed it back.

Chapter 36

Bing-bong.

Roxanne's doorbell rang, and she jumped up from the couch in her apartment. When she opened her front door, a small brown box was lying on the stoop.

She snatched it up hungrily, carried it inside, and closed the door behind her. When she tore the box open, there was a small booklet inside. It was titled, *Setting Up Your Magnetic GPS Tracker.*

Roxanne flopped down on the couch, set the box down beside her, and leafed through the booklet with a smile on her face.

Thank you for buying this magnetic GPS tracker, it read. *Just attach the strong magnetic case to the underside of any vehicle to track its location in real time from your cell phone.*

Roxanne tossed the booklet aside and pulled a small, card-sized plastic case out of the box. It was black and heavy and had two industrial-strength magnets on one side, and she smiled and rolled it between her fingers.

I'm going to nail that snake, she thought in fierce glee, and tucked the black plastic case into her bag. It was just thirty minutes before the start of her shift, so the tracker had arrived just in time to be attached to Sebastian's car.

Maybe if she could track him, she could catch him selling stolen goods to his buyer. The buyer who'd threatened him for flaking last time.

Roxanne reached for her cell phone, checked its camera and battery strength, and then slipped it into her jeans pocket as she left for work.

It was almost five o'clock. The sky over her apartment building was a hot, hard blue, and the heat blasted her as soon as she stepped out the door. She hurried down a flight of concrete steps to unlock her beat-up car. She slid in and cranked up the AC before pulling out of the parking lot and into the street.

Roxanne turned her radio up to blasting, lit a cigarette from the dash lighter, and blew out an angry cloud of smoke as she drove. Sebastian was a slick one, and he'd gotten away with murder so far, but his luck was about to run out.

Her eyes narrowed as she imagined the pleasure of busting him in front of Kate and everyone else at the restaurant. It'd be sweet to have video evidence of the creep selling stolen goods; and she was sure she was close to getting it.

The Stonehouse was only a couple of blocks from her apartment, and she swung in, looped around the building to the employee parking lot at the back, and zoomed into her usual parking space. The screaming radio died abruptly as she killed the engine, and she crushed out her cigarette in the ashtray as she jumped out.

Roxanne scanned the lot for Sebastian's car, made a mental note of where it was parked, and settled down to wait until her mid-shift break. It was good and dark by eight p.m., and Sebastian had conveniently parked his car in a corner of the building that got very little light. It would only take her a few seconds to walk over, slap the tracker under his car, and then scoot back inside.

Roxanne frowned as she hurried up the loading dock steps. It was probably illegal to track someone's car without them knowing, but she didn't care. Sebastian had hit her on the back of the head, she was sure of it. He'd accused her of being a thief and was trying to get her fired.

That was a declaration of war; and she was determined to inflict heavy losses on the enemy.

She blew through the kitchen and out into the main hall to the greeter's station. Roxanne stowed her handbag behind the counter and was glad to see that Kate wasn't working for the night. That was one less pair of watchful eyes.

Everybody else was going to be too busy to notice what she did.

The customer traffic that night was heavy, and by the time her evening break rolled around, Roxanne was ready for it; but she wasn't going to allow herself to rest until she took care of business.

She traded off with Trina at the greeter's station, and walked out the front door past the people talking and laughing at the entrance. She didn't want to go through the kitchen past Sebastian's suspicious eyes; and the crowd of customers in the front didn't know what she was doing, or care where she went.

She slipped through them, out into the warm summer night, and around the front corner of the brick warehouse, She passed the employee picnic table and a long row of parked cars on the side of the building, and rounded around another corner to the loading dock in back.

Roxanne paused there in the shadows and scanned the dock and parking lot warily. Sebastian's car was in the same place, and she didn't see anyone else around.

It was her chance.

She was clutching the tracker in one hand, and she gave the lot one more once-over before slipping out of the shadows and across the line of parked cars. She scanned the lot as she walked toward the car, and she shot the kitchen door a wary glance as she passed the loading dock. It was open and the light in it glowed a bright gold, but it was empty.

Roxanne took a deep breath, then hurried over to the passenger side of Sebastian's car. She knelt down quickly, extended her arm under the door, and pressed the tracker to the metal underside. There was a heavy, solid *clink,* and Roxanne smiled as she pulled her hand back.

"Hey Roxanne!"

Roxanne straightened instantly and whirled around. She put a hand to her hair and walked quickly back to the loading dock, where a frowning waitress was standing with her hands on her hips.

"I, um, lost my contact lens," Roxanne mumbled as she swept past. The girl watched her as she went, then barked, "Trina said to come get you. She had to take over for a sick waiter and she needs you to cover the greeter station."

"Sure," Roxanne mumbled, and hustled herself out of the kitchen and back to the front of the restaurant. Her heart was pounding like a drum, and she flicked a glance at the other girl's face; but the waitress just sighed and turned back for the dining room.

"Thanks, Roxy."

"Sure."

Roxanne watched the other waitress go. Once the girl was gone, Roxanne pulled her phone out of her jeans pocket and tapped a few buttons. The tracker software flicked on, and to her delight, a flashing red dot appeared on a map of Sandy Creek.

I got you now, you reptile, Roxanne thought grimly, and glanced up in the direction of the dining room. She'd gotten away with planting the tracker, as long as the other girl didn't blab about what she'd seen.

If she got caught, she'd probably get fired and maybe even charged with a crime or something, but Sebastian would have to find the tracker first, and her money said he wouldn't. He probably wouldn't give her enough credit to even suspect her of such a slick move.

Sebastian always thought he was the smartest cookie in the room; and that was what was going to make busting him so much fun.

The look on his face when he finally realized she'd nailed him.

That mental image put Roxanne in a good mood, made her hum to herself and beam at guests as they walked into the restaurant.

Chapter 37

"Now Roxanne, the private dining room is booked tomorrow," Kate informed her evenly. "I want you to show our guests right back when they arrive. I don't want them to have to stand in the lobby."

Roxanne nodded. "Am I going to be the server?"

Kate shook her head. "I'll be taking care of them myself," she replied briskly.

"Gotcha."

Kate sighed and seemed to relax. "Other than that, everything else will be the same as always. So that's tomorrow's schedule. Thanks for pinch hitting tonight, Roxanne. "

Roxanne nodded with an expression of relish. "Just like I always do, and no problem. When then is all over you'll see that I was telling you the truth."

Kate shot her a keen glance but only replied, "I appreciate it. I'll be upstairs if anybody needs me."

Kate turned on the words and walked away, and Roxanne watched as her slender form disappeared through the dining room archway. But as soon as Kate was gone, she pulled her phone out of her bag, flicked the screen, and pulled up her new app.

A map of the neighborhood popped up, and Roxanne watched as a small red dot slowly moved away from the restaurant. She already knew that Sebastian lived in a condo three blocks over, that he often shopped at the most expensive clothing boutique in town, and that he sometimes visited the local park. That last bit of information was one she was monitoring, just in case he went there to move something besides his feet; but she had to be patient.

The whole thing would blow up on her if she wasn't careful.

She watched as the little red dot moved toward the condo complex, and then slowly moved past it in the direction of the park. Roxanne pursed her lips, flicked the phone off, and tucked it back into her bag.

She called out toward the kitchen. "Kate, I'm heading out. See you tomorrow."

There was no reply, and Roxanne slung her bag over her shoulder and hurried out of the main door. She'd parked her car near the front that night in the expectation that she might need to follow Sebastian, and sure enough.

She unlocked her car door, slid in, and cranked the motor. She stuck her phone into a plastic holder on the dash and pulled out of the lot and into the street. The little red dot on the map was moving steadily toward the park just outside of town, and it was almost midnight.

Roxanne turned right at the first red light beyond the Stonehouse. At that late hour, the little town square was almost empty. She reached for a cigarette and lit it as she drove past the dark, shuttered storefront shops and cafes. She was careful to cruise slowly, to keep her distance. Sebastian's car was about three blocks ahead of hers, and she didn't want him to see her headlights in his rear view mirror.

He was going to the park to fence stolen merchandise, she could feel it in her bones. If she could catch him on camera taking money in a darkened park at midnight, maybe she couldn't prove he'd stolen from Kate, but it'd be suspicious enough to attract the attention of the cops.

Maybe enough to justify a search warrant at his condo.

Roxanne glanced at the blue screen propped up on her dash. Sure enough, the red dot was turning into the little park, and she turned off all but her running lights as her own car got nearer to the park. It made it hard to drive in the dark, but she knew the way, and she wasn't likely to meet anyone else on that stretch of road after midnight.

Roxanne sputtered smoke into the air and crushed out her cigarette. What was that boogeyman saying her mother had always used on her when she'd wanted to go out with her friends?

Nothing good happens on a road at night.

It looked like her mother's warning was going to be proved true after all; only Sebastian was going to be the one that it hit right between the eyes.

Not her.

Roxanne flicked off the running lights as her car rounded the last curve. She cut off the motor at the last minute, turned into the park, and let her car glide soundlessly into the paved lot. She pulled into the deep shadows under a big oak tree and let her car roll to a silent stop.

She pulled up the parking brake and peered through the windshield. Sebastian's little car was parked three hundred feet away, halfway down a long drive that ran from the front lot to the edge of a hiking trail. That whole end of the park was as dark as pitch, and she could only see his fender glimmering there because the anemic parking lot lights barely grazed it.

Roxanne cracked the driver's side door and peered into the darkness. It was a hot, humid night, and the air was heavy with the moist, heavy scent of wet earth. The air was still and quiet, and if she didn't already know better, she would've sworn there was no one else out there.

But there was.

She grabbed her phone off the dash, opened the camera app, flicked on the night vision function, and slipped it into her jacket pocket. She was all in black that night, and her sneakers had rubber soles; so she was as invisible as she could be.

Roxanne slid out of the car, crouched down, and pushed the car door quietly shut. She rose warily under the shade of the oak tree and walked to the edge of its dark canopy. She tilted her head and listened intently. The night was deep and still, but now she could just detect the sound of muffled voices. They were faint and far off, but they jolted her like a live wire.

If there was a buy going on, she was missing it.

She stuck one hand into her jacket pocket, then emerged from the shadows into the lighter darkness at the edge of the parking lot. She moved quickly from one tree to another, pausing each time to gauge the direction of the voices.

Roxanne paused at the third tree lining the drive and leaned against the trunk. Sebastian's car was just a stone's throw away and she could see that it was empty. She listened again.

The voices were closer now, but still hushed and indistinct. They seemed to be coming from the other side of the driveway near the trail head. She lifted her phone, pointed the camera side in that general direction, and stared at the screen. The night vision took an instant to adjust, but then flicked on.

Two small, glowing figures were standing in the middle of the shaded path. She pressed the record button and zoomed in as one of them passed something to the other.

Roxanne bit her lip and scowled. *The cops are going to say this is a drug deal*, she fumed. *But maybe it won't matter. This should be enough to get Sebastian's place searched. Maybe enough to get him fired. I can show it to Kate and...*

A flash of pain abruptly struck her left temple, followed by a shower of stars and a heavy fall. Roxanne hit the ground, rolled over and over in the grass, and came to a stop facing the sky. The phone slid out of her fingers as her dazed eyes darted around her.

She'd forgotten about the lookout.

Roxanne mustered her strength, grabbed the phone back up, and scrambled to her feet. She couldn't see who'd hit her, but it didn't matter.

The only important thing now was to run like—

Something swung through the air so near her head she could feel the breeze, and she whirled and ran for her life. She felt dizzy and sick, but she made herself fly. If she got caught now, she'd get beaten to death.

Roxanne sped toward the car, fumbling in her pocket as she ran. She found the key fob and jammed the unlock button. Her car lights flicked on as her feet pounded the grass, and she prayed that there was nobody else out there waiting for her by the car.

She could hear her attacker running after her, panting and grunting, but he was falling behind.

Maybe she had a chance to reach the car.

The thought had no sooner crossed her brain than one of her feet hit the ground wrong. The next thing she knew she was on the ground, and she rolled, then scrambled up again; but now she was limping, and every time she put her weight on her left foot, pain branched up her leg.

Her attacker was at her back now, and the man was so close that Roxanne sobbed as she half-ran, half-hopped across the blacktop to her car. It was only a few yards away.

Something grabbed her hair from behind, and Roxanne screamed in pain as her pursuer ripped a handful out of her scalp, but she threw herself on the car door, scrambled inside, and slammed the door shut. She locked the door and scrabbled for the key as a dark shadow ran up and threw itself against the car with a *wham*.

She sobbed again and turned the key in the ignition. The engine growled to life, her window shattered with a *bang*, and she yanked the gear shift. The car jerked backwards, the hand grabbed her shoulder through the window, and she turned the wheel and gunned the motor. The hand jerked back with a hoarse yell, and the car scratched away and roared out of the parking lot and down the road.

Roxanne flicked the headlights on, shaking and sobbing as she clutched the wheel. Her window was broken out, glass was everywhere, her head was throbbing with pain, and her scalp was on fire where the hair had been yanked out.

I could've bought it just now, she thought in panic. *I could've died!*

Nothing good happens on a road at night.

Her eyes rolled to the rear view window. Nobody was following her yet, but that could change any second. She yanked the wheel and turned off onto the first side street she could find and gunned the motor in fear.

No job is worth this. I could've been killed. No job is worth getting killed over!

She sent the car roaring down the side road, then turned again at the next intersection, before her panic faded enough for her to think about strategy.

I can't go back to my apartment. Sebastian might tell them I was the one who saw them.

Somebody could even be waiting for me if I go back. They might be a gang or something.

Roxanne reached for a cigarette with a shaking hand.

I'm getting all the way out of Dodge. I'm never coming back here.

Sebastian can have it. He'll get his one day.

Roxanne turned again to enter the back alleys of the town square. She wanted to head for the interstate without being seen by anyone waiting on the main drag. Her only goal at that moment was to get so far out of Sandy Creek that no one could ever find her again.

A deep wave of fear shook her, and as she skirted the town, Roxanne caught a glimpse of the Stonehouse across the street through the gaps in the brick buildings. The only regret she felt, as it slid into her past, was a fleeting pity for Kate.

Kate had no idea what was going on in her own place; or that it was serious enough to shed blood for.

Chapter 38

"Did she say anything to you about having to take a night off?"

Kate leaned against the greeter's station and stared into Trina's puzzled face, but the girl shook her head earnestly. "No, nothing! I'm worried about her. Roxanne's been different lately. We used to talk about everything, but the last few days, she kind of clammed up. Like she was mad about something."

Kate sighed and put a hand to her head. "Well, we don't have time to worry about it now. Call that friend of Sebastian's and ask him to come in tonight. Maybe he can sub for her."

Trina gave her a sympathetic look. "Sure, Kate."

"And after that, I want you to start setting up the conference table in the private dining room. We have a large group coming in there tonight."

"Okay."

Kate watched as Trina scuttled off to make the phone call and sighed deeply. Sebastian had called in sick, Roxanne had disappeared, and now she was going to have to scramble to find replacements on the night the whole Spade clan was coming to have dinner at the Stonehouse.

Buck had invited her to join them, and she'd wanted to impress his family; but now she was wondering if she was going to have to beg off just so she could get their dinner on the table.

She glanced at her watch. It was a bit past three, so she still had time to get everything in gear if she hustled.

She was just turning to go back to the kitchen when to her astonishment, the front door opened and Sebastian breezed in. Kate squashed her split-second of surprise to demand, "Are you working tonight?"

Sebastian gave her a sickly smile, but his eyes flicked to the empty greeter station. "Yes. I have a splitting headache, but I'm going to suck it up. I knew you need me here." He glanced past her.

"Is Roxanne working tonight?"

Kate crossed her arms. "She was supposed to, but she hasn't showed. She's not answering her phone. I don't know what's going on."

Sebastian's lips curled up in a sour smile. "Well. I guess she flaked, then. But I've got your back, Kate. I'll be in the kitchen."

Kate watched him sympathetically. "I appreciate you coming in, Sebastian," she murmured, and crossed her arms, thinking:

I'm glad I can count on somebody.

Trina came bustling back and reported, "Steve says he's coming in, Kate. I think we're okay."

"Good. Let me know if there's anything else."

"Sure."

Kate took a deep breath and headed off to her little office. She'd ordered fresh floral arrangements for the private room, and the florist had just delivered them. The special crystal dinner set and silverware was in the dishwasher, and her finest linen napkins were clean and fresh and ready to go.

She walked in and was greeted by the glorious spray of sunflowers, peach roses, and bluebonnets sitting on her desk. The arrangement was as big as a bushel basket, crammed with blooms, and had been delivered in a huge terra cotta bowl.

She picked it up and carried it through the restaurant to the private dining room. As she set it down on the big table, she looked up to see Sebastian in the doorway.

"Are you feeling alright?" Kate frowned.

"Just fine," he replied with a smile. "Trina told me you wanted help setting up in here, so I thought I'd lend a hand. I'm not busy yet in the kitchen."

Kate nodded gratefully. "All right. You can unload the dishwasher and wipe down the dishes and silverware, then bring them in here."

"Got it."

Sebastian turned on his heel and left, and Kate glanced around the room, ticking off all the things she still needed to do. One of them was to make sure Molly was safely tucked away upstairs, and she abandoned the room to go check on her daughter.

She walked into the hall, passed the greeter's station, and turned into the main dining room. She crossed the room and climbed the stairs at the far end to the open hall at the top. Her own door was the end of the brick-walled corridor, and she unlocked it with a sigh.

"Mollykins?"

To her relief, Molly was curled up on the sofa, munching on the last bits of her dinner and watching cartoons on television. Kate closed the door behind her and walked over to give Molly a peck on the brow.

"Are you going to be okay here alone, Molly?"

Molly looked up at her and nodded. "I'm big enough now to stay up late," she replied proudly.

"Hmm. Now what are you going to do?"

Molly sighed and rolled her eyes. "I'm going to stay inside the apartment, and not open the door to anybody, and watch t.v. until nine o' clock."

"Then what?"

"Brush my teeth and go to bed," Molly mumbled in a disappointed voice.

"That's right. Remember, if you behave this time, Mamma might let you stay up late again, but it depends."

"I'll remember," Molly sighed, and Kate laughed and kissed her again.

The phone rang, and Kate walked over to pick it up. "Hello?"

Buck's rumbling voice was on the other end. "You ready for a bunch of roughnecks in your place?" he teased.

"I'm ready," she sighed. "One of my waitresses flaked on her shift, so it's been interesting, but we adjusted. Come on over."

"I want to introduce you to everybody tonight," Buck went on. "It's hard to get my brothers all together in one place at one time, so this is probably the best chance I'll have."

Kate's tone softened to a murmur. "That's sweet of you, Buck. I'd like to meet your brothers. How many of them are there?"

"There's seven of us," Buck laughed. "And it gets pretty loud when we're all together. Just wanted to warn you ahead of time."

"You're welcome to be as loud as you like," Kate replied with a smile. "That private room is all yours."

"Well, that's good news, because there's likely to be shouting. It's kind of a business meeting," Buck explained, "and Eugene's coming up too."

"Is it about the water rights case?"

"Yeah. Eugene's going to give us a damage report."

"Not too bad, I hope," she frowned.

"Oh, no. It'll be alright. Eugene always has to look at the dark side. It's his job."

Kate laughed and twined a sprig of auburn hair around her fingers. "Why don't you come over a little early, Buck? We could have something to drink before dinner."

"That sounds great. I'll be right over," he promised.

"Good. Maybe you can help me set the table," she teased. "See you then, Buck."

"Looking forward to it, Kate."

Kate hung up with a sigh, then turned to Molly. "All right, baby. I'm going to work now. I'll be back late, so I'll see you tomorrow morning."

"Night night, Mamma."

Kate kissed her again, then walked out of the apartment and down the stairs. It was shaping up to be a big night, and she hoped she was as ready for it as she'd told Buck she was.

Chapter 39

Eugene leaned over the table and pushed a pile of papers across it. "There it is," he muttered. "Read it and weep."

Kate glanced from the graying, bushy-haired lawyer, to Buck, to his six brothers. Her initial impression had been that she'd never seen so many handsome men in one place in her life. None of them were under thirty, but most had ink-black hair, and all had varying shades of blue eyes and muscular physiques. Buck was the tallest and largest, but a couple of his brothers were almost as big as he was.

Buck turned to her and gestured to the row of relatives seated around the table. "Before we get started, I need to introduce Kate to everybody," he announced. He leaned toward her, pointed to Morgan and began, "Morgan you've already met, and, um, Carson," he muttered with a dismissive flick of his finger. "This boy next to Carson is Luke."

Kate turned to the man sitting beside Carson. He was the only fair brother, with sandy blonde hair, and he looked as if he'd be more at home on a beach than a ranch. He appeared young, barely over twenty, though Kate guessed he was older, and his pale blue eyes jumped out in contrast to his tanned face.

He grinned at her and nodded. "Nice to meet you," he mumbled, and Kate repressed a smile, because Luke had the same Texas drawl as Buck, only slower and more pronounced.

"That mean booger next to him is Jesse," Buck went on, and Kate felt herself going warm in embarrassment; but she had to admit that Jesse looked the part. He was a big, handsome man with a thick head of gloriously unkempt black hair and a neat spade beard; but his eyes were piercing and narrow, and he had a brooding, almost badgerlike look.

"How do you do," Kate murmured in awe, and Jesse grunted and gave her a curt nod.

"Will's our soldier boy," Buck drawled, and pointed to a trim, severely-groomed man with a buzz-cut and a close-shaven face. "He's an Air Force pilot stationed over at Langley in Virginia. He flew in special for us."

Will nodded and smiled, and Kate couldn't help smiling back. Will was as trim and bright as a new penny.

"Last over there is lover boy Chance," Buck drawled, and a tall, gorgeous, even better-looking-brother than Carson lifted a glass in salute and flashed a row of even white teeth. Kate felt her mouth dropping open, because though all of them were handsome, Chance was box-office beautiful, with gloriously clear blue eyes, jet black hair, and a perfectly-proportioned, masculine face.

"H-hello," she stammered, and Buck reached out to put a hand on hers. She snapped back to herself and shot him a chastened look

"All right," Buck told the room at large, "everybody ready to get down to business?"

Each brother reached out to grab a copy of the report, and they leaned back in their chairs to study it. Carson pulled a hand over his face and muttered from the corner.

"The problem is that Big Russ' original water rights contract is missing," he sighed. "Without it, we can't beat off Buster's lawsuit, because after the fire back in—what year was it, 1988?—there's no record of it at the courthouse either."

Buck looked up sharply from his copy. "Big Russ had that contract," he retorted. "He would've taken care of it. We just need to find where he put it."

"Fine," Carson shrugged. "Where is it?"

"I don't know yet," Buck mumbled. "But I'll find it."

"We don't have long," Eugene warned them, as he sat back down in his chair. "The hearing's been scheduled for next week, and if we can't prove you own senior water rights, then they go to the applicant with the next-oldest claim. Per my research, that would be Buster Hogan."

"He's lying through his teeth!" Buck burst out, and Eugene sighed and glanced at him over his glasses rims.

"We'll certainly make that argument in court," he replied. "But we can't expect the judge to accept it without consideration of evidence."

"Evidence," Jesse rumbled darkly. "When did Buster ever care about that?"

An angry grumble eddied around the table, and Chance asked, "Where have we checked for that contract?"

Carson looked up. "I cleaned the house when Miss Annie died," he replied. "She had a coffee can with all her papers in it. I found the deed to the ranch, the house, and that old beater truck she drove, but nothing else."

"What about their lawyer, that fellow we used before?" Luke piped up.

"He died three years ago," Buck mumbled, and flipped a page. "His office shut down. And Miss Annie wouldn't have given him her papers anyway. She was just like Big Russ that way."

"That's true," Jesse agreed. "Both of 'em kept their own stuff around that house. If we find those papers, it'll be because we dug 'em up."

Will looked up. "Let's get some ground-penetrating sensors," he suggested, and tossed the papers onto the table. "That should tell us if they buried the papers, one way or the other."

"I'll get on that," Buck promised. "I'll find somebody this week."

As he spoke, the door behind them opened softly and Kate glanced back over her shoulder. Sebastian slipped in with a small cart and wheeled it into a corner. He lifted a pitcher and began moving down the table, refilling glasses.

Carson glanced around the table. "Did anybody ever hear Big Russ or Miss Annie mention that contract?"

The others glanced at him, and then at each other. "No," Will replied, and the others shook their heads.

Eugene sighed and rubbed his eyes. "Well, gentlemen, I suggest you do everything you can to find that rights renewal, and as soon as possible," he muttered. "I don't look forward to walking into that courtroom without it."

"How did we lose it in the first place?" Jesse grumbled. "Buck, you're supposed to be running the Seven. Why don't you know where it is?"

Buck scowled at him. "You better believe I'm running it," he growled.

"It's not Buck's fault," Carson put in. "After Miss Annie died he sent me up to the house to collect their papers."

Jesse turned to stare at him. "It's your fault then," he replied coldly, and the room broke up into angry muttering.

Eugene put up his hands. "Gentlemen, please! Let's address the issue at hand. Now I hope you can produce that contract, but as your lawyer I have to help you prepare for what might happen if you don't."

"I told you we'll get it," Buck told him, and Jesse retorted, "Oh, shut up, Buck!"

Kate's eyes widened as Buck stood up suddenly. "You wanna come over here and make me?"

The room broke out into loud arguing as Buck slowly sat down again, and it got so bad that Eugene leaned over in his chair and beat on the table with his shoe.

"Calm down!" he yelled.

The fighting stopped instantly, and a startled silence fell over the room as everyone turned to look at him. Eugene took a deep breath and went on,

"Gentlemen, if we can't produce that contract, how do you want to go about getting water rights for the Seven?"

Carson rubbed his eyes. "We'll have to take Buster's leavings, and truck in water from the outside."

"That'll break us," Morgan put in quietly, and several others nodded.

"That would only be a short term fix anyway," Buck added, and his face looked so weary and stressed that Kate had to restrain herself from putting a hand on his arm. "We could drill for water. We have the legal right to pump all the ground water we can find, isn't that right Eugene?"

The attorney nodded. "That's right. If you can find enough to make that worth while."

"That might tide us for a year or two, but it isn't long term either," Morgan put in glumly.

"Well, it's the best I got right now," Buck muttered.

Eugene adjusted his round glasses. "The ranch is set up as a limited partnership, if I remember correctly?"

"That's right," Buck replied.

"Your bylaws require a vote on all major decisions," the attorney reminded them. "Shall we put it up for a vote, then? If we fail to find the rights contract, you'll drill for water and failing that, truck it in."

"Until the money runs out," Morgan put in glumly.

Eugene glanced around the table. "All yeas?"

Kate's glanced flicked around the table. Five hands slowly went up.

"Nays?"

Jesse and Luke put up their hands, and Eugene nodded. "The record will show that the partners voted yea," he murmured.

A soft clinking announced Sebastian's departure as he rolled the beverage cart out, and Kate watched him go in relief. *I don't know what I would've done without Sebastian tonight,* she thought gratefully. *It looks like he was telling the truth after all, and that Roxanne was the thief.*

An innocent person doesn't run.

Anger flicked in Kate again as she remembered Molly's ransacked room, but if Roxanne's absence meant that their troubles were over, maybe it was just as well.

The mention of her own name snapped Kate back to the present. Buck had turned in his chair and was smiling at her.

"Let's all thank our hostess tonight," he was saying. "Kate, it was a fine meal."

A jumbled murmur of agreement eddied around the room, and Kate smiled at her handsome guests as they lifted their glasses to her.

"It was a pleasure to meet everyone," she murmured. "I hope you'll all come back again."

"I will," Eugene promised, and lifted his drink to his lips. "I haven't had steaks like this even in Dallas."

"We all will," Chance grinned, and sipped from his glass with a mischievous glance over the rim. "Watch out, Buck!"

Buck shot him an exasperated glance, but to Kate's amusement, he also stretched an arm around the back of her chair.

Chapter 40

"I want to go up to the old ranch house tomorrow," Buck was saying. "I'm going to take the copter. Want to come with me?"

Kate was chopping carrots on the counter in her kitchenette, and she nodded in the general direction of her phone. "Love to," she answered. "I'll just have to find someone to watch Molly."

"Bring her to the house," Buck suggested. "She could stay at Morgan's place and play with Kit. The two of 'em seemed to hit it off at the pool the other day."

"Are you going to ask Morgan what he thinks about it?" Kate sputtered, but Buck's voice sounded faintly puzzled.

"I don't have to," he replied mildly. "Morgan'll be happy to watch Molly for us."

"Okay then," Kate smiled and shook her head. Buck came from a big, tight-knit family like she'd always wanted. She'd been an only child, and her parents had divorced when she was Molly's age; and so it was a treat to meet Buck's sprawling family.

"Great. I'll be over about noon to pick you up."

"Not in the helicopter, I hope," Kate teased. "I don't think the town has gotten over the last time you brought it here."

She could almost hear Buck's grin on the other end of the phone. "Well," he drawled, "if you don't want me to, I guess I'll just have to bring the truck. It won't be as much fun, but I always give a lady the last word."

"You're spreading it on thick now," she sputtered, and Buck laughed with her.

"I'll be by tomorrow at noon," he promised. "See you then."

"Bye, Buck."

Kate murmured, "Hang up," and the little red light on her phone flickered once, then went dark.

Molly came running in from the back of the apartment, and laughed in shock to see her daughter dressed in a pink tutu and tights.

"Where on earth did you get that?" she demanded, as she wiped the carrots off the cutting board and into a bowl.

"Daddy bought it for me," Molly replied proudly, and Kate's hand froze in the air. She glanced at her daughter over her shoulder, slowly recovered, and wiped her hands on her apron.

"That's right," Kate murmured, as Molly twirled around in her spangled costume. "I'd forgotten about that. Daddy bought it for your fourth birthday."

Molly skipped through the living room with her arms raised over her head. "It's a little tight," she confessed, and suddenly stopped to pull the leggings up. "But I can wear it."

Kate gave her daughter a wan smile and turned back to the counter. *It never fails,* she marveled. *Just when I think I'm getting a little better, something happens to remind me that Kevin's dead.*

It always hits me like a hammer. Right between the eyes.

She had been looking forward to going out with Buck, but her anticipation was fast darkening into guilt. It tinged her question as she asked, "Molly, Buck….Buck's invited us back over to the ranch. Would you like to go over and play with Kit?"

"The little boy at the pool?"

Kate smiled and reached for a jar of mayonnaise. "Yes, the boy at the pool."

Molly stopped twirling to consider. After a judicious silence she sighed, "I suppose. He's all right. I don't much like boys, but he can put his fingers in his mouth and whistle, and he promised to show me how if I came back."

Kate glanced at her again, this time in amusement. It seemed that Molly was destined to become a tomboy if she kept hanging around the Seven Ranch.

"Good," she smiled. "Buck's going to come and take us to his house tomorrow, and then we're going to let you play with Kit until we come back. Buck and I are going to visit his old home, way out at the far corner of the ranch."

Molly tilted her head like a bird. "Mamma, is Buck a cowboy?" she demanded.

Kate smiled, raised her brows, and thought to herself, *He's probably their king;* but she only sputtered, "Yes he is, baby."

"I thought so," Molly nodded. "I like cowboys."

Kate smiled more to herself than to Molly and murmured, "So do I, baby." Guilt suddenly stabbed her again, and she shot her daughter a frowning look.

"Go change your clothes, baby. You don't want to rip your ballerina costume."

She watched as Molly scampered away, then closed her eyes and leaned against the sink.

Kate marveled as Texas grassland stretched out beneath them all the way to the horizon. The glittering, oak-lined Big Sandy snaked across the earth at their feet; and around it on every side, green meadows dotted with brown cattle rolled on forever.

The shadow of the helicopter sped across the earth beneath them, across pale green pastures veined by silver creeks, dotted by dark green groves of oak and mesquite trees, and marked by brown dirt roads that crisscrossed one another like tiny threads.

Kate stared down in wonder. She'd never get used to the fact that everything she was seeing—*all* of it—was the Seven Ranch.

Her eyes moved to the horizon. Something huge and blue was slowly opening up on the edge of sight, and she turned to question Buck's calm profile.

"What's that up ahead?"

He turned to smile at her, and his voice crackled through the intercom. "That's Thunder Lake," he replied, and pointed toward it. "It's right on the northern edge of the Seven."

Kate stared at it. The sheet of water glittered vast and silver-blue in the distance.

"Is it part of your ranch?"

Buck shook his head regretfully. "No. I wish it was! We wouldn't be fighting tooth and claw with Buster Hogan if we had all that water. That lake belongs to the state. It's a park."

"Oh, I see."

Kate watched as the lake became steadily larger and closer. Buck pointed at a low cluster of hills on the southwest edge of the lake. "There's my old stomping grounds," he told her with a smile. "The old ranch. It's right in between those hills."

"I'm looking forward to seeing it," Kate told him. "You've told me so much about it, I feel like I've already been there."

Buck's smile faded. "It probably isn't much to look at now," he murmured slowly. "I haven't been there in years. I should've, but running the Seven's a full time job. It's hard to get away."

"You remember where it is, though?" Kate asked, with a flicker of concern. The landscape rushing below them looked uninhabited, overgrown, and a little wild.

Buck's smile shone out again. "Oh, no fear of that," he laughed. "I know this country blindfolded. I could set this helicopter down and walk home from anywhere within ten miles."

Kate glanced at him and smiled a touch nervously as Buck swung the copter in a wide circle on the final approach to a circle of oak-covered hills.

Buck set the helicopter down in a grassy clearing on the crown of the foremost rise. Kate squinted at the forested descent ahead as the rotors slowly wound to a stop. The hollow at the foot of the hill was thick with the massive trunks and gnarled branches of ancient oaks, and the grass had grown up to their mossy knees.

Buck slipped the earphones off. "There's a little creek down at the bottom of this hill," he explained. "The ranch house is on the other side of it."

Kate turned to stare at him in alarm. "Are we going to have to wade across?" she asked, but Buck grinned and refused to placate her.

"I expect."

Kate stifled an exclamation and didn't know whether to laugh or be exasperated with him as she climbed out of the helicopter. Buck came walking over and held out his brown hand, and Kate took it as they picked their way through the broom grass and brambles on the hill.

Buck led her down the clearing and under the huge oak trees. Kate glanced up through the branches as they walked. The sky had been mostly clear, but the clouds were beginning to huddle together, and a sudden gust of wind through the leaves smelled of approaching rain.

"Hold on," Buck warned her and tightened his fingers around hers. "The ground under these trees is mossy, and the hill drops off quick. I wish I had a dollar for every time I've slid down it."

Kate gripped his hand tight, and Buck stepped sideways down the slanting hill over twisted tree roots and moss-slick rocks. Kate followed him one careful step at a time, never taking her eyes off her own feet. They slowly worked their way down the steep descent, and when they reached the foot of the hill, Buck had to clear a path to the creek bank through a chest-high tangle of brambles.

"This place has grown up sure enough," he grunted as he used his arms to push the bushes aside. "I can't even see the water yet. When I was a kid, you could see the creek from the top of the hill." He chuckled a bit and shook his head. "I spent most of my childhood on this creek bank with a fishing pole in my hand."

Kate shot him an affectionate glance. *Yes, I can see that*, she smiled to herself. Her imagination served up the picture of a barefoot ten-year-old perched on a fallen log with his jeans and his sleeves rolled up. She saw him lick his line, thread it through a hook, and throw it into the still water with a *plop.*

"Well, there it is at last," Buck panted, and dragged his arm across his brow. He pushed through a screen of bushes to reveal a calm, shallow sheet of water, fifteen feet across. The opposite bank was also a tangle of brambles and oaks, and when she looked, Kate couldn't make out anything that looked like a house.

She glanced at Buck in doubt, but said nothing as he reached for her hand again.

"Wait just a minute," she told him, and stooped over to take off her shoes; but Buck put a hand on her arm.

"I've got a better idea."

The next thing she knew, Buck bent down and scooped her up in his arms, and to her alarm, he began to slowly descend the muddy creek bank as she dangled over the water. He half-slid suddenly, and Kate shrieked and clutched his shirt; but he smiled at her, regained his footing, and stepped out into the stream.

"You're awful skittish," he observed with a grin. "Ain't you ever been in a creek before?"

Kate rolled horrified eyes to his face and tightened her grip on his collar. "Buck Spade, if you dunk me I'll murder you!"

"You need to relax," he replied easily, as he stepped from one rock to another. "It wouldn't be the end of the world if we both fell in."

"Buck!"

He laughed softly as he crossed the stream, then paused to glance up at the overgrown bank. "The last time I was here this whole bank was a long, sandy spit," he thought aloud. "I'm going to have to clear all this out. Tidy the place up."

Kate gripped his shirt like a terrified cat. "Get us across first."

Buck laughed again and set one big boot into the underbrush, found a foothold, and brought the other one even. He balanced precariously on the lip of the bank, then shouldered through the brush and up the opposite bank with her in his arms. Kate sputtered and turned her head as branches swiped her face. To her alarm, another sudden blast of wind came swirling through the trees, and when she raised her face to the sky, she was spattered by raindrops.

"Oh, Buck, it's starting to rain!" she moaned.

"Hold on," he told her. "We're almost there."

Kate closed her eyes and pressed her face into Buck's shirt as raindrops pelted her. She felt a sudden heave and surge, and when she opened her eyes again, they were at the top of the bank.

Buck set her gently down on her feet. They were standing on a broad, flat, grassy overlook under the canopy of a ring of massive oaks, and they were facing a long, low, wooden house. The dark green paint was peeling off, and the tin roof was rusted. Wild vines were curling up the porch posts and the yard was overgrown, but the house was still intact.

Buck's keen eyes clouded over at the sight of it, and Kate bit back what she'd been about to say. Buck's expression was faraway and a touch sad, and she let him have his moment.

It didn't last long. He inhaled sharply, then took her hand. "Let's go have a look," he murmured, and they walked across the yard and up the sagging steps to the porch. Kate hurried under the shelter of the porch as the rain spattered down on the tin roof: first one drop, then two, then a dozen, then a downpour. It was already cool under the shade of the oaks, and the rain-cold breeze raised goosebumps on her arms.

"Let me go inside first," Buck muttered, and opened the screen door, then the wooden door behind it. They both creaked loudly, and his big boots echoed across the plank board floor as he walked into the house.

Kate stood in the doorway, hugging herself with the cold; but she was curious enough to peer inside as Buck flicked a lighter and held it up. He walked across the room, and she got a glimpse of a big stone fireplace as he reached for a lantern on the mantle. The faint scent of kerosene and ashes eddied to the door as he lit the lamp.

An instant later a soft circle of yellow light bloomed in the dim room. To Kate's surprise, the interior of the house was furnished and tidy, as if the owners had just stepped out for a while. There was a rag rug on the floor in front of the fireplace, and a pair of rocking chairs facing it.

Buck turned and held the lantern up, and Kate could make out old paintings on the wall, an old piano, and an ornate Victorian bookcase that she would've killed for.

"Huh," Buck grunted. "It looks a lot better in here than I thought it would, Everything's clean, and some of this furniture is new. Or at least, it wasn't here when I was here last. Morgan's probably been coming here to keep the old place up. Might even be bringing Kit here to stay the weekend."

Kate turned to glance over her shoulder at the yard. She noticed an old well under one of the oaks, with the bucket still dangling from an old rope.

Thunder suddenly growled right overhead, and a flick of lightning pushed Kate inside the house. She closed the screen behind her and watched in awe as the sky opened up and rain poured over the edge of the porch roof like a waterfall.

When she turned back again, Buck wasn't there any more, but a faint radiance glowed from an open doorway on the far side of the room. There was a faint *clink,* followed by the sound of Buck's wandering boots.

"I was right about Morgan," he muttered. "He's put a little refrigerator in the kitchen, and it's still got some stuff in it." There was a pause, and a soft sniffing sound. "It still looks good."

Kate glanced at the fireplace. "There's wood in this fireplace," she called. "Could we start a fire, and maybe warm it up in here? It's a little chilly."

The light bobbed back into the room, followed by Buck. "Sure, Kate," he replied. "Sorry about that. I got a little distracted. You just sit down. I'll get a fire going."

Kate sank gratefully into the rocker as Buck set the lamp on the mantle, knelt down, and began to build a fire.

"You said there was a refrigerator," she murmured. "Does the house have electricity?"

Buck glanced back at her over his shoulder. "Not any more. Morgan's rigged the fridge up to run off a battery, but the battery isn't here. He just left a couple of apples in there, and they last forever."

Kate's hope deflated. "Oh."

A small flicker in the fireplace threw Buck's craggy profile into gold highlights and black shadow. Kate let her eyes linger on the glossy black curl that drooped over his brow as he worked, on his proud nose, on the little muscle in his square jaw. She tilted her head and considered him as he stacked firewood over the little bloom of fire.

Buck was a big man, a man's man. He was a hunter, a fisher, a man who knew how to build a fire and fly a helicopter and run a ranch. He was brash and blunt and opinionated, then gentle and courtly and tender. Sometimes he made her laugh, sometimes he made her furious, sometimes he made her mouth go dry.

But if she had to sum him up in one word, she'd say that Buck made her feel *safe*.

After the disasters of her recent past, that feeling was as luxurious as snuggling into her down pillow, of pulling her faux fur blanket up around her ears.

Kate glanced down at her hands and rubbed her thumb over her bare ring finger. She could take care of herself and Molly, she loved running a restaurant, and she knew Kevin would've been proud of the job she'd done. But she'd been driven mostly by necessity, and sometimes she felt more harassed than empowered by all the things she had to do.

It was wonderful to relax and let someone else take over for a change. And if there was anyone on earth who knew how to take over, it was Buck Spade.

He stood up, clapped the wood smudge off his hands, and glanced down at her. "There! The fire'll be going good in a few minutes."

Kate stretched her hands out toward it. "Thanks, Buck."

He jerked a thumb toward the back of the house. "I'm going to poke around and see what else I can find. Maybe Morgan left something behind we can use."

He turned on the words and disappeared through the far door. As soon as he was gone, a ferocious peal of thunder shook the house, and a loud *pop* and brilliant flash followed instantly. Kate's shoulders jerked in alarm, and Buck's voice yelped from the adjoining room.

"*Wooo*, that was close! You alright in there?"

"Yes," Kate called back, but she put a hand to her chest just the same. Her heart was galloping.

A fresh downpour of rain hit the roof, and Kate rocked slowly in her chair as it drummed overhead. The rocking chair, the dim yellow glow of the glass lamp on the mantle, and the flickering firelight on her arms made her feel almost like a pioneer woman. As if stepping into the old house had somehow transported them back two hundred years.

Kate closed her eyes and sputtered softly. With Buck, that wouldn't be a big stretch of the imagination. He would've made a fine pioneer. Her, not so much with her art gallery in LoDo, her bohemian friends, her love of frilly, feminine things. She probably would've fallen off the back of the prairie schooner and never even made it to Texas.

The heavy sound of Buck's boots on the floorboards announced that he was returning, and Kate looked up in time to see him appear in the doorway with blankets in his arms.

He walked over and draped a pretty blue patchwork quilt over her shoulders. "I found these in the main bedroom," he rumbled. "Pull this one around you. It should keep you warm."

Buck sank down in the chair beside her, and the wooden rocker creaked and groaned as he settled in. He tossed another blanket over his lap and stuck his boots up to the fire.

Kate snuggled thankfully into the quilt. It smelled faintly of cedar chips and wood smoke, and it was very pale and soft and worn. She wrapped herself in it up to her chin, because the rain was falling harder than ever, and the house was cool.

Another *pop* of lightning made Kate twitch again, and she glanced back at the door. "It doesn't sound like the storm's going to let up soon," she thought aloud.

Buck nodded absently as he stared into the fire. "I wouldn't want to take us back up in this lightning," he muttered. "We might have to ride the storm out here."

Kate glanced at Buck and was comforted by his big, solid presence. The house was old and dark and isolated, it was true, and if she hadn't been with Buck, it might've felt lonely or even frightening. But with Buck, the old house somehow felt snug and safe and homey.

Everything would be alright as long as he was there.

And it came to her then, in a small moment of insight, that the reason Buck had seemed so casual about his palatial home was that it was just his surroundings. Now that she'd seen him in both places, he'd seemed ten times more at home in that tumbledown house than he had in that multi-million dollar ranch complex.

He glanced up from the fire and sighed. "I need to turn this place upside down," he muttered. "I just got a bad case of lazy right now."

"You, lazy?" Kate laughed.

Buck folded his hands on his chest and slumped down in his rocking chair. "Yep. I don't wanna get up from this chair."

"Why do you think you need to?" she asked curiously.

Buck rolled his eyes up to the ceiling. "Oh, it's about the water rights case," he grumbled. "Eugene says we need to prove Big Russ' lease is still in force. The contract we have says it expired."

Kate's mouth dropped open slightly. "Oh."

Buck pulled a big brown hand over his mouth. "Yeah. We'll find it, but right now it's lost." He raised his head and glanced around the room. "I wouldn't be surprised if Big Russ socked it away on this place somewhere we haven't looked."

Kate smiled at him. "Was he the sort to keep his valuables in his mattress?"

Buck laughed into his hand. "Big time. Can't say he was wrong, come to think of it."

Kate's eyes roamed around the softly-lit room as the rain poured down on the roof. "There isn't much furniture here to hide something in," she observed.

Buck followed her gaze and nodded. "That's a fact," he agreed. "But he wouldn't have hid it in the house, most likely. Probably stuffed it in a mason jar and buried it someplace in the yard."

Kate stared at him in sympathy. "I'm sorry, Buck. I hope you find the documents."

Buck nodded. "We will. There's only so many places he would've likely hid it. I know he had the contract updated. Big Russ wouldn't have left us in the lurch. He probably stuck it away someplace safe and meant to get back to it."

"He sounds like a character," Kate smiled, and Buck nodded.

"He was that. I miss him," he replied softly. "Especially coming back here. There's not an inch of this place that doesn't have a thousand memories for me. It still doesn't seem real that Big Russ and Miss Annie are gone."

"I know what you mean," Kate murmured, and her eyes drifted to the dancing fire. "The people we love never really die, do they? They live on as long as we do."

The faint crackling of the fire was the only reply, and the two of them slowly settled down into silence. The rain pelted down outside harder than ever, and the wind moaned around the corners of the old house, but the heat from the fire and the warmth of the quilt around her shoulders almost lulled Kate to sleep. The room was slowly getting dark.

The touch of Buck's fingers on her hand roused her up again. Her fingers curled around his instinctively, and they sat there hand in hand in silence as the fire burned.

Buck looked up at her, and his bright blue eyes glinted in the firelight. "Kate, I want to court you," he announced.

She glanced up at him in surprise and swallowed a spurt of incredulous laughter. "*Court* me?" she teased.

"That's right," he replied softly. "I want to be the only man you're seeing, and for you to be the only woman I see. We've been billing and cooing a little while now, but I want us to have a plain understanding."

Kate gave him a look of exasperated affection. "Is this about Carson again?"

"Mostly," he replied evenly. "But not all about him." He looked back at the fire and added, "I want us to be exclusive."

"You don't beat around the bush, do you?" she smiled.

"I don't see the use of it," he answered. "Well, now I've told you what I want. What do you want, Kate?"

Kate squeezed his hand. "Before I tell you, answer a question for me, Buck. *Why* do you want us to be exclusive?" She turned to stare at him, to plead with her eyes. What she wanted was what any woman wanted from a man: a plain and simple declaration of love. But she knew Buck well enough by that time to doubt she was ever going to get it.

Buck adjusted his shoulder and glanced away, and Kate sighed. "Is it so hard to say that my eyes are like sunlight through the leaves? That my hair is red silk? That you want to kiss me?"

Buck sighed and looked away again, then turned back to challenge her with his vivid eyes.

"I'd a lot rather show it," he rumbled, and leaned over to kiss her. Kate met him halfway and luxuriated in the soft, strong, reassuring kiss that she was beginning to need. *I love this man,* she thought with a slap of surprise. It had come to her as suddenly as a flick of lightning tapping her shoulder, and it branched through her like fire.

I love him.

But as her fingers curled through his hair, Kate found that she was as reluctant to say so as Buck was. Even though the touch of his lips set her nerve endings on fire, even though his voice and his laugh and even the calluses on his hands were becoming familiar and dear to her.

She knew why '*I love you,*' got stuck in her throat. Maybe it was the same for Buck.

It still felt too soon, even though that made no sense at all. It was one thing for her to kiss a handsome man, to go out with him, to have fun. But for some reason, getting serious about Buck felt like she was betraying her husband's memory in a deeper and more profound way.

It felt like she was replacing Kevin in her heart, like she was forgetting him. Like she was consigning him to history and closing the book.

Buck's voice brought her back to the present. His lips lifted from hers and he caressed her cheek. "What's wrong, Kate?"

She leaned back into her chair and looked away. "Nothing's wrong."

He gave her a puzzled look. "Yes, there is something wrong, I can tell."

Kate frowned down at her hands, then looked up at him. She searched his face with her eyes.

She hadn't confessed to anyone that she'd been trapped in limbo since Kevin died. That she wasn't dead, and yet not fully alive. It was hard even to admit to herself.

"I was just thinking about Kevin," she stammered. "It's a crazy thing, Buck, but—you're the first man I've gone out with since Kevin died, and—being with you makes me feel guilty. Like I didn't wait long enough.

"Like I didn't love him enough."

Kate looked away, suddenly horrified that she'd admitted it. Tears stung her eyes, and her face burned with embarrassment. She hated to admit her own weaknesses, Kevin had always teased her about it; and it seemed she still did.

She didn't like making herself vulnerable to criticism; but Buck didn't criticize her. He kept staring into the fire, listening.

Kate picked at the blanket and murmured, "Kevin and I were college sweethearts. I was an art major and he was in pre med. We shouldn't have had anything in common, but we just clicked somehow. He was smart and curious and funny and compassionate. He was truly gifted, and he cared about people. He wanted to make the world a better place."

Buck stirred in his chair. "Sounds like a heck of a guy," he mumbled.

Kate looked down at the quilt sadly. "He was. But he's gone now. I need to let him go, but I feel so guilty about letting him go."

She turned to him with tears in her eyes. "Can you understand that?"

Buck looked up at her, and his eyes glinted in the firelight. "Sure. And it's not about how much you loved your husband, Kate. It's about how good a night's sleep you got, and what kind of mood you're in, and if something hit you wrong that day." He turned back to stare into the fire. "It's about time, and putting one foot in front of the other."

He sighed deeply and shook his head. "You know what helps me the most? Knowing that my wife would want me to live life as strong and full as I can. She was a firecracker. Full of life.

"I was lucky in one way," he sighed. "I had time with Delores before she passed. She told me that if I moped and dragged my bottom around after she died, she was going to come back and haunt me."

Kate uttered a shocked crack of laughter, and Buck smiled a bit. "That was Delores."

He paused and sighed. "I miss her every day, Kate. I guess that won't ever go away, and maybe it shouldn't. But she helped me see that if I let that get in the way of living life now, I've missed the point of being alive."

He coughed a bit. "Big Russ was like that, too. He told me that if I ever missed him, just to go have a beer and remember him falling in the creek, or Miss Annie pinching him just as the preacher walked in, or us fishing together.

"It was the best advice about grieving I ever got."

Kate pulled her mouth down slightly and blinked back tears. Buck's words had been wise and warm and kind, and she reached out for his hand.

"Thank you, Buck," she whispered. "You make me wish I'd known your wife and your grandfather."

He turned to give her a crooked smile. "In a way, you do," he replied softly, and squeezed her hand.

He fell silent for a while, then added, "And it's alright if you want to take things slow, Kate. I understand. Delores always told me that I only have two speeds, rocket and stop. I know my own mind, and I make it up quick." He shrugged.

"I'm willing to wait, if you need time."

Kate's heart melted as she stared at him. In that moment, she thought she glimpsed Buck's heart. It was simple and strong and true, and she was sure enough of her own to murmur:

"Yes."

Buck raised his brows and looked over at her, and she added, "You heard me. I just answered your question. It's yes. I'm willing to let it be just us, Buck. I don't promise how fast I can go, but I know that much." She met his eye and whispered, "It's you."

Buck tightened his fingers around hers, and Kate leaned over to meet him as he pulled her to him. As she tangled her fingers in his hair, she was thinking, *Yes.*

Yes, this may be hard for me, but it feels right. It's you, Buck Spade.

Chapter 41

The storm crashed on outside, and lightning branched across the sky as the daylight faded into evening. But the two of them sat there in front of the fire, hands clasped, until the heat and the gentle motion of the rocking chair made Kate drift off into a warm, comfortable drowse.

When she roused up again, Buck was gone. She glanced around the room in confusion, but it was impossible for such a big man to be hidden in a house with creaking floorboards. Buck's heavy footsteps announced his presence from the far side of the house.

Kate closed her eyes, reassured, and snuggled back into the quilt. She slipped back into a light drowse, sometimes seeing the little fire flickering in the dark, and other times half-wandering in her dreams.

So she wasn't sure she was awake or asleep when she heard Buck murmur, "I'll say it right out. I love you, Kate." He fell silent for a moment or two and added, "You don't have to tell me anything back. I know you're not sure in your mind. But I can say it. It's just how I'm made. I always know my own mind right away."

Kate saw him rise from his chair and chunk up the fire. The firelight painted a red sheen across his coal-black hair, and outlined his profile in light. A shower of little sparks sprayed across the brick fireplace floor as he threw a log in.

The next thing she knew, Molly sat down beside the fire and propped her chin in her hands as she stared into it.

"Mamma, are we spending the night here?"

"Yes, baby. Go and brush your teeth," she murmured.

Buck sat down in his rocking chair and turned to take her hand in his again. His thumb caressed her fingers.

"I think I knew I loved you when you fell off that horse," he whispered. "I thought you might've broken your neck, and I panicked."

He caressed her fingers again. "And when you looked up at me, I felt like shouting, I was so relieved." He shook his head. "Sometimes you can just tell. I felt that way almost from the first, Kate."

Kate inhaled, opened her eyes, and roused up. She turned to look at Buck with a yawn.

"Did you say something, Buck?"

He smiled a bit sadly, gave her fingers a squeeze, and shook his head. "No," he murmured.

She yawned again and felt herself slipping back into sleep. She was so warm and comfortable that she didn't care if they stayed there all night; but Buck glanced up at the roof. "It's stopped raining."

Kate followed him with her eyes as he stood up, stretched, and walked over to a window to glance out. "I think the storm's over now," he murmured.

He turned to glance back at her. "I think we should be getting back to the ranch," he added softly. "I love this old house, but it's not the most comfortable place to spend the night. At least, not like it is now."

Kate rocked in her chair slightly and snuggled into the quilt. She was warm and drowsy and not in a hurry to move. "I'm not complaining," she murmured sleepily.

Buck's voice was warm with affection as he looked down at her. "You're mostly asleep," he rumbled.

"True."

"Come on, Kate," he muttered, and put a hand on her rocker. "We've got to get back. They'll be thinking something happened to us."

Kate snuggled her chin into her blanket and giggled softly, and Buck laughed with her. "Oh, now, let's not encourage gossip," he teased, and grabbed her hand. "Come on, Kate. We got to go."

"All right," she sighed, and rolled her head back reluctantly as she let Buck pull her to her feet.

"Get your things. You may have to tie 'em on you. I'm gonna have to carry you back across that creek. It's twice as high after all that rain."

Kate opened one eye. "Is it safe to cross?" she asked in alarm.

"It will be, if you hold on tight," he replied, and put a hand under her arm.

Buck led her out onto the porch of the old house. It was black as pitch, but the air was cool and moist and smelled of wet grass. Frogs sawed from somewhere out in the trees, and Kate could hear the creek water rushing past in the darkness. She frowned and put a hand on Buck's arm.

"I don't think it's safe," she told him. "There's no light. We can't cross that creek in the dark, Buck."

The words were no sooner out of her mouth than a full summer moon shone out from behind the scudding clouds. A wave of bright silver light flooded the countryside, and she could make out the broad contours of the lawn, the tangle of bushes beyond, and the creek bank.

And just as she'd feared, Buck brightened.

"There it is!" he grinned. "I know every inch of this place. I could walk it in the dark, and specially in the moonlight."

Kate frowned. "I don't want to go across that creek in the dark, Buck."

"It'll be fine, I promise," he told her. "Do you trust me, Kate?"

Kate stared at him in dismay. "W-well, yes, but—"

"Come on, then."

The next thing Kate knew she was dangling from Buck's big arms, and her feet bobbed in the air as Buck walked down the porch steps with her and began to cross the wet lawn.

"Buck, put me down!" she cried, and rolled anxious eyes to the dark creek bank that was coming steadily closer.

"Don't be a baby, Kate," Buck replied easily. "I could carry three of you easy, and I know the way."

"Put me down!"

"We'll be across before you know it." Buck strode through the darkness to the edge of the lawn, then sidled through the wet bushes. Kate gasped to feel something cool and wet slap her face, then slap it again as Buck carried her through the underbrush to the lip of the bank.

The sound of the unseen water was like a waterfall, and Kate clutched Buck's shirt like a terrified cat as he stuck one boot out and began to feel for a foothold on the treacherous bank.

"Buck…"

Buck's foot slipped suddenly, and Kate gasped as they both got a short, sharp slide down the muddy bank to the water's edge. "It's all right," he grunted, and found a foothold again at the bottom. "I got it. Even if we go into the water, it'll be me, not you."

"I don't want you to go into the water, either!" she retorted.

"Too late," he grinned, and stepped far down into the darkness. Kate gasped and pulled her feet up as high as she dared as Buck sank into the creek. Kate could feel the cold breath of the water rushing under her, and she could only imagine how Buck must feel. She clung to him as he took one slow, careful step after another as the current roared all around them.

Here and there the moonlight sifting down through the trees glimmered off the water, and she could see that the rain-swollen stream was practically frothing. But Buck held her high up above the water, and though she was freckled by its cold spray, her foot never touched its surface.

Buck stepped across to the far bank, swayed, then took a fresh grip on her with one arm as he reached up to grab a limb with the other. Kate watched in round-eyed terror as his hand slipped off the first branch, then grabbed the second.

Kate turned her face into Buck's shirt and closed her eyes as they teetered there, then tightened her grip as Buck pulled them up by one hand, found a foothold, then hauled them up the bank in three giant strides.

"There," he panted, and slumped against a tree. "We're across."

Kate opened her eyes and looked down. They were under the branches of the giant oak grove at the top of the far bank, and she could see the creek rushing below, pale in the moonlight.

Buck let her slip to the ground, and as soon as her foot touched the grass, she turned to sputter: "You're soaked to the skin, you endangered us both, and I told you I didn't want to go across in the dark."

Buck nodded and pulled his forearm across his mouth. "That's right. But I told you it'd be okay.

"And it is."

Exasperation whisked up in Kate's heart like sparks from a lighter. "Buck, you're impossible!" she sputtered, "You're the most stubborn, bull headed man I've ever met! Did you listen to a single word I said? Did you—"

Her words were cut off abruptly when Buck pulled her to his chest and crushed her to his mouth. Kate frowned and mumbled into his lips, and pulled her hands into fists against his chest; but as he kissed her, slow and soft and tender, her eyes slowly closed, and her hands unclenched. Her irritation slowly melted away, and she let herself be smoothed down.

Buck's lips moved to her ear. "You're welcome," he whispered, and Kate's brows rushed together again.

"Now come on. Let's go back to the ranch."

Buck took her hand, and Kate grumbled under her breath, but let him pull her along through the waist-high grass and up the hill to the helicopter. It stood there, a darker black shadow against the night sky.

Buck walked her up to the craft and released her hand. "Give me a minute to dry off and get in," he mumbled. "I got a blanket back there somewhere, and I'm going to towel off. Then I'll light up the cockpit and help you in."

Kate crossed her arms and waited; and a minute later the dash lights in the helicopter winked red and blue. She could see Buck's big silhouette in their dim light as he leaned over and stuck a big hand out of the open doorway.

"Ready?"

"I'm ready," Kate replied and grabbed his hand. He pulled her up as she climbed in and settled into the passenger seat.

Buck turned the key, and the copter's motor roared to life. The rotors were still for a moment, then began to move slowly.

Kate glanced up at the sky. The storm had blown over, and a round, full moon had sailed out from behind its last tatters. Its white nimbus rimmed the clouds with silver and painted the countryside below like white chalk on gray paper.

Buck turned to her and his voice crackled over the intercom. "Here we go," he told her, and the craft slowly floated up into the air, then gradually turned and nosed back toward the south.

Kate gazed out over the nightscape. Everything immediately below and around them was dark, except for the subtle highlights painted by the moon: a swipe of silver off the tin roof of the ranch house, a faint glitter in the creek as it escaped the cover of the trees and meandered off to the huge lake in the distance.

Buck nudged the accelerator, and the craft began to move, to slowly pick up speed. The air pouring in through the open door was moist and heavy and smelled like rain, and Kate smiled into the darkness. It was the nearest thing to flying that she could imagine, and it made her feel as light and free as if she was skimming the earth in a dream.

Buck lifted the copter up suddenly, and the earth and sky abruptly opened up before them. A million stars spattered the inky sky overhead, the moon glowed like a silver dollar, and as they ascended, the lights of Sandy Creek glittered in a bright, glittering starburst off to the southeast. She could see the lights of trucks as they traveled on the interstate on the far side of town, and even the glow of the smaller, nearby towns off to the south and west.

She glanced toward Buck. She could barely see him in the dim glow of the dash lights, but they glimmered faintly in his eyes and traced the fringe of his dark hair and his profile: the straight slope of his nose, the contours of his lips, his stubborn chin. His face was calm and unreadable, focused on the sky beyond and the dashboard displays.

Kate gazed at him in wonder. Buck wasn't the man she'd always dreamed of. She'd always seen herself with a man like Kevin: a highly-educated, idealistic professional. A crusader, a teacher, a man who loved art and learning and who cared about the big picture.

Buck was the opposite of all that. He was focused like a laser on his home and his ranch and his family. He was very physical and intensely practical. He was the first man she'd ever known who could ride a horse and start a fire and fly a helicopter. Buck gave her the sense that if something went wrong in the middle of nowhere, he'd know what to do and be able to do it.

Kate rubbed her arms. It troubled her, but Buck stirred her in ways that felt absolutely new. Buck was the most masculine man she'd ever met, and she responded to him in a way she never had to Kevin.

Maybe that's what makes me feel so guilty, she mused with a frown. *I adored Kevin. I always will. I thought he was the love of my life.*

But maybe he's not.

Maybe the love of my life is...someone else.

That had feeling been growing on her ever since she met Buck; and at that moment it was so strong that she wished Buck could let go of the controls and take her in his arms.

Her guilt and her sense of caution kept her from telling him so; but she couldn't help what she felt. The best she could do was question her own heart and breathe a prayer as the rain-washed air rushed beneath them, and a million stars smiled down from the night sky.

Chapter 42

"Sleep tight," Buck murmured, and leaned in to kiss her. Kate twined her arms around his neck and kissed him back long and slow.

They'd arrived back at the Seven ranch house a little after one in the morning, and they were standing outside the guest room door. Kate sputtered and wriggled in his arms. "Buck, you're still damp," she smiled. "And I still can't believe you carried me across that creek in the dark. You're a crazy man."

Buck reached down and played with a tendril of her hair. "I'm glad you came out to the old house with me today," he whispered. "I wanted you to see it."

"I'm glad I came," Kate told him softly. "You're right. It is special."

Buck sighed deeply, then nodded. "Well…good night, Kate. I'll see you tomorrow morning."

"Good night, Buck."

Kate reluctantly withdrew her arms from around his neck as he stepped back, turned, and walked down the hall to the big stairway. She watched his broad back as it slowly disappeared, then sighed and opened the door to the guest suite.

The lights were out, and Kate didn't turn them on for fear of waking Molly. She kicked off her shoes and padded across the marble floor to the door connecting to the next room.

Kate opened the door softly and peeked in. The moonlight streaming in through the big window showed her that Molly was snuggled up in bed and sleeping soundly.

Kate smiled and closed the door silently, then drifted to the big wall of glass that overlooked the valley below. It was by now deep night, and a million stars spattered the sky like diamond dust blown across black velvet. She gazed out across the night, then her eye fell on a white handle in the middle of the window.

She pulled the handle, and a section of the glass wall slid aside to open out onto the balcony outside. Kate walked out into the cool air, right to the low wall of the balcony, and rested her hands on the wooden railing.

The rolling pasture lands that stretched out below were serene and still and slumbering under a silver dollar moon. The Seven Ranch nestled in a gorgeous river valley, and the view at night was magical. Kate crossed her arms, leaned over the rail, and let the peace of deep night seep into her soul.

She closed her eyes and relived the delirium of Buck's kisses. The lightest touch of his lips set her skin on fire, skittered up and down her spine like electricity, and Kate lingered over that delicious memory with a sigh of pleasure.

The two of them had mad chemistry, she couldn't deny it; and she'd seen enough of Buck to understand that he was a good, decent man. But to her, there was a more important consideration than either of those things when she weighed her relationship with him.

The most important thing was how Molly would respond to a new man in her life. Not just a friend they visited, not just an occasional guest at their home.

A serious suitor, a man who might one day become part of their family.

Kate tilted her head and questioned her own heart. It was full of the memory of Buck's profile in the firelight, of his soft, deep voice telling her his secrets; and was it still tingling with his kisses. It told her that she was falling in love with Buck as irresistibly as she'd slipped down that muddy creek bank. She couldn't stop herself if she tried.

But would Molly bond with Buck as easily as she had?

Kate searched her memory. Everything she'd seen suggested that Buck and Molly were friends. Molly was relaxed and happy and secure around Buck. That was a hopeful sign, but before she committed to more with Buck, she had to be satisfied that Molly would be okay with it.

Molly's father had only been gone two years, after all.

Kate sighed deeply and bowed her head. The thought of Kevin stabbed her with guilt, made her wonder what he'd say if he could know what she was thinking.

That while she'd loved him, she might end up loving someone else better. She couldn't shake the feeling that it was shameful, a betrayal of her husband.

Even though that made no sense.

She could only hope that Buck would understand her need to go slow; but from what she'd learned about Buck, she believed that he would. Buck might be impulsive and opinionated and stubborn and brash; but he was also tender and sweet and strong and caring, and he knew what it was to lose someone dear.

What was it that he'd said to her—that remembering the good times was the best antidote to grief?

Kate sputtered and shook her head. She'd gone to therapy for over a year, and if she had to distill her therapist's advice into one sentence, that would be pretty close.

I wish I'd met Buck sooner, she thought wryly. *I could've saved myself a lot of money and time.*

Maybe I can start taking his advice now.

She lifted her eyes to the sky, and as she watched, a shooting star flicked across the night sky and was gone. Kate smiled up into the darkness and thought:

I'm going to take that to mean that you forgive me, darling, she thought with a crooked smile. *I tried not to fall in love with Buck, but I can't help myself.*

I'll always love you, but I can't follow you. I have to go on.

Tears sprang to her eyes; but they didn't prevent her from seeing a second shower of stars that flared out, then disappeared. Kate stood staring at them in disbelief, and raised her face to smile up into heaven.

Chapter 43

Buck closed his bedroom door and walked across it, unbuttoning his shirt. His bed faced a glass wall, and the lamplight inside the room was so dim that he could make out the traffic lights out on the interstate.

Buck walked over to the bed, sat down on it, and pulled his boots off. He frowned suddenly, leaned over, and picked a wet leaf out from between his toes before standing up again. He came out of his jeans, tossed them onto the gleaming wooden floor, and stared at them wryly.

Kate was right; he was still mostly wet. He needed a warm shower and shave, but he was too weary that evening to fool with it.

He flicked the huge brown coverlet back and climbed into bed, then crossed his arms behind his head and stared out at the night.

Well, I've said my piece, he sighed to himself. *It's up to Kate now.*

He saw her again in his mind, wrapped up to her ears in Miss Annie's old blue quilt, with her sleepy eyes closed and that beautiful, dark red hair spilling over her shoulders. She'd dropped off to sleep in that rocking chair as sweet and natural as a little child, and something about that just melted his heart.

It meant that he'd won her trust, and that meant a lot to him.

Buck smiled and licked his lips. The taste of Kate's lipstick was still on them, something sweet and smooth and vaguely like lilacs. He could still feel her soft hands curling around his neck and gently running though his hair.

And when those lovely green eyes had smiled up at him, they were full of that soft look that always set him on fire.

The soft, warm look of love.

Buck closed his eyes and saw Kate's eyes again in his mind, the way they'd looked at the old house: emeralds glossed over with the golden sheen of firelight. He saw the way Kate's eyes had studied him in the helicopter on the way back home when she thought he wasn't looking. He saw the way they'd looked just now, out in the hall.

That warm, dreamy, drowsy look in Kate's eyes was just for him, because back in that cabin, she'd told him it was; but he knew it without having to be told.

Maybe Kate wanted to take things slow because she needed time to let herself love again. To give herself permission. He understood that.

Buck turned and reached over to his nightstand. His favorite picture of Delores was on it in a little wooden frame, and he picked it up and stared at it. Delores' big, warm brown eyes smiled down at him, and he stared into them sadly. She'd been the most beautiful brunette in all of Texas.

The most beautiful on the inside, too.

Buck brushed her picture softly with his hand. *Well, darlin',* he told her, *I've done what you always said I'd do. I've fallen in love again. I didn't believe you then, but turns out you were right.*

You always did know me better than I knew myself.

I think you'd like Kate. She might not love rodeos and a good beer, or be as good with horses as you were; but I think the two of you would've been friends.

Buck stared into Delores' smiling eyes and sighed. *Thanks for giving me your blessing, Del. For giving me that gift. I didn't want to hear it at the time, because it meant that you were telling me goodbye. I didn't know then how important it was.*

I do now.

He pressed the picture to his lips, then placed it carefully on the nightstand and turned his eyes back to the night sky beyond his window.

As he did, he saw Big Russ again in his memory, saw his shaggy head of thick white hair, that face that was as brown and wrinkled as a paper bag, and those bright blue eyes.

Some day son, he was saying, *you're gonna meet a woman who hits you like Miss Annie hit me. You're gonna fall in love.*

He saw his child self turn toward his grandfather as they sat fishing on the creek bank outside the old house.

How will I know I'm in love, Grandpa?

Big Russ had chuckled and tossed his line into the water with a *plop*.

Oh don't worry, boy. You'll know.

A fond smile curled Buck's lips as he closed his eyes. Big Russ had been right, as usual. He knew he was in love, all right.

Maybe it was the way of love, to fall deeper every time.

Chapter 44

Bing bong.

The next morning, Buck raised his head from his computer and frowned to hear his doorbell. It wasn't yet ten o'clock.

He ran a hand through his dark shock of hair, rose from his desk, and sauntered out of his office and across the great room to open it.

To his astonishment, his elderly lawyer was standing on the other side. "Eugene! What are you doing here at this hour?" he asked in surprise.

Eugene shouldered right in. "Buck, I have bad news."

Buck blinked at his attorney's grim face, then walked to his leather chair, settled down into it, and nodded toward a nearby drink cart. "Well then, you get something tall and cool, Eugene, and tell me about it."

Eugene stared at him grimly over his glasses, and there wasn't a flicker of humor in his tired eyes as he sat down.

"I didn't drive all the way up from Dallas to make jokes, Buck. We're going to be slaughtered in court," he stated flatly. "You're not going to like this, but I just got a call from Hogan's attorney, and he knows that we don't have the contract. Somebody at your family meeting talked."

Buck stared at him in frowning disbelief. "That's impossible," he objected. "Me and my brothers might fight amongst ourselves, but when it's something from the outside, we stick together. None of us would rat about something like this, Eugene. This is about whether we can keep our home!"

"I'm just your attorney," Eugene replied tightly. "I can only work with what I'm given. If someone breaks confidentiality, my hands are tied."

Buck scowled at him. "I tell you, none of us would rat the family out, and especially not to Buster Hogan. Not one of us, Eugene!"

The lawyer raised his eyes again. He nodded grimly. "All right then, Buck. Buster had to find out somehow. Who else was in that room when we discussed it?"

Buck stared at him in dawning outrage. "What are you saying, Eugene?" he growled.

Eugene planted his arms on the table and leaned over it. "There were only nine people in that room, Buck. You and your brothers, myself, and Kate."

"Now you wait just a minute!" Buck roared. He half-rose from his chair and jabbed a brown finger in his attorney's face. "Kate wouldn't breathe a word of what she heard and you know it!"

The older man met his eye. "I know no such thing," he retorted. "You just told me that none of your brothers would talk about this, Buck. I believe you, because that wouldn't make sense.

"That leaves only one other possibility. Now I'm not saying Kate did this maliciously, or with the intent of ruining your chances. But at this point her motives are irrelevant. The outcome is going to be the same."

He shook his shaggy head. "I told you at the time that it was ill-advised to invite an outsider into such a sensitive meeting. It wouldn't be the first time a client of mine had lived to regret such a decision."

Buck narrowed his eyes and stuck out his chin. "Kate knew it was important to keep that meeting a secret. She wouldn't betray my trust, Eugene," he insisted stubbornly, but Eugene just shook his head.

"I'm just a simple country lawyer, Buck," he sighed, and closed up his briefcase. "I don't presume to advise you about love, but the law is simple enough. You need to prove you own those water rights. Now Buster knows you can't prove it. We can assume he also knows our Plan B, because we discussed it in Kate' presence.

"If Buster Hogan gets those water rights, he can drive you out of business. And now he knows not just how to do it, but what to do afterwards to make sure you never recover.

"If I were you, Buck, the first thing I'd do is bid the lovely Mrs. Malone farewell."

Buck pulled his brown hands over his face, then glared at his attorney over them.

"Get out, Eugene," he growled.

"All right, Buck," Eugene sighed, and stood up. "I knew this wouldn't be welcome news. But you're a longtime client of mine, and you pay me a great deal of money to tell you the truth."

He walked to the door of Buck's suite, but paused at the door for a parting shot. "If I'm being unfair to Mrs. Malone, I'll be the first to apologize. But on the other hand, Buck—you wouldn't be the first man in the world to lose everything he's got because of a beautiful woman."

He walked out on the words, and Buck scowled at the door after it closed and sank deeper into his chair. He frowned into space.

It took a long time for his outrage to cool down; but it finally did. After he'd smashed his emotions down long enough for his brain to wake up.

As much as he hated to admit it, Eugene had reason to be suspicious. It was true that Kate was the only other person in that room beside the family to hear all their secrets and plans.

I can't believe it, Buck brooded. *I won't. Kate knew what that meeting meant to us. She wouldn't stab me in the back.*

Still, his brain was telling him that, given this unwelcome news, he now had a choice to make.

He had to decide whether he was going to risk the Seven and his family home for Kate; or whether he was going to give her up to protect them.

Though now that Buster knew their plans, the damage to the Seven was already done. Buck sighed and rolled his eyes to the ceiling.

The only question still left was, how much damage had Kate Malone done to his heart.

Chapter 45

Sebastian skipped up the steps to the Stonehouse loading dock and hurried to the back door of the kitchen. He unlocked it with a flick of his wrist and slipped in quickly.

Monday was such a slow business day that the Stonehouse was closed to the public; but Kate was short-staffed and had asked for a volunteer to come in anyway to set up for Tuesday.

He'd been glad to oblige.

Sebastian breezed into the kitchen and tossed his keys across the big table. He was only going to stay long enough to pour himself a glass of Kate's best wine and whip up an expensive lunch with the Stonehouse's gourmet provisions. Then he was going to clean up all traces of what he'd been doing there before blowing that hick town for good.

Sebastian sputtered as he reached for a frying pan and turned on the big stainless steel stove. It was ironic. Roxanne had the brain of a chihuahua, but she'd sniffed him out, like the little rat dog she was.

She was absolutely right that he'd been up to no good. He'd had a good paying chef gig in Austin until he was fired, and he'd been forced to take a pay cut to work at the Stonehouse. So he'd found a way to more than make up the difference by taking bribes from some redneck at a nearby ranch. Good money, too.

Sebastian poured oil into the pan and pulled a loaf of bread from a nearby cupboard. It had been local politics—something stupid between the local yokels. He remembered vaguely that it had been about water somehow, but he didn't care.

He giggled under his breath when he remembered Roxanne's outraged face. She'd set herself up beautifully. He'd been able to clock her across her thick head for snooping in his work locker; then he'd broken into Kate's apartment and deflected all the blame onto her.

Stupid cow, he thought to himself, and reached for a wine bottle. He poured himself a generous drink and sampled it with relish.

Still, all entertainment aside, the important thing was that he finally had enough money to get to Portland and set up there in style. Now that he'd wrung the last drop of money out of this backwater job, he was ready to return to his rightful place as the chef of an elite urban restaurant.

And once he'd enjoyed a fine, leisurely meal, he was going to the private dining room to pull the little bug from underneath the table. The last bit of evidence against him. Then it was—*sayonara, suckers.*

A blur in the corner of his eye made Sebastian frown and turn his head. Something had streaked past in the hall outside, and to his irritation, it was Kate's kid.

That spoiled brat little girl that set his teeth on edge.

"I'm going to hide!" she called out from the hall. "Try to find me, Sebastian!"

He made a face and stifled an impatient expletive. As far as he was concerned, that kid could hide and never come out again; but he called out in a dull voice.

"Okay, darling."

He turned back to his wine; but an instant later his head snapped up again. He could hear the sound of a door opening.

The door to the private dining room.

He set the wine glass down and hurried out into the hall. As he passed the entrance to the main dining room, he glanced warily toward the stair and the upper hall on its far side. Kate doted on that brat, and if she caught him so much as frowning at her kid, she'd show him her claws.

Not that he couldn't handle that, too; but he saw no reason to complicate his lunch.

He hurried out into the front foyer, and to his annoyance, the door to the private dining room was just closing.

Trust that kid to go straight to it, he thought angrily. *I'm going to tie her eyebrows together.*

"Come out, come out, wherever you are," he called in a flat tone, and followed to the private room.

Sebastian opened the door and stuck his head in. There was no sign of the kid, and that could only mean one thing. She was hiding under the table.

Under the table, where the bug was.

"Come on out, darling," he called warily, and began to circle the table. "Your Momma's calling, I heard her. She wants you back upstairs."

There was a rustling sound from beneath the table, then Molly's puzzled voice. "What's this?" she piped up.

Terror prickled up and down his spine, and he bent over to peer under the table. To his horror, Molly's frowning eyes were focused on the little plastic bug he'd stuck to the underside of the table, and as he watched, she pulled it off with a little *pop.*

"Give that to me," he barked, and stuck out his hand; but Molly smiled and scrambled out the other side of the table.

"You have to catch me first!" she laughed, and darted toward the door. Sebastian cursed under his breath and lunged after her. He swiped at her pink shirt, caught the hem, then lost it as she dashed out into the hall.

"Come back here, I mean it!"

Molly's giggling laughter was the only reply. Sebastian ran out into the hall and saw her turn into the big dining room.

"Where are you going? Come back here!"

He chased her around the tables as she darted away. She leaned one way, laughing, then dodged the other when he lunged at her.

Sebastian watched in helpless defeat as Molly zoomed up the stairs and flew along the upper hall. She twisted the door lock, slipped inside, and shut the door tight after her.

He stared at it in shock; but only for an instant. The second Kate saw that bug, it was over for him.

He had to get away.

Sebastian scrambled out of the dining room, across the hall, and into the kitchen on the way to the parking lot. He rushed past the hot stove and jostled the pan full of oil with a *clang* as he passed. Fire flashed up from the stove, but he didn't stop.

He could go to jail if Kate put two and two together; and he wasn't going to stick around to find out.

Chapter 46

Be sure to catch Mia Thompson's sultry jazz stylings at the Stonehouse this weekend, Kate typed into her computer. *Friday and Saturday nights, seven to closing.*

Kate hit a few keys to upload a photo of her guest performer to the restaurant's social media account. Mia was a hometown girl, and she liked to showcase local artists at the Stonehouse when she could.

Kate watched in satisfaction as the new post appeared on the screen. *That should guarantee a nice turnout this weekend,* she thought, and was just closing out of the account when the sound of Molly's running footsteps rushed up the stairs.

"Mamma," she called, "look what I found!"

Kate's eyes were still on the screen. "What, baby," she murmured absently.

Molly came running into her office, slightly out of breath. "Look, Mamma," she said proudly, and held a small object out in her little palm. "Guess where I found it?"

"I don't know, baby. Put it down on the table, and I'll look at it in a little while."

Molly sighed in disappointment, dropped whatever it was on the table, and sat down patiently. Kate tapped on her computer for another fifteen minutes before Molly picked her prize up again.

"Momma, look what I found! What is it?"

Kate glanced at it, then glanced again. She frowned and picked it out of Molly's hand. "I don't know, baby," she frowned, as she turned it over. She wasn't an expert, but the thing looked suspiciously like a...bug.

Who would put a bug in my restaurant, she wondered in puzzlement.

"Where did you find it?" she asked, and turned her eyes to Molly's excited face.

Molly swelled up in excitement. "I was hiding under the big table in the front room," she confided breathlessly, "and it was stuck to the bottom!"

Kate frowned. Molly called the private dining room the 'front room.' She turned the little plastic disc over in her hand. She couldn't imagine why anyone would want to eavesdrop on her customers in the private dining room. The only ones who ever used it were local civic clubs and—

Buck.

Buck Spade, the richest man in the county. Buck, who was in the middle of a bitter lawsuit.

Kate turned to Molly. "Are you *sure* it was the front room, chickadee?"

Molly nodded vigorously. "Yes, it was, Mamma! And Sebastian was downstairs and saw me find it. We played hide and seek. He chased after me, but I ran up the stairs fast and closed the door before he could catch me!"

Kate stared at her in horror, then in dawning comprehension. *Of course,* she thought slowly. *Roxanne was right all along. It was Sebastian. And he wasn't stealing money, or even my jewelry. He was stealing…*

Kate jumped to her feet and stormed out toward the door, the plastic bug still clenched in her hand. "You stay here, chickadee," she replied tightly. "Mamma is going downstairs to talk to Sebastian."

"Are you going to play hide and seek, Mamma?" Molly giggled, and Kate bit her lip into a hard, straight line.

"No, baby," she muttered. "Mamma's already found what she's looking for!"

She stormed down the steps to the hall, then out into the living room. *Just wait until I get my hands on him,* she fumed, and she stomped to the apartment door and yanked it open in anger. But to her horror, as soon as it swung open, billowing smoke rolled in.

Kate rushed out into the open hall outside her door and looked down at the big room below. There was no sign of Sebastian, and the entire middle section of the dining room was a wall of fire. Tables and chairs were crackling as they burned, the tablecloths were sheets of fire. As she watched, a glass exploded with a sound like a gun shot.

The restaurant was engulfed. There was no escape for them that way.

She gasped and turned on her heel, shouting, "Molly, where are you? Molly!"

She rushed back into the apartment. Molly came running out into the living room, and Kate grabbed her hand and darted to the patio door to escape. She snatched the knob and yanked it; but to her panic, the door wouldn't open, and it was hot to the touch.

She dropped Molly's hand and yanked at the knob, but it was jammed tight.

"Mamma, something's on fire!" Molly cried, and rolled frightened eyes to the doorway. "Look, Mamma, there's smoke!"

Kate wrestled desperately with the doorknob. "What's wrong with it?" she cried, and yanked it again with all her strength. She put her whole weight on the knob as she pulled backwards, but it was frozen.

They were trapped.

Oh God, Kate prayed frantically, *God help us!*

Chapter 47

Buck sat in the driver's seat of his big red truck with his brow pressed against the wheel and his brown fingers curled around it. He'd stayed up all night, standing at his big window. He'd spent those dark hours questioning his heart and the stars; and now he had his answer.

Oh Lord, he prayed, *help me. I may be making the biggest mistake of my life, but I can't help it. I'm in love with Kate, and I can't help believing in her.*

If I'm wrong, I'll crash and burn, but I knew that going in.

All I'm asking is, if I'm wrong, please just put me back together after.

He sat up, sighed, and turned the key in the ignition. The truck growled to life, and he slowly turned the wheel to nudge it around the courtyard and out into the long drive.

The time it took him to get to town felt endless. His whole future, and Kate's and Molly's, was hanging on what happened next, and the suspense felt like torture.

By the time he turned onto the main drag through town, every nerve he had was on edge; but when the restaurant swam into sight, his worry jerked sharply from the future to the present. There was a thin stream of gray smoke curling from the roof of the Stonehouse. Buck gunned the truck's motor, and it roared down the street and spun into the parking lot of the restaurant in a spray of gravel. The truck jerked to an abrupt stop, and Buck stared up at the roof in disbelief.

Oh Lord, he gasped, *the place is on fire!*

Buck's heart gave a sickening jerk as he scrabbled at the seat belt, burst out of the truck, and pelted to the entrance. He grabbed the heavy handle and yanked hard, but the big door was locked up tight. He pressed his hands to the glass and looked inside. To his horror, orange light was flickering off the foyer ceiling inside.

He pounded on the glass and yelled. "Kate! Kate!"

There was no answer, and as he stood there, smoke and the scent of burning curled out from underneath the door. He threw himself at the door again, and it trembled under the blow, but stood fast. He threw himself against it again and beat it with his fists.

"Kate!"

There was no answer, and the inside was empty; but the orange glow was brighter and closer now. He could see billows of smoke rolling out into the hall from the direction of the kitchen.

Buck backed up a pace, then kicked the glass door with his boot. The door trembled, but held; and he kicked it again.

A loud splintering sound from somewhere inside spurred Buck to kick the door a third time, and a crack branched up the glass.

Buck pulled back and kicked it again with all his strength, and it gave way.

He reached in to grab the handle and was inside a second later. He rushed into the foyer and yelled: "Kate? Kate, are in you in here?"

The smell of smoke was overpowering, it stung his eyes and his nose, and he tugged his shirt up over his face as he hurried down the hall and into the dining room.

As soon as he cleared the entryway, he saw where the orange glow had come from. The ceiling of the dining room was hidden under a cloud of thick smoke, and a wall of fire spread from one side of it to another like a dancing curtain.

"Kate!"

"Buck, we're up here!"

Buck coughed and fought his way through the heat and smoke. It was hard to see through the flames, but when he looked up the stairs, to his horror, he could see Kate and Molly huddled at the top.

They were trapped.

"Go to the patio door!" he yelled, and Kate sobbed, "We can't! The apartment's on fire!"

Buck cast about him, then grabbed up a tablecloth and tried to beat a path to the stairs through the wall of fire, but it lit up instantly, and he threw it down in disgust.

Molly screamed a high, childish scream of terror, and Kate sobbed, "Buck, we're trapped!"

Buck coughed, bent over, and willed his mind to clear. He shut out his own panic and pictured the building in his mind. The big windows on the back side were on the third floor, but the second floor roof was just below.

He straightened up, took a deep lung full of smoke and yelled, "Kate, can you get to your bedroom?"

Kate's sobs were his only answer, and he yelled out, louder: "Can you get to your bedroom?"

"I don't know!"

"Try," he shouted. "I'll climb up on the roof and break the windows out!" The throat full of smoke doubled him up again with coughing, but he looked up to see Kate hustle Molly down the hall and back into the apartment.

He turned around and swam through the smoke, out of the dining room into the hall. He dodged aside just in time to avoid a blast of flame from the kitchen door, lunged through the smoky foyer, and out into the sunlight. He gasped for air as he ran around the corner to the back side of the building. When the roof patio swam into view, to his relief, it wasn't yet on fire.

Buck sprinted to the stairs and took them three at a time, gained the patio, picked up a chair, and brought it down on the door with all his strength. The chair broke under his hands, he made a dent across the metal door, but when he threw himself against it, it held fast.

Buck spat out a frustrated exclamation and stared up at the roof above the patio door. It was smoking in a dozen places, but it was within reach. He turned to grab the patio table, pushed it up against the wall, and climbed up on it. It cracked under his weight, but he grabbed the smoking roof and pulled himself up onto it just as the table gave way under him.

Buck grimaced as he hauled himself up. The roof was hot as a griddle, but he slowly pulled himself up onto it, and then scrambled upright. The heat seared his feet through his boots, but he moved sideways, step by careful step, to the big warehouse windows to the far left of the patio door.

He got as close as he dared to peer through them, but he knew better than to touch them with his hands. He looked down into a big bedroom.

"Kate, are you in there?"

Kate's panicked voice jumped up to greet him. "Yes!" she shouted, and then dissolved into a fit of coughing.

"I'm going to kick the window in," he yelled. "Get back!"

Buck glanced around for something to hold, but the walls were too hot. He widened his stance, put out his arms to brace himself, and kicked the window with all his strength. It cracked, but he swayed backward and almost stumbled off the roof.

Buck caught himself with a gasp, then glanced back over his shoulder. There was a dizzying, 30-foot drop to the pavement below.

Kate's scream clawed at the glass. "Buck!"

He turned and kicked the window again. This time it shattered with a splintering crash, and he kicked it again to clear out the jagged remnants of glass. He knelt down and poked his head through the opening, and smoke came pouring out. Terror stared out of Kate's pale, pinched face as she raised it to his.

"Take Molly!"

Kate lifted her up, and Buck grabbed the sobbing six-year-old and pulled her out. He hurried across the roof to the patio, still carrying her as she cried. He grabbed her hands and lowered her down by her arms.

"I'm going to drop you down, doodle bug," he gasped. "Get ready!"

"I can't!" Molly screamed, but Buck grunted, "You got to, Molly. It's only a few feet. Now!"

He leaned down as far as he dared and dropped her on the patio. She landed on her seat with a bump, then looked up at him. Buck turned to hurry back across the smoking roof to the big warehouse windows.

"Kate?"

White smoke was billowing out of the broken window, and his heart jumped into his throat when there was no answer.

"Kate, are you all right?"

There was no response except a heavy *thump*, and Buck grabbed the hot window sill and jumped down into the bedroom. The room was full of choking smoke that stung his eyes and his lungs, and he coughed and waved it away with his arms.

"Kate, answer me!"

He turned around and to his horror, Kate was lying crumpled at his feet with her auburn hair falling over her eyes. Buck knelt down and lifted her up into his arms.

"Kate," he muttered, "Kate, wake up!"

Her head lolled back from his arm like a rag doll's, and Buck looked up at the broken window, then lifted her up, slung her over his shoulder, and climbed up to the opening.

Buck grunted with the strain of pulling himself and Kate through the window, but he summoned all his strength and powered up and out onto the roof. The shingles were now so hot that he could barely stand on them. He hurried across the roof, but fire suddenly burst through a hole in the shingles, and he staggered sideways, then slid almost to the lip of the gutters as Kate dangled precariously from his arms.

Molly's scream clawed at the air. "Mamma!" she shrieked, as Buck gasped and scrabbled for a foothold on the smoking ledge. The parking lot swam three stories below him as he swayed back and forth, fought to regain his balance, and stumbled again. Molly's head lolled in the air over the brink, and Buck grimaced, hoisted her up more securely in his arms, and leaned backward.

Slowly he regained his footing, and he turned to carry Kate across the roof, step by step, until he stood high over the patio. Molly stood below with her terrified face turned up to his.

"Get back!" Buck warned her, and Molly danced backwards. Buck hoisted Kate up in his arms, grabbed her by the wrists, and lowered her over the ledge. She hung there limply, with her feet dangling, and he lowered her down as gently as he could before letting go. She crumpled up instantly, and he sat down hard on the roof, then jumped off after her.

Buck landed hard on the patio pavement beside Kate and grimaced in pain. His feet and his hands were burned and throbbing, and every inch of exposed skin felt sunburned. But he leaned over Kate and pulled her up into his arms. To his relief, she groaned and coughed.

"Kate," he murmured urgently, "Kate, wake up." He shook her lightly. "Kate, look at me."

Kate suddenly doubled up and was racked by a convulsion of coughing. Buck's heart crumpled in pity as he stared down into her anguished face. He held her shoulders as she gasped, and the distant wail of a siren curled in the air.

Thank God, he thought, and closed his eyes in relief. *It's the fire department.*

Kate opened her eyes and looked up at him. "Where's Molly?" she gasped in a raspy voice.

"Right over there," Buck replied softly, and nodded toward Molly's anxious face. Kate struggled up on one elbow to look, then collapsed against his chest in relief.

"Are you hurt?" he asked, and scanned her in worry. "Are you burned?"

She shook her head. "My lungs hurt," she croaked, and coughed again. "I got so dizzy all of a sudden. I must've passed out for a minute."

Buck took her by the shoulders. "We need to get away from here," he grunted, and looked up at the smoking roof above them. "Can you stand up?"

"I don't know."

Buck helped her sit upright. "I'll help you. We need to get down off this patio. Come on."

He stood up and half-pulled her to her feet, then threw an arm around her shoulders as she slumped against him. He pointed at the stairs and called, "You first, Molly. Get down the stairs. Hold the rail, now!"

He glanced up in time to see a fire engine turning into the parking lot of the restaurant with its siren blaring and all its lights flashing red. When he glanced back over his shoulder, to his horror, the whole warehouse roof was engulfed. Billows of black smoke were belching into the sky.

"Hurry, now!"

Molly's eyes were wide and dark with fear, but she hurried down the steps ahead of him. Buck took a new grip on Kate and helped her down the stairs as fast as she was able to go. When they reached the ground at last, he hoisted her up into his big arms and carried her around the back of the building and out to the front parking lot.

The fire engine was already pulled up in front of the burning building, and a couple of paramedics came running over as soon as they caught sight of him. Buck set Kate down gently on the ground, and they immediately pushed in front of him.

"Get back," one of them commanded curtly, and Buck stepped back just enough to watch as they clapped an oxygen mask over Kate's mouth and nose. He looked over his shoulder to demand, "What about the little girl?"

"She was in the smoke too," Buck replied, and the other paramedic rose and hurried over to check her.

"Are they going to be alright?" Buck asked anxiously. Kate's eyes were closed and she looked very still.

"We're taking both of them to the hospital," the paramedic announced, then glanced back over his shoulder at Buck.

"What about you?" The man's eyes flicked to his hands, and Buck glanced down at them. They were red, blistered, and swollen.

"Let's have a look at you," the man offered, but Buck scowled and stepped back a pace.

"You just tend to them," he replied curtly. "I'll be behind the ambulance." He turned on the words and hurried across the parking lot to his truck. But his heart was in his throat, and as he climbed in and cranked the engine, and he was praying:

Oh Lord, please let her be alright!

Chapter 48

Kate opened her eyes sleepily, then had to close them again. There was a bright light shining into them, and it hurt. She felt disoriented and her lungs hurt. She was cold and uncomfortable, and there was a steady, irritating *beep, beep, beep* in her ear.

Buck, she murmured, but her breath clouded over, and she frowned. There was an oxygen mask over her nose and mouth, and no one could hear her.

I want Buck, she whispered, and closed her eyes; but then the last few hours came rushing back to her memory, and she opened them wide in alarm.

"Where's my daughter?" she yelped and sat bolt upright. A nurse came hurrying over and put a calming hand on her shoulder.

"Lie down, ma'am," the girl murmured, but Kate tore the mask off her face.

"Where's my daughter?" she coughed, and the nurse frowned and took the mask in her hand. "Your daughter's being treated in the room next door," the girl told her. "Lie back now. It's important that you keep the oxygen mask on for now."

"Is Molly all right?" Kate asked in rising panic. "She's probably terrified, in a hospital room all alone. I want to see her!"

"Mrs. Malone, you have to lie still and keep the mask on," the nurse insisted. "Your daughter's stable and alert and receiving oxygen therapy. Please lie back now."

Kate pushed the mask away. "Get this off me," she insisted. "I'm going to see my daughter!"

"Mrs. Malone, you can't remove the mask," the nurse objected, and grabbed her shoulder in an attempt to hold her down.

"Get your hands off me!" Kate cried, and then broke into a fit of coughing.

The nurse turned toward the bay door. "Can I get some help in here?" she called loudly. "I need help with this patient!"

Kate kicked off the sheet covering her and tore the mask away as the nurse wrestled with her. "Get off me!"

"I need help in here!"

The bay door opened abruptly, but instead of another nurse, Buck filled the opening. Kate looked up at him and burst into tears; but the sight of him was like a balm to her heart.

Buck sank down into a chair beside her. He took her hand in his, and there were tears in his bright eyes.

"Where's Molly?" Kate cried.

"Molly's just fine," he assured her softly, and caressed her palm with his thumb. "I've been with her this whole time. The doc says she's all right. They're just watching her to be extra careful." He nodded at the oxygen mask dangling around her neck. "You need to settle down."

"I want to see Molly," she told him, but in a whisper; and Buck nodded.

"You'll see her. But right now you both need to rest up. Come on, now." He released her hand long enough to pull the sheet back up around her chin, then clasped her fingers again.

"I won't be smoothed down," Kate told him, with a flash of her usual self. "I won't be managed. I want Molly!"

Buck pulled his mouth down slightly and gave her a look of sympathy. "Well, you don't always get what you want, do you?" he murmured in commiseration; and Kate stared at him, unsure of whether to be outraged or to burst into sputtering laughter.

The nurse pushed in and tried to elbow Buck out of the way, but only succeeded in pressing up against his chest. "Sir, I need you to move so I can get this mask back on her," she informed him; and fire flared in Kate's heart.

"I'm talking to him right now," she growled; and Buck glanced up at the girl in sympathy.

"Can we have five minutes?" he asked softly, and the nurse sputtered, turned on her heel, and left. Buck watched her go, then turned back to Kate with a wry smile.

"You're not the best patient in the world, are you, red?" he teased, and brushed a tendril of hair back from her brow. He gave her a long, tender look and squeezed her hand.

"How are you feeling?"

Kate leaned back on one elbow. "Groggy," she whispered. "I don't know what they whacked me up with." She put a hand to her head.

Buck's smile faded as he searched her face, and he put up a big hand to caress her cheek. Kate stared at it in dismay.

"Buck, your hands," she murmured, and took his swollen fingers in her own. "Your poor hands! They're—"

Her eyes flicked up to his face. "You should be getting treatment, too," she murmured in rising alarm. "Your hands are burned and I know you inhaled smoke and—"

Buck's expression was unmoved. "You let me worry about that. You lie back now."

"But—"

"Lie back."

She sighed at last, then pressed her brow against his and murmured, "Buck, I want to go home."

He tightened her to his chest. "All right then, Kate," he whispered. "I'll take you and Molly home."

Kate nodded and closed her eyes in relief; and she had no doubt at all that *going home* meant going to the Seven.

She knew Buck well enough by now to understand that he meant it that way, too.

Chapter 49

"You lie back and rest, now."

Kate looked up at Buck as he pulled the silky red quilt up around her chin. He'd taken her and Molly straight home to the Seven and up to the guest rooms, just like she knew he would. He'd actually carried Molly upstairs in his arms, and she was sound asleep in the adjoining bedroom.

But Buck had deposited her in the big, luxurious bed in the main guestroom—the one with the antique furniture and the glass wall overlooking the ranch.

"I'm all right," Kate assured him and picked at the quilt. She felt guilty about all the trouble Buck had gone to, and had objected all the way back from the hospital; but as usual, Buck had to have the last word.

He'd just brought her home with him anyway.

Kate struggled up a bit on the pillows. The bed was as big as a houseboat, and she felt swallowed up by its huge covers.

Buck looked down at her and laughed softly. "You look like a newborn calf," he teased.

Kate looked up at him in exasperation. "You don't have to say so," she sputtered.

He sat down on the edge of the bed, then leaned in to brush a tendril of hair away from her brow. The tender expression on his face made Kate's heart beat faster and made all her objections die on her lips.

"You don't have to worry," Buck replied softly. "You couldn't look bad if you tried."

She glanced up at him, and he leaned down to kiss her. Kate closed her eyes and yielded up to the touch of that kiss on her lips, and to her delight, Buck used his mouth to tell her all the things that he'd been too stubborn to say out loud.

Still—a girl always wanted to hear the three most important words in the world.

Kate pulled back from Buck's lips and brushed a lock of his dark hair back from his brow. "Buck," she whispered, "did you mean it when you said you loved me?"

He raised an eyebrow and looked away. "What are you talking about, Kate?" he mumbled.

"Back at the cabin," she replied softly, and reached out to take his hands. "You thought I was asleep, but I heard every word. In a moment of terrible weakness, you admitted that you love me."

Buck had been looking away, but at that, he turned back and gave her a sheepish look. "Well…"

"Admit it Buck," she teased him, but she was only half-joking. "I won't ask you to say it ever again, but I want to hear it now. Tell me I'm radiant. Tell me that you've lost yourself in my eyes. Compare me to Guinevere, to Helen of Troy, to Delilah. Tell me that you're my slave forever and kiss me like a crazy man."

A reluctant smile dawned across Buck's lips and he rubbed the back of his neck with one hand. "Who's Guinevere?" he teased. "And I don't know anybody named Helen."

"Oh, you're impossible!" she sputtered, but she didn't have a chance to say more, because Buck snatched her up in his arms and stared down at her from his vivid eyes.

"I'm not big on poetry, Kate," he smiled. "But I think I can manage the crazy man part."

He bowed his head to kiss her, but Kate pressed a finger against his lips and held him at bay.

"Say it," she demanded softly.

Buck's glowing eyes held hers for a second, but only a second.

"Shut up woman," he whispered, "and let me show you."

Kate stifled a sigh and resigned herself to failure as Buck's lips closed over hers. He'd probably never say the words that she wanted to hear; or at least, he'd never say them on command. But he was kissing her so delightfully that she had to admit that his way had a lot going for it.

As usual, Buck chose to be practical.

When their lips parted Buck looked down and pulled something out of his shirt pocket. He reached for her hand and slipped a ring on her finger, and Kate put her other hand to her mouth.

"There you go, Kate," Buck told her solemnly. "That's everything I wanted to say. Now I'm asking you.

"Do you love me?"

Kate was struck to the heart. She glanced up quickly into Buck's clear eyes, but she wasn't seeing them. Her memory was showing her Buck's heart, replaying every kind and loving thing he'd ever done for them.

She saw Buck kneeling down beside her in the grass after she'd been thrown, felt him lifting her up in his arms. She saw him smiling behind that bouquet of red roses in the guest bedroom, saw him laughing as he made the helicopter circle over their restaurant. And when she thought of him climbing up on the roof of the restaurant to lift Molly through her broken bedroom window, and remembered his face bending over hers when she came to on the patio roof, she was robbed of words.

Buck didn't like to confess his feelings, but he'd shown them in a thousand ways. He was a plain man who valued actions over words; and when Kate questioned her own heart, she discovered that she did, too.

A wave of love rose up in her throat so hot and strong that it almost choked her; and she put a gentle hand up to Buck's cheek to brush it with a feather-light caress.

"Shut up, Buck," she whispered, "and let me show you."

His face split into a sharp white grin, and when he bowed his head to kiss her, Kate made good her words. She leaned over to give him the most heartfelt kiss of her life. She poured all her love into that soft, passionate, tender kiss; and her eyes blurred with tears as she did. If she'd ever doubted that she loved Buck Spade, the last shred of that doubt vanished as his fingers curled around her shoulders, and her lips wandered over his neck.

Chapter 50

The next morning, Kate woke up, yawned and stretched; but when she looked up, something winked and glittered on her hand. She frowned, then smiled as the memory of the previous night twined its arms around her.

I'm engaged, she told herself in wonder, then hugged herself in delight. She could truly say that she was happier than she'd ever been in her life.

She loved, and was loved by, a wonderful man.

Kate smiled, threw off the covers, and rose to meet the new day. She was still sore and shaky, but she was feeling much better; and she had no doubt that the Spade family's personal doctor would soon be by to check on her and on Molly.

She went to the bathroom and took a quick shower; then she wrapped a fluffy white bathrobe around herself and slipped down the hall to the guest room. She rapped softly on the door.

"Molly, are you awake?"

There was no answer, and Kate rapped again. "Molly?"

She pushed the door open and found Molly sound asleep in bed. Kate drifted across the room to sit down on the bed beside her daughter. She leaned over to press a tiny kiss to Molly's smooth brow.

"Wake up, wake up, Molly bird," she sang softly, and smiled to see Molly's eyes flutter open.

"Good morning, baby," she whispered. "How are you feeling?"

Molly looked around in confusion, and then, to Kate's dismay, her mouth crumpled up.

"Mamma, our house burned down!" she cried in a quavering voice. "All our things burned up!"

Kate opened her arms and Molly went into them. Kate rested her cheek on her daughter's hair and hugged her close.

"I know, baby. But it's going to be alright, I promise."

"No it's not," Molly sobbed on her shoulder. "All my clothes are burned up, and my bed, and my dolls!"

Kate suffered an answering echo of grief for all their family photos, for the things Kevin had given her, even for the Lichtenstein. Their house and their possessions had been insured, but Molly was right: there were some things that could never be replaced.

Still, they had only one choice.

To go on.

"I know, baby," Kate crooned. "But we'll get you new clothes and new dolls."

"It's not the same," Molly hiccuped, and Kate stroked her hair and rocked her back and forth.

"No, it's not," she sighed. "But we're still here, and that's what matters. We're going to be alright, you'll see." She pressed a kiss to Molly's flushed cheek.

"But where are we going to live, Mamma?" Molly quavered, and Kate held her breath before replying:

"Buck is going to let us stay here at his house, baby. For as long as we like. Isn't that nice of him?"

To Kate's overwhelming relief, the mention of Buck seemed to calm Molly down. She watched as the cloud lifted from her daughter's brow.

"Y-yes," she stammered.

A wave of mother love surged through Kate, and she hugged Molly fiercely. Her little daughter was shaken by their narrow escape from the fire and the loss of their home. Her silky hair still smelled faintly of smoke. It was too soon for Molly to hear that Buck was going to be her new father. But she liked him, and for the moment, that was enough.

"Are you hungry, baby?" Kate whispered tenderly.

Molly nodded. "A little bit."

"Why don't we get dressed and go down to breakfast? I bet Conchita has something yummy all ready for us."

Molly considered, then nodded, and Kate smiled; and when they walked out of Molly's bedroom at last, and out into the big main room, Buck was there to greet them.

Molly took one look and ran to him, and Buck knelt down to take her into his arms.

"Well, well, doodlebug," he murmured, and closed his arms around her. "It's going to be alright."

Kate gazed at them through a sheen of quick tears. *It is going to be alright,* she thought in relief. *Buck and Molly adore one another.*

When we finally tell Molly that we're getting married, she's going to accept it.

Buck gave Molly a smack on the cheek and stood up suddenly. He held out his big hand, and Molly took it.

He smiled down at her and winked. "Let's go get some breakfast," he suggested; and Kate smiled and followed them out.

Chapter 51

"Hoo-hoo-oo!"

Buck crossed one arm over his eyes and groaned. Somewhere on the other side of the old ranch house window, an owl was calling for its mate and had woken him from a sound sleep.

Buck rolled over and buried his face in the pillow. The deadline to find that water rights contract was only a few days away. He'd torn himself away from Kate when they'd just got engaged, and when Molly needed him to stay close.

Because of Buster Hogan's foolishness, he'd had to drag himself out to Big Russ and Miss Annie's place one last time. They'd already had a team of professionals come out and scan the ground with radar, they had metal detectors comb all around the house, and they'd still come up snake eyes.

Now it was crunch time. He'd spent days combing the house himself, and he still didn't know where that rights contract was.

Buck mumbled into the pillow. He'd tried everything: pulling out the fireplace bricks, tearing up the floorboards, climbing into the attic, even getting down on his hands and knees and crawling under the porch with the spiders.

Nothing.

Despair curled its sharp fingers around his shoulders. *We're going to lose the Seven,* he thought darkly, *and it'll be my fault.*

How am I going to face my brothers when we lose the ranch?

How am I going to face Kate?

He rolled over restlessly and stared up at the ceiling. *Oh Lord,* he prayed, *if there was ever a time for you to throw in, this would be it. Please help me find that piece of paper!*

There was no immediate answer, except for the distant, answering call of the owl's mate, somewhere in the big oaks beyond the creek. Buck groaned and turned over to bury his face in the pillow again.

He plunged instantly into the dark void of unconsciousness. He drifted in the blackness for a long time, but gradually the veil lifted. He saw Kate's laughing green eyes, heard her happy laughter as she reached up to run her slender fingers through his hair.

I love you, Buck, she whispered, and his lips moved soundlessly in reply.

Kate's lovely face faded, and was replaced by Buster Hogan's angry red one. Buck's brows twitched together in his sleep and his hands clenched into fists.

Liar.

He murmured and turned his head on the pillow, and he moved further back in time. He saw a gray-haired Miss Annie standing at her old cast iron stove, and as he watched, she turned and smiled at him over her shoulder.

"I guess you'd like a biscuit, *mmm*? I swear, you got the biggest appetite of any boy I've ever seen," she declared and wiped her hands on her apron. She smiled at him, picked a biscuit out of a pan, and handed it to him hot from the stove.

He gobbled it up and licked his fingers, and looked up just in time to see Miss Annie smiling down at him with her wry blue eyes. "I guess it's time for your allowance, too, ain't it? What did we say—a quarter for mowing the lawn and taking out the trash?" She turned and reached up to pull a pale yellow pot down off the top shelf of the stove, and she pulled out a quarter and handed it to him with a smile.

"There you go, Buck. You've earned it."

Of course.

Of course.

Of course!

Buck woke with gasp and sat bolt upright in bed. His heart was pounding like a jackhammer and he felt like he'd been shocked by a live wire.

I've been looking in the wrong places, he thought wildly. He threw off the covers and slapped his bare feet on the floor.

I've been looking for that paper where Big Russ would've hid it, but Miss Annie outlived him by five years.

Buck jumped up and hustled across the bedroom and yanked the door open.

I got to look in Miss Annie's hiding places!

He stumbled out into the dark main room, then flipped on the switch. A solitary light bulb burned in a lamp on the ceiling, and in its weak light Buck rushed to the window overlooking the back yard and ran his hand along the top of the frame.

Nothing.

He whirled around, searching the room with his eyes; then he lurched to the kitchen door and stumbled in. He turned on another light and hurried to the old cast iron stove. It was still there, and he glanced up hungrily.

Sure enough, the old yellow pot was still there. He grabbed it and turned it upside down, then peered into it; but it was empty.

Buck turned around and around in frustration, wracking his brain to remember where Miss Annie had hidden things; and he closed his eyes.

He stood there for a long, frowning, moment; then he opened his eyes and drifted across the room to stare at a 1981 farming calendar hanging on the wall. He lifted it up with one finger, then peered underneath.

A small, barely visible crack branched out in the faded wallpaper, and Buck picked at it with his fingernail.

A little fold of wallpaper peeled back, and tucked underneath it was an old, faded sheaf of paper. Buck pulled it out slowly and unfolded it with a trembling hand: and then he rolled his head back and whooped like a crazy man.

Chapter 52

Buck settled into the polished wooden seat at the county courthouse and adjusted his tie. He was dressed in his best gray suit and hat, and he was thoroughly uncomfortable. He glanced at the big brass chandelier hanging from the ceiling and then all around at the paneled walls of the courtroom.

Eugene leaned over from the next chair to whisper, "Now let me handle this, Buck. Buster Hogan would love nothing better than to get you to show out in front of this judge. No matter what Buster says or does, you hold your temper."

Buck shot him a short, angry glance. "I'll try."

"*Try* doesn't get it," Eugene retorted. "You need to just sit there and let me—"

The bailiff called out, "All rise. The Honorable Judge Henry Collins presiding."

Buck stood up slowly and adjusted his black string tie as the white-haired, moustached judge entered the courtroom. He sat down behind the bench, shuffled papers, and barked:

"So Mr. Blevins, this is a case about who owns senior water rights on the section of the Big Sandy River along the border of the Seven and the Lazy H Ranches, is that correct?"

The opposing counsel, a tall, young, bushy-haired man that Buck guessed to be a particularly hungry shark from Dallas, stood up.

"That's right, your honor."

"And Mr. Blevins, you're counsel for the first party"—the judge adjusted his glasses and peered at a sheaf of papers—"the Hogan family of the Lazy H Ranch."

"That's correct, your honor."

The judge scanned the papers in his hand and grunted. "The Hogan family is claiming that the late Mr. Russ Spade, the original owner of the Seven Ranch, sold his senior water rights to the late Homer Hogan, per the attached copy of the original contract provided to the court."

Buck stirred and shot a resentful glance at the other side of the courtroom. Buster Hogan was sitting there looking as smug as a cat licking cream off its whiskers. He was all tricked out in a blinged-up suit that looked like he stole it from a singing cowboy, and his hard red face was scrubbed Sunday shiny.

The judge went on, "The Hogan family has therefore submitted a claim for the senior water rights to this portion of the Big Sandy."

"That's correct, your honor."

The judge studied the documents for an instant longer, then called, "Who's the counsel for the second party?"

Eugene stood up. "I am, your honor."

The judge glanced at him over his glasses. "Oh, yes, Eugene. Very well. So you're claiming that the contract document the Hogan family has provided is"—he paused before adding—"not valid?"

"That's right, your honor."

The judge scratched his nose and asked, "Do you have any documentation to prove your own claim?"

Eugene coughed. "Yes, your honor. We have the original contract, which shows that the Spade family claim to senior water rights is current. We therefore maintain that the 'contract' provided by the other party is fabricated."

Buck rolled his eyes to Buster's face to enjoy the sight of it going even redder than usual. Buster grabbed the arms of his chair and shouted: "That's a lie!"

Buck twisted to point at Buster's scowling face. "You know you forged that contract, you sidewinder!"

"Order!" the judge cried, and pounded his gavel. "Another outburst, and I'll clear the courtroom!"

Buck muttered under his breath and glared at Buster as he turned around in his seat.

The judge sighed heavily and fixed Eugene with a grim stare. "Let me see your documents."

Eugene opened his briefcase and handed the contract to the bailiff, who carried it to the judge. The older man studied it in frowning concentration, and Buck held his breath. The silence seemed to stretch out for hours.

Finally the judge tossed it down on the desk. "Counsel, approach the bench."

Buck followed Eugene and the Hogan lawyer as the two of them walked to the bench. They both leaned close, and the judge bent over to murmur something to them. Buck frowned and pricked up his ears, but he couldn't make it out.

At last the judge straightened and barked, "The court finds in favor of the Spade family claim. Court dismissed."

A triumphant whoop jumped from the back row of the courtroom, where all six of his brothers were sitting. Buck slapped his hands against his knees and jumped to his feet with a bursting heart. He hurried to meet Eugene and slapped him on the back, and Eugene looked up at him.and smiled.

"Congratulations, Buck."

Buck pumped his hand. "I can't thank you enough, Eugene," he murmured fervently. "That was too close." He paused for an instant and added, "What did the judge say to you up there?"

Eugene shook with silent laughter and rubbed his nose as he bent down to close up his briefcase. "He congratulated me. Then he told the other attorney to come back to his rooms to explain why he was pushing a forged contract," he chuckled. "He told him to bring Buster with him. I'd give a hundred dollars to be there when Buster discovers the penalty."

Buck broke out laughing. "Me, too, Eugene. But right now it's time to celebrate. Come on out to the house. I'm gonna throw the biggest party the Seven's ever seen!"

Eugene smiled up at him and nodded. "I'd be glad to, Buck. I'd like to rest for a change."

Buck slapped him on the back again, then turned to look for Kate. She was waiting for him on the second row of benches, and he walked out to meet her and give her a kiss on the cheek.

She looked up at him with stars in her eyes. "You did it, Buck," she beamed. "I knew you would!"

Buck gave her a crooked smile, but felt his chest expand just a bit anyway. Morgan, Carson and his other laughing brothers pushed in just then and slapped his back sore.

Buck looked around at all the smiling faces surrounding him and felt a bloom of gratitude in his chest; and just for an instant, an old, familiar feeling, like a well-known and well-loved hand on his shoulder.

Chapter 53

"Thank you for calling. I feel so much better now that I know what happened."

Kate hung up the cell phone and tossed it back into her bag. She and Buck were enjoying a late breakfast by the pool, and Buck propped one elbow on the glass table and gave her a look of mild curiosity from the other side.

"What was that all about?"

Kate sighed and looked down at her hands. "That was the police detective," she murmured. "He was calling to let me know what Sebastian told them."

She shook her head sadly. "They caught him about an hour after he skipped town. They got a confession out of him. He's going to jail, the detective said."

Buck frowned and reached out to take her hand. Kate shot him a grateful glance and took it.

"Well, don't let it upset you, Kate," Buck murmured and stroked her fingers with his thumb. "It's over now anyway."

Kate paused for a long, reluctant moment before she answered: "No…it's not, Buck. Sebastian told the police that he was…taking money from Buster to spy on you."

Buck's hand yanked out of hers in outrage. "What!"

Kate nodded. "That's why he planted that bug in the private dining room at the Stonehouse. Buster told him to. He knew you liked to go there to talk to Eugene."

Buck's blue eyes blazed. "Why, that cheating, sneaking, dirty—"

Kate laughed and reached for his hand again. "Who's upset now?" she chided gently.

Buck grumbled under his breath, and Kate leaned over to kiss his cheek. "Settle down, big boy," she teased.

"Settle down my big toe," he fumed. "I'm gonna call Eugene and have him sue that crook for cheating and spying and lying and every other stinking thing he's done since he was born. And that's *if* I don't find him and punch his lights out first!"

"But we're about to be married, remember?" Kate reminded him softly. "A bride doesn't want a husband who runs off and gets all busted up in a fight."

Buck glanced away with a stubborn expression, and Kate took his jaw in her fingers and gently turned it back to her.

"A groom has more important things to do than fight, don't you think?" she smiled.

Buck looked away. "Well…"

Kate leaned over the table to tickle his ribs. Buck jumped and sputtered, then laughed. "You might have a point there," he rumbled, and leaned over to kiss her. Kate giggled and turned her face up to receive a long and very communicative kiss.

"*Mmm*," she murmured, and traced his lips with a pink forefinger. "You know, I'm glad I dumped that pitcher of beer into your lap," she murmured.

"You are?"

Kate smiled up at him. "*Mm-hmm*. If I hadn't, Carson might not have come by the restaurant and invited me over to the ranch. And then I'd never had gotten to know you." She caressed his jaw with her fingertips.

"I've never been more wrong about anybody in my life than I was about you, Buck," she whispered. "I thought you were rude and pushy and a lot of other things, but you're…you're the sweetest, most decent man I've ever known."

Buck's eyes snapped to hers, and the startled look in them told her that he understood all the implications of what she'd just confessed. He nodded soberly.

"Thank you, Kate," he whispered. "I treasure that. And I want you to know that I feel the same way about you. Sometimes the best things in life…just take their time."

Kate's eyes blurred with tears, and suddenly, she was just too far away from her fiance. She scurried over to plop down beside Buck and snuggled against him.

She looked up with a mischievous twinkle. "That's true," she nodded. "That's why I'm not letting you out of here any more. No more running off to search for documents, or to go to court, or to fight Buster Hogan.

"You're all mine from now on, cowboy."

Buck's face split into a wide, white grin. "Yes, ma'am," he told her solemnly, and he turned to take her in his arms as Kate shrieked with laughter.

Chapter 54

A month later, Kate stared at her reflection in the old vanity mirror and adjusted her hair. She'd swept her shining auburn tresses up on top of her head, and two curling tendrils spilled down over her ears. The woman in the mirror was glowing and looked better than Kate had ever seen her, in her pearl earrings and off-the-shoulder white gown.

Kate's eyes wandered from her reflection to the room around her. She was in the old ranch house, in Big Russ and Miss Annie's old bedroom, and she was sitting in front of Miss Annie's old vanity. Somebody out on the porch was strumming a guitar, and another somebody picked up a violin and joined in a sweet, simple melody as she prepared to marry Buck Spade at the old ranch house.

The Spade men had spent most of that month transforming the old place. They'd descended on it in a roar of truck engines, swept it out, cleaned it up, and restored it to the charming backwoods cottage that it had been when Big Russ had first carried his bride over its threshold. Kate glanced around the little bedroom. It was sparkling clean and tidy. A simple cherry wood bedstead with a white quilt was pushed up against one wall, a matching chest of drawers and vanity lined the side wall, and a big rag rug covered the floor. A pair of big windows were hung with sheer lace curtains, and the little stone fireplace was cleaned out and ready for wood.

Kate breathed a tiny sigh. Buck had wanted to be married in his old home place, and while it hadn't been her first choice—she'd have preferred a proper church wedding—she'd been happy to yield. It had been her gift to Buck, and when she saw how happy it made him, she was more than rewarded.

A little knock made Kate turn her head.

"Come in."

A side door opened slightly and Molly slipped in. Kate smiled and held out her arms, and Molly hurried into them. She was as pretty as a little doll in her pink satin gown and crown of fresh daisies.

"They sent me in to ask if you're ready," Molly murmured. "Everybody's out there."

"All right, I'm coming. Just let me get my bouquet ready."

Molly looked down, and then up again before asking quietly: "Are you happy, Mamma?"

Kate reached out and caressed her daughter's pink cheek. "Yes, baby," she whispered. "Mamma's very, very happy."

Molly studied her face solemnly for a moment, then smiled. "Then I'm happy, too."

Kate blinked at her daughter, then pulled her into her arms. She hugged Molly fervently, then kissed her cheek.

"Thank you, Mollykins," she whispered brokenly. "You just gave Mamma a beautiful gift." She leaned back and smiled at her little daughter through her tears. "Go on out now, and get ready. I'm coming."

Molly withdrew from her arms and walked to the door. She turned there and gave her a shy smile.

"You're beautiful, Mamma," she murmured, then slipped out.

Kate watched her go, then brushed a tear from her cheek before she picked up her bouquet and rose to her feet. She looked down at the glorious profusion of perfect pink roses and daisies for a long, silent moment, but she wasn't seeing them.

She straightened, walked quietly to the door, and put a hand on the knob. She stood there, motionless, for one more moment of prayer.

Thank you, she whispered. *I never saw this coming, and it hasn't always been easy; but it's so much better than anything I could have planned. Buck is perfect for me and for Molly.*

I'm going to do my very best to be perfect for him.

Kate took a deep breath and opened the door to the main room; and as soon as she stepped across the threshold, a dozen smiling faces turned to beam at her and someone started strumming "The Wedding March" on a guitar. She was dimly aware of Molly, her pink face beaming as she stood beside the elderly minister in his gray suit and wire glasses; Morgan, standing tall and handsome in his black go-to-meeting best; and Carson, dapper as ever in a tailored leather jacket and designer dress slacks. Luke, Jesse, Will and Chance's smiling faces grinned at her from behind them, but Kate's eyes skimmed them all to rush to Buck.

He was standing there, waiting for her, with his Stetson in his hands and his head bowed. He was all slicked up, with his dark, wavy hair swept back from his brow, and his shoulders broad and square in a beautiful gray wedding suit. Kate's heart swelled with love as she glided toward him. Buck was the tallest man in the room, and the tallest in her heart. He'd saved her life more than once, and in more than just one way.

When she'd first met him, she'd felt only half alive; and now she was whole, glowing with life, and free to love again.

Buck raised his eyes, and Kate's locked on his as she glided to his side, took the hand he extended, and turned with him to face the minister.

The elderly man smiled at them, raised his Bible, and murmured: "Dearly beloved, we are gathered together here in the sight of God, and in the face of this company, to join together this man and this woman in holy matrimony."

Buck squeezed her fingers gently, and Kate turned to smile at him. The preacher's words slowly slipped away to a distant buzz, and all she could see was Buck's eyes—those beautiful pool-blue eyes—and the love shining through them.

Her mind spun back to the first day she laid eyes on Buck Spade. He'd been big and brash and his voice had filled the little dining room. She saw his wide blue eyes, almost comical with outrage, when she'd dumped that pitcher of beer into his lap. At the time, she thought she knew all she needed to know about Buck Spade.

How wrong I was, she thought, and tightened her fingers around his.

She was so deep in Buck's bottomless eyes that she hardly heard the minister until Buck turned from her to pull a ring out of his jacket. He stared into her eyes, slipped it on her finger, and rumbled:

"I, Buck, take thee, Kate, to be my wedded wife, to have and to hold from this day forward. For better, for worse; for richer, for poorer; in sickness and in health; to love and to cherish, till death do us part, according to God's holy ordinance; and thereto I pledge thee my faith."

Kate's heart melted, and she blinked back tears as Buck slipped the ring on her finger. She turned to the minister as he intoned, "Repeat after me."

Kate pulled Buck's ring out of her bouquet, turned to smile up into his eyes, and slipped it on his big finger as she murmured:

"I, Kate, take thee, Buck, to be my wedded husband, to have and to hold from this day forward. For better, for worse; for richer, for poorer; in sickness and in health; to love and to cherish, till death do us part, according to God's holy ordinance; and thereto I pledge thee my faith."

The elderly minister beamed at her and murmured, "By the authority vested in me by the state of Texas, I now pronounce you husband and wife. You may kiss the—"

Kate heard no more, because she was already in Buck's arms. His hand cradled the back of her neck as he bent down to give her a long, vigorous, and wildly communicative kiss. Kate's bouquet dropped out of her hands as she sent them around Buck's broad back. She was dimly aware of muffled laughter in the background, but she didn't want to ever let go of that magical, perfect moment in time.

It seemed only a few seconds later that the preacher put a hand on Buck's shoulder, and they looked up to see him beaming at them. "Congratulations," he smiled.

To Kate's disappointment, Buck released her, though slowly and reluctantly. He reached out to shake the minister's hand. "Thank you for coming out here, pastor," he nodded. "We appreciate it."

"It was my pleasure. I have another wedding, so I have to get back to town, but I wish you every happiness."

"Thank you," Kate smiled, and the elderly man patted her hand and turned for the door. As soon as he stepped away Kate was dimly aware of being mobbed by Buck's brothers, of being congratulated, of smiling faces. Carson leaned in and gave her a quick peck on the cheek.

"Congratulations, pretty lady."

Kate took his hands. "Thank you, Carson," she murmured.

The brothers lingered with them for a few moments, but to Kate's relief, they soon broke up and began to drift toward the door. She saw Morgan lift Molly up and carry her out the door on the way back to the main ranch house. The others winked at Buck and smiled at her, and shouldered through the door after him. The sound of their big voices and heavy boots shook the walls, but gradually faded across the lawn.

As soon as the last one had gone, Kate turned to Buck and twined her arms around his neck. He leaned down to kiss her, then suddenly hoisted her up into his arms and smiled down into her face as she shrieked with laughter.

His expression sobered, and his smile faded, then shone out again. "I love you, Kate," he whispered, and she stared up at him in wonder.

"I love you, too," she breathed; and then added, with a spark of mischief, "But since you finally told me, does this mean you aren't going to show me?"

"Oh, no ma'am," Buck assured her, as he whirled her around in his arms and carried her into the bedroom. "I'm going to show you," he promised, and kicked the door shut behind them as Kate giggled and kicked her high heels into the air.

Chapter 55

Red and bronze autumn leaves fluttered outside the big glass wall as Buck sat down beside his brother on the couch, clasped his hands in his lap, and stared at him in frowning concern.

Morgan shot him a look of wintry gratitude. "Thanks for coming down here, Buck. I hate to interrupt you and Kate's honeymoon."

Buck adjusted a pillow behind his back and settled in. "It's all right," he rumbled. "Kate and I are going to be on our honeymoon for a month at least.

"I came as soon as I got your message. Something bad must've happened to make *you* want to talk, Morgan," he added, in a gentle attempt at humor. "What's wrong?"

Morgan looked away from him, and Buck could tell that he was struggling to contain himself. He shook his head bitterly and waved an impatient hand in the air.

"I just got a text from Cecily," he rumbled.

Buck frowned. "Cecily? I thought you and her weren't talking any more. What did she want?"

Morgan rubbed his long hands over his face. "What does she always want," he mumbled bitterly. "She wants to make my life a living hell. But this time, she's really outdone herself." He turned to fix Buck with an angry stare.

"Do you know what she told me, Buck? She texted me to tell me that Kit wasn't my *son*. Just like that." He waved an angry hand in the air. "I know she's a witch, but even I didn't see this coming!"

Buck's frown deepened. "Has she given you any proof of—of what she says?" he stammered.

Morgan glared at him. "Do you think it makes any difference to me?" he growled. "Kit is my son regardless, and I'm not giving him up to anybody." He tensed his shoulders and added, "Cecily's just mad that the court awarded me custody after the divorce. This is her way of getting even."

Buck put a hand on his shoulder briefly and coughed, "I'm sorry, Morgan. You're probably right, this is just Cecily getting payback for you fighting her in court. Kinda the last twist of the knife. Forget it. You won custody of Kit. There's nothing more she can do."

Morgan tilted his dark head, as if to concede the point, but muttered, "If she can prove that Kit's not my son, the biological father might sue for custody."

Buck leaned toward him and muttered, "Not likely. He's not likely to win, anyway, since if he was the father, he sure didn't step up before now. Forget it, Morgan."

His younger brother rubbed his face with a brown hand and mumbled, "I'll try, but I didn't get a wink of sleep last night. All I can think about is somebody coming over here to take Kit away from me."

Buck put a hand on Morgan's shoulder. "You want me to call Eugene?"

Morgan shook his head. "I don't see the use of calling a lawyer right now," he replied reluctantly. "If Cecily tries something, then it'll be a different story."

"Well, if she does, we'll be ready for her," Buck replied in as bracing a tone as he could muster. "Don't pester yourself about it, Morgan. It's just one last little trick to make you sweat. Don't let it work. Come on down to breakfast."

Morgan grumbled and looked away. "No, I couldn't eat anything."

Buck stared at him in sympathy. "She's probably lying anyway, Morgan," he said softly. "It wouldn't exactly be the first time, would it? And seems to me that if you weren't Kit's father, she'd have hit you with it before now."

"That's a fact," Morgan agreed glumly. "She sure didn't care what she said to me when we fought." He sighed and shook his head.

Buck looked away uncomfortably and glanced around his brother's big living room. Morgan's apartment suite was warm and homey, with its paneled walls and hanging Indian blankets, but there was no little boy playing in it.

"Where's Kit?"

Morgan followed his glance. "Aw, I sent him downstairs," he confessed, and rubbed his brow as if it hurt him. "I don't want him to see his daddy like this. I'm a wreck, Buck."

Anger whisked up in Buck's heart as he stared at Morgan's haggard face. He'd known when Morgan had married Cecily Cooper that she was a gold digger and a tramp. Everybody in the family had seen it except Morgan, but they'd all known better than to tell him. It wouldn't have done any good.

But seeing Morgan's strained eyes still made Buck suffer a flick of guilt. Maybe he should've sucked it up and told Morgan the hard truth when it might've helped.

Maybe it would've been better to let Morgan hate him, than to see his brother like this. Buck frowned and looked down at his hands, and Morgan glanced at him.

"You go on down to breakfast, Buck," he rumbled. "There's nothing you can do. I just needed to get it off my chest."

Buck shot him a stricken glance. "You're sure you don't want to come down and eat?"

Morgan shook his head. "I'm sure. You go on."

Buck sighed deeply and stood up. "Come on up to my place if you want to talk, Morgan," he said quietly. "Anytime. And if you need help, I got your back."

Morgan glanced up at him. "I know it, Buck," he replied softly. "Thanks."

Buck gave him a crooked smile and walked slowly to Morgan's front door. He paused there with his hand on the knob and looked back over his shoulder.

"I'll keep Kit busy for awhile downstairs," he promised.

Morgan nodded. "I appreciate it, Buck."

Buck gave his brother one long, last glance before he opened the door and walked out into the hall of the big ranch house that he shared with his brothers. It was the hub of the Seven Spades Ranch, and it was probably what had first attracted Cecily Cooper to Morgan.

Buck bit his mouth into a hard, straight line. Cecily was a greedy little leech, and she'd never loved anybody but herself: not Morgan, not even Kit. The day Morgan had divorced her had been the best day he'd had in years.

And as Buck descended the big staircase, he made up his mind that he wasn't going to let her come back and haunt them, not if he had to spend a fortune on fences, firewalls, or legal fees.

As the eldest, Buck considered himself the protector of his family; and now that Morgan had divorced Cecily, he was free to do more than just sit back and watch.

And that was just what he planned to do…

Enjoy the next Spade brothers' book

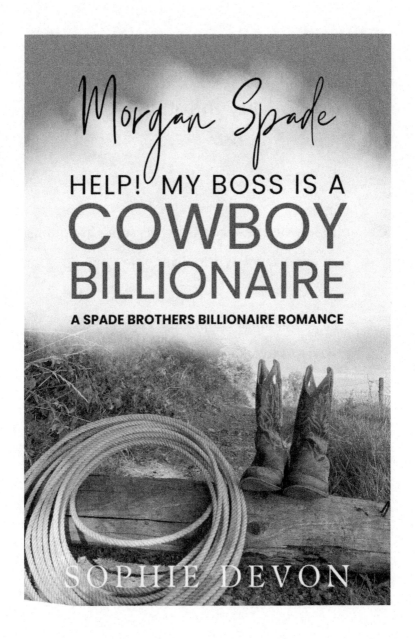

Stay in touch

Get notified when new books in this series are published
here: www.writtenbysophie.com

Follow Sophie on Tiktok:

www.tiktok.com/@sophiedevonbooks

Printed in Great Britain
by Amazon

57713048R00205